MAGIC STORIES
FROM AROUND THE WORLD

MAGIC STORIES

FROM AROUND THE WORLD

Translated and retold by
Veronica Lawson and Pamela Waley

Illustrated by
Luděk Maňásek, Karel Teissig
and Vladimír Tesař

TREASURE PRESS

First published in 1986 by
Treasure Press Limited
59 Grosvenor Street
London W1

Text © by Octopus Books Ltd. 1986
Illustrations © by Artia Prague 1986
Graphic design by Pavel Helísek

ISBN 1 85051 084 9
Printed in Czechoslovakia by TSNP Martin
1/18/09/51-01

Contents

THE MAGIC HORSE
OF KU-SUK-SEIA

This is an old story told by the Red Indians.

Once upon a time, before the white men drove them away to Oklahoma, the Pawnee Indians lived in Nebraska, where their sworn enemies were the Sioux. There they lived all the time in villages, where they were skilled farmers and potters.

In one of the Pawnee villages lived a poor woman with her grandson Ku-suk-seia, which means 'left-hand'. She was a helpful old soul, and the boy was pleasant and friendly. Yet the two of them were not well thought of in the village, for while there was no shame in being poor, there was no glory either. And they had practically nothing: no horses, no cattle, nothing worth mentioning at all. Their clothes were clean enough, but much patched. When Ku-suk-seia's father had died in a hunting accident, he had no fine head-dresses to leave to his son. Even their tent was small and badly placed, and when Hotoru the storm god swept over the prairie the modest shelter shivered on its poles as if it might collapse at any moment.

As soon as the bison began to move in the autumn, the Pawnees went hunting. For the northern winter would be long and bitter, and before it came they must have enough dried fish, pemmican and bison skins to see them safely through till spring.

So when the chief gave the order to set off, the Pawnees gathered together their tents and everything they needed for the journey. Even the old woman and her grandson tied up their few belongings. They had neither a mount nor a beast of burden, so they loaded their baggage on their own shoulders and trotted after the long caravan of people.

They were so poor that their people would not let them join the caravan. Instead they trudged miserably along a little way away. Humans can be very cruel, and the contempt of their people weighed heavier on the couple than the burdens on their shoulders. The Great Spirit couldn't be very kindly disposed to them if he let them suffer so.

One fine morning the rest of the group left the campsite before the poor couple had gathered their belongings together. The old woman and her grandson were nearly dying of hunger, so they searched through the site looking for cast-off food. At that moment a broken-down old bay horse slipped into the stockade on the same errand. Catching sight of them, the old nag breathed in sharply, and snorted. But then he walked up to them and made friends, for the poor soon recognize the poor.

'Poor animal,' said Ku-suk-seia. 'I expect his owner got rid of him once he wasn't fit for work.'

The poor creature was half-blind, deaf and lame. His ribs stuck out under his dull stained coat, which was covered with sores.

'What a pitiful sight,' thought the grandmother to herself. 'The poor creature is as useless as I am!' But the animal would not stray more than an inch from her side.

'Son of my son,' she confided at last to her grandson. 'We are going to keep this old nag and feed it. With two of us already starving, a third poor wretch won't make much difference.'

Ku-suk-seia and his grandmother began to load their baggage on to their shoulders. But the horse knelt down and began to whinny.

'Just look at that!' laughed the boy. 'I think he wants to make himself useful, the brave animal.'

So he put the baggage on the horse's back, and the beast followed them at a gentle trot, limping all the time. The rest of the tribe had disappeared long ago, but the grandmother knew the way of old.

That evening they reached the bend of North Plate, where the water spirit Chahuru had hurled an enormous boulder into the river. Every year the Pawnees set up their main camp there before scattering across the prairie. The bison rarely strayed from their ancient trail, and so the migrating herds almost always passed through North Plate.

The rest of the Pawnees had set up camp on the river bank earlier. Scouts had been sent on ahead, and in the evening they returned.

'There is a big herd of bison moving westwards,' they reported, 'and a white female is close behind the leader of the herd.'

This was exciting news. The skin of a white bison was the most precious thing an Indian of the prairies could imagine. White bisons were very rare, and no Pawnee had ever been known to fell one.

The chief of the Pawnees prayed a long prayer, calling on the helpful spirit Awahokshu and begging all the other good spirits to come to his aid.

'He who brings me the white skin shall have the hand of my daughter,' he promised his people.

Now the chief's daughter was the prettiest girl in the tribe and all the braves wanted to win her. Next morning, when the sun rose behind the boulders of Hotoru, the hunters scattered far and wide over the prairie to hunt the white female.

Ku-suk-seia too mounted his skinny horse, but the warriors mocked him.

'Just look at this hot-headed steed, everyone!' they jeered. 'Which is

8

carrying which, the horse or the rider?' And they elbowed each other in the ribs, laughing fit to burst.

Their jeers cut Ku-suk-seia to the quick, but he did not show it. He lagged behind, partly to escape the others' taunts and partly because his old mount could go no faster. All alone they sauntered along through the high grasses of the prairie.

Suddenly the horse began to talk. 'Take me to that little valley,' he said. Ku-suk-seia was startled, but he obeyed. A talking horse was certainly out of the ordinary, but who knew what the Great Spirit might have in store? Soon they came to a stream.

'Cover me with mud!' the horse ordered his rider. 'Not a tuft of hair must show, or the spell won't work.'

Puzzled, Ku-suk-seia did as he was told.

'Now climb on my back,' said the old nag. 'But don't move yet. Let the hunters go on ahead.'

The Pawnee warriors galloped after the bison in a cloud of dust. Then they split into two groups and rode off in different directions, to surround the bison and cut out some of the herd.

At that moment the old horse began to move. Hurling himself onwards like a tornado, he charged the herd from the side. The warriors watched open-mouthed. Wasn't that Ku-suk-seia on his blind old nag? What magic made it gallop fast as a prairie fire?

The horse forced its way straight to the white female. Ku-suk-seia's spear shone in the morning light. He took aim calmly and hurled it with all his strength. The white bison sank to the ground as if struck by lightning, and the horse gave a whinny of victory.

Ku-suk-seia jumped down and dismembered the dead animal, while the rest of the herd fled in all directions. He loaded the meat on to his mount, wrapped himself in the white skin and rode back to the camp.

The news of his triumph had reached it ahead of him, and the chief was waiting in front of the main tepee.

'Awahokshu was with you,' said the chief kindly. 'The spirit brought you luck, or you could never have felled the white bison. Give me the skin.'

'All in good time,' replied Ku-suk-seia. 'First I must go to my grandmother, for she is hungry.'

It was not a wise thing to say to a chief, and an angry gaze followed him as he rode over to his tepee. He unloaded the meat himself, though that was usually squaw's work.

'A miracle, a miracle!' cried his grandmother, clasping her hands. 'H'uraru the earth spirit must have been with you, my brave boy. Now we shan't be hungry any more.'

'Cook us some meat, grandmother,' said Ku-suk-seia, 'while I give this horse water and something to eat. For a rider must see to his mount before he thinks of himself.' The horse gave a whinny of contentment. When it had eaten its fill, it watched Ku-suk-seia and his grandmother feasting on bison meat.

Before he went to bed, Ku-suk-seia walked over to stroke his mount.

'Tomorrow, at sunrise, the Sioux will attack the camp,' said the horse. 'Ride me right into the enemy. Have no fear, but kill the Sioux chief, and hurl yourself at the enemy three times. Nothing can hurt you. But after that turn back, or one of us will die.'

Everything happened just as the horse had said. At the first glimmer of dawn, the Sioux war cry rang out. An army of braves had surrounded the Pawnee camp.

The boy mounted his horse and rode fearlessly into the enemy ranks. Arrows and spears hailed down on him, but some unseen shield seemed to be protecting him. He rode up to the Sioux chief, brandished his tomahawk and killed the chief with a single blow.

Twice more he hurled himself on the enemy, killing many of the Sioux warriors. But he became over-confident, and forgot the horse's advice. A third time he spurred the horse on, and now the Sioux weapons met their mark. Riddled with arrows, the horse sank to the ground. Ku-suk-seia escaped, but his brave mount was dead.

When he reached his tent he threw himself down, beating the ground with his fists. Why, oh why hadn't he taken that advice? Now he had lost his companion forever.

The Sioux cut the magic horse into countless pieces, scattered them to the four winds, and fled.

Weeping, Ku-suk-seia searched the battlefield from top to bottom. He gathered up all the pieces and collected them in a heap on a hill. Then he sat down beside them and wrapped himself in the white bison skin. His heart breaking, he prayed to the Chikoos, the forces of nature. He called to Tirawa the Great Spirit and to the helpful Awahokshu. He cried to Shakuru the sun god, H'uraru the earth spirit and to Uti Hiata the harvest goddess, on whose fruits his horse had fed. He prayed to the wind god Hotoru and the water spirit Chahuru.

Suddenly the sky darkened. Lightning flashed across the clouds, and thunder rumbled. Huge water spouts gushed out across the prairie. The river rose, and a great storm raged. Volleys of hailstones come crashing down. It even snowed; something unheard of at that time of year. For three days and three nights Ku-suk-seia sat there under the skin of the white bison. Then at last the veil of blackness was torn apart, and darkness gave way to broad daylight. The sun shone in all its brightness,

10

and there in place of the scattered bones stood the bay horse, strong and healthy.

'Tirawa, the Great Spirit, has brought me back to life,' he said to his master. 'Why did you disobey me?'

'I forgot, and I am truly sorry,' replied the boy. 'Tell me what I must do.'

'Promise to follow my counsel at all times, for it comes from the Great Spirit himself,' said the horse.

The boy promised gladly. He handed the white skin over to his chief, and received the hand of his daughter. When the chief died, he himself became a famous chief. He followed the advice of the bay horse at all times, and ruled the Pawnees with great wisdom and skill.

At last Ku-suk-seia died. The Pawnees intoned their death chants, wrapped their chief in the white bison skin and laid him on the litter of the dead. But when the warriors went to find his mount, to kill him on the altar of the dead so that he could go to the Happy Hunting Grounds with his master, the bay horse had disappeared.

THE PIRATE BROTHERS

Once upon a time there were two brothers who came from a village in the mountains of southern Serbia. Their names were Lepa and Tchernyegor, and they were fierce, bold men. They served for a time in the king's army and learned to fight and be tough, but they were also badly paid and badly treated, so they deserted. They went up into the mountains of Macedonia and gathered around them a band of fearless desperadoes. Soon they were the scourge of the land. They had a fleet of boats and they would sail along the river in the darkness of night to attack the vessels of rich merchants. They robbed the villas of noblemen in the country and the houses of the idle rich in the towns. They lived well on the proceeds, but they never forgot what it had been like to be poor, and so anyone in need could be sure of being helped by them, just as anyone who was well-off could not hope to be spared by them.

The King offered a large reward for their capture, but the poor people would never betray their hideouts, and the soldiers who went in search of them did not know their way about the mountains. As time went on, the pirate raids of Lepa and Tchernyegor took them as far away as the Aegean sea and the coasts of Greece and Turkey.

The two brothers married two sisters: Lepa took as his wife the haughty Jevekhimia and Tchernyegor wed the fair-haired Nastasie. One day the pirates captured a merchant vessel. Among other things, they found a most beautiful dress, embroidered with gold and richly decorated with pearls. It was a dress for a princess.

'I'm going to take that dress to my Jevekhimia,' Lepa said to his brother. 'I saw it first, as soon as I came into the cabin.'

'Oh no you're not, brother,' said Tchernyegor. 'That dress is for Nastasie. I was the first to board the ship, so I have a better claim to it.'

They argued, and the argument turned into a quarrel, and the quarrel into a fight. Tchernyegor pulled out his pistol and fired at his brother. He missed, but instead he shot his brother's page dead. Then they both drew their swords, and the blades crashed and sparks flew from them.

There was an old singer who used to sing ancient songs of great deeds as they sat round the camp fire at night. When he saw them behaving like that he scolded them.

'You stupid men!' he cried. 'Fancy fighting over a rag!' He snatched it up and tore it in half.

No one dared to harm the old singer. Lepa put his sword back in its scabbard and said, 'He's right, of course. Let's be friends again, brother.'

Tchernyegor agreed. But Lepa did not forget that his brother had killed his favourite page, and he meant to have his revenge for that. Before his brother got back home, Lepa had already been there and had carried off Nastasie, and sold her as a slave to the captain of a Turkish ship.

When he arrived home and heard what had happened, Tchernyegor was beside himself with rage and grief. He seized his gun and strode off to Lepa's house. 'You come with me,' he ordered Jevekhimia, and he made her go with him to the Turkish ship.

'Here's a beautiful slave,' he said to the Turk. 'I'll let you have her for only six hundred ducats.'

The captain laughed. 'I've just bought one for five hundred,' he said, 'and she's a blonde. I like blondes better than brunettes.'

'All right, you can have this one for five hundred. But let me see the one you've got,' said Tchernyegor.

So he sold Jevekhimia, and the Turk sent for the fair-haired slave to be brought up to the bridge. 'Lift your veil!' he ordered her. As soon as she did so, Tchernyegor saw that it was Nastasie. Trembling with emotion, he said to the captain, 'Let me buy her from you. That is my wife.'

The Turk laughed contemptuously. 'She pleases me,' he said. 'Business is business. And now go, before I have you whipped and thrown overboard.'

Tchernyegor was absolutely furious, and he jumped into his boat and made for the shore, intending to get his men together to attack the Turkish ship. On the shore he met Lepa, who was looking for his wife, anxious and unhappy.

'Forgive me, brother,' said Tchernyegor. 'I have sold Jevekhimia to the Turk.'

'And forgive me, brother,' replied Lepa. 'I sold Nastasie as a slave. Let's forget our quarrel and rescue our wives. Separately we may be defeated, but together we are strong.' They embraced, then hurried their men aboard their ships and went to attack the Turkish vessel.

'Give us back our wives, captain,' they shouted.

When the Turk realized that the combined forces of the pirate brothers were more than a match for his own men, he ordered the wives to be brought up on deck, and he let them go. Tchernyegor and Lepa welcomed their wives back on their own ships and were about to hurry away when the Turkish captain shouted, 'Stop! I want my money back!' The two brothers burst out laughing. 'The slaves are ours, and the money is ours too! Or would you like us to set fire to your boat?' The

Turkish captain did not like that idea at all, and he quickly raised his anchor and sailed away.

Lepa and Tchernyegor went home with their wives, and there was never again a quarrel between the captains of the pirate band. And for many years they raided land and sea.

14

THE TREASURE OF STALAC

Udbina is in Yugoslavia, in the Kapela mountains between the river Una and the sea full of islands, along the Dalmatian coast. Near Udbina there is an old Turkish ruin, known as Stalac. This story is about a treasure that is supposed to have come from there. The Kapela mountains are full of caves, and one night, at the beginning of the last century, a young man of Udbina had a dream. In his dream he saw a cave, and in the cave there was a fine hoard of treasure.

When he woke next day, he went up into the mountains, found the cave he had dreamt about, entered it and saw inside a stone table. On the table lay two Turkish scimitars, one across the other. Hanging on the walls all around were necklaces of pearls and precious stones, and in one corner there was a great heap of gold coins. The young man filled his pockets till they would hold no more, and then turned to go home. But when he tried to get out of the cave, he could not find the way. The entrance had disappeared. He thought, 'This must be the work of the spirit of the mountain, angry that I have taken what is not mine.' Frightened to death, the young man quickly emptied his pockets of everything he had taken, but still the cave remained closed. He searched round and round the cave, again and again, but it was hopeless.

Suddenly a thin little voice said to him, 'If you leave behind all the gold you took, you can go.'

He searched his pockets again, and then his clothes, and he found a little piece of gold sticking to his stocking. When he had put that back with the rest, he found the way out easily.

He fled home, very relieved at having escaped, because he valued his life more than all the gold in the world. When he got to the village, he told everyone what had happened to him, and they were all much too scared of the spirit of the mountain to try to do better than he had.

At that time, the chief town of the district, Gospic, had a troop of soldiers garrisoned there. The story of the treasure of Stalac reached the officers, and the captain, Filipovic, decided to go and collect the treasure with the help of some of his fellow-officers. Soldiers are always short of money, and this adventure was all the more interesting because it might be very profitable. These officers were not afraid of spirits, and they took along the priest, Kovacevic, just in case they met the devil himself.

When they reached the cave, they found everything just as the young man had described it. 'That's fine,' said Captain Filipovic. 'We'll have all of that. Put it into the sacks.' Kovacevic the priest raised his hand in

protest. 'Wait a moment,' he said, 'perhaps the place is haunted. I'll say a prayer first, to be on the safe side.'

He put some candlesticks on the table, and candles in them, which he lit, and then opened his prayer-book. But before he could utter a word, the voice of the spirit of the mountain spoke. 'That will do you no good. If you do not have the key to the earth, you will never succeed in taking away the treasure.'

Captain Filipovic tried speaking to the shadowy voice. 'Are you the spirit of the mountain?' he asked.

'I am what I am,' the voice replied.

'Well, stay that way,' laughed the captain. 'We will take the gold, and you won't stop us. Come on, comrades.'

The voice said, 'You have been warned, captain.'

The priest started saying prayers to ward off evil spirits. But when the

16

soldiers approached to lay hands on the gold, a gust of wind swept through the cave, putting out the candles. In the darkness were heard shrieks and roars, screeching and howling, which filled the cave with hideous noise.

'Let's get out of here,' cried the captain, scared out of his wits. 'These are evil spirits!'

Then the men, forgetting how brave they were, took to flight. They groped their way around the cave, seeking the way out, and from all sides blows rained down upon them. It hurt them a great deal, and soon they were black and blue all over. When at last they reached the freedom of the open air, the priest noticed that he had left his prayer-book behind, so very bravely he went back into the cave to find it. Again he was hit over and over again before he was able to find it, and the candlesticks, and return outside.

As white as a sheet, the men left that terrifying place and returned to Gospic in silence. None of them survived the adventure by more than a few months except the priest Kovacevic, and he would only rarely speak of his fearsome experience. Since that time no one has ever found, or even looked for, the treasure of Stalac.

ROBERT THE DEVIL

Duke Hubert of Normandy was a wise, brave and just ruler, his country flourished and his people were happy. He lived with his wife in the castle at Rouen. They were much loved and respected, but their happiness was incomplete because, although they wanted one very much, they had no child. The Duke, even more than the Duchess, was saddened by the fact that he had no heir to succeed him. One day the Duchess overheard him murmuring to himself, 'God must hate me to be deaf to my prayers. Other men have beautiful and healthy wives, and they give their husbands children, but mine gives me none.' She was very unhappy when she heard this. They were no longer young, and she was afraid that he would think that their marriage was a failure. In her distress, she thought within herself, 'It seems that God will not help us. If ever I do have a child, I shall owe it to the devil rather than to God!'

Nine months later, in the middle of the worst storm that Normandy had experienced for centuries, she gave birth to a son. The proud parents decided to call him Robert. He was an amazing baby. When he was born he was already the size of a year-old child. When he cried he could be heard in the remotest parts of the castle, when he was christened, his howls echoed through the cathedral. His first teeth began to come through when he was only a few days old, big, strong ones, and no matter how often he was fed, he always cried and demanded more.

By the time he was a year old he was like a five-year old, both in mind and in body. And he went on growing in the same way. No one could control him; he was an absolute plague and pest to grown-ups and he would hit any children that came within reach. They used to run away as soon as they saw him coming. They called him Robert the Devil, and the name stuck.

When he was seven, his father found a tutor for him, who was supposed to teach him to read and write and do sums. But when he was having lessons, Robert behaved as though he were quite crazy: every day he invented new lies to tell, new tricks to play. He splashed ink all over the walls, tore up every scrap of paper and smashed up the schoolroom furniture. One day when the unfortunate tutor threatened to punish him, he pulled out a knife and killed him. Then he ran to his father shouting: 'I don't want a tutor, I don't want to have any lessons!'

Robert need not have worried, because no one in the whole country was willing to try to teach him anything. He grew more and more ferocious, and his parents, who had longed so much to have a son, now fervently wished he had never been born. It was impossible to educate him in the way that a future duke of Normandy should be educated, and they could only hope that one day, when he was old enough to be a knight, he would show his true worth in tournaments.

Soon after his eighteenth birthday there was a tournament on the feast of Pentecost. The day before it, Duke Hubert said to his son, 'You know that tomorrow all the knights of the country will come to the court for a tournament. You must take part in it, and show that you are able to do all the things a knight should do. A tournament is really a practice for fighting wars, and you ought to be good at fighting! But remember that there are rules, and good knights do not break them.'

Robert only laughed and said, 'Just as you like, father. I don't care whether I am a knight or not. I like my way of life, and I have not the least intention of changing it.'

In spite of his misgivings, the duke knighted Robert before the assembled company during the ceremonies next morning. Then the tournament began. Robert the Devil lived up to his name: he took no notice of the rules, he knocked the knights he fought off their horses, breaking their arms or legs, and he throttled three of the most important barons in the country. Robert paid no attention to the pleas and reproaches of his parents or of anyone else, and his mad behaviour continued until there was no one left for him to fight. Then he mounted his horse and rode away.

After some time, news of Robert reached Rouen. He had joined up with a band of robbers and brigands, and they had built a fortified house deep in thick forest and were making raids from there into the surrounding countryside, robbing churches and farms, attacking travellers, carrying off girls. Nothing was safe from them, and they seemed impossible to stop.

The Duke and his wife were the unhappiest people in the world. For years and years they had done everything they could to ensure the peace and prosperity of Normandy, and now it was all being destroyed by their own son.

One of the knights at the Duke's court suggested to them that they should send messengers to Robert, asking him to return to Rouen because they wanted to talk to him. 'If you can make him change his mind and stay here, preparing himself for the day when he will succeed to the dukedom, then all that has happened can be forgotten. But if he refuses, you must forget that this man is your son. He must be brought to justice, and you must treat him as a stranger.'

This seemed wise advice to the duke and duchess. They agreed that it should be done, and the messengers set off. As soon as they set foot inside Robert's stronghold, he put out their eyes. Then he sent them back with a message for his father. 'Tell him I did this to help you sleep better, and so that he will know he must leave me in peace.'

The duke then ordered that he must be captured, at whatever cost.

Robert and his band barricaded themselves in their lair, and only went out at night by secret underground passages, in search of what they needed — food, drink and money. They were like ravaging wolves.

One day Robert saw from their watch-tower a party of seven unarmed men riding peacefully through the forest, and it was easy to see that they were pilgrims. Robert leapt on his horse and galloped after them, and when he had caught them up, killed them, one after another, although he had no reason at all for wanting to harm them. It was as though he was mad, or drunk. Then, exhausted by the fury of his attack, with his face, hands and clothes covered in blood, he rode out of the forest and wandered through the fields. After some time he came across a shepherd, guarding his flocks, and asked him where he was. Terrified by Robert's appearance, he managed to stammer out an answer. He told him that he was not far from the castle of Darques, and that the duchesss herself was due to arrive there that evening.

Robert the Devil went to the castle that evening to see his mother. All along the road, the men who saw him coming fled as fast as their legs would carry them, and for the first time in his life he did not enjoy the sight. For the first time in his life he wondered, 'What have I been doing? Why am I so cruel?' He entered the castle courtyard and dismounted, but no one came forward to welcome him or to take charge of his horse. With his bloody sword still in his hand, he made his way to the hall, and found himself face to face with his mother. When she saw her son so wild and blood-soaked, the duchess could not control a movement of fear. But Robert threw down his sword, and earnestly begged her to give him an answer.

'Tell me, mother, why am I so cruel and wicked?'

It was a question the duchess had always dreaded, but she realized that only the truth could help her son, so she told him everything. Robert the Devil fell to the ground as though struck by lightning, and lay motionless for a long time. Then he got up, bowed respectfully to his mother and said, 'I shall make a pilgrimage to Rome, and there I shall confess all my sins. Perhaps God will take pity on me.' It was the first time that the name of God had ever passed his lips.

He left the castle and went back to the house in the forest, where he found all his band feasting. They gave their chief a noisy welcome, but when Robert explained what he meant to do and tried to persuade them

20

to follow his example, they grew very angry. 'You're the worst of us all, and now you try to tell us we should behave like good little boys! We certainly will not, we'll go on the way we're used to!'

When Robert heard this, he bolted the door, took a heavy cudgel that stood in the corner, and killed them all, one after the other. There were many of them and there was only one of him, but no one was anything like as strong as he was. Then he went out of the house, locked it and took the key with him. He rode southwards, in the direction of Rome. At midnight he came to a monastery which he had often attacked with his band of followers. The monks all feared and loathed him; even the abbot, who was his cousin, detested him. To his surprise, Robert knelt down before him and told him what had happened. He gave him the key of the house in the forest and asked him to take all the treasure stored up there and to give it back to the rightful owners from whom it had been stolen. At dawn he set off on his journey south, on foot. He had left his horse and his blood-stained sword in the monastery.

News of Robert the Devil and his misdeeds had reached even the Pope's ears. But the Pope welcomed him and listened to his story. Then he advised him to go to see a hermit at Montalto, three leagues to the south of Rome. 'He is my confessor,' said the Pope, 'and he will tell you what penance you must do to atone for your sins.'

Robert found the hermit living in a simple wooden hut. He confessed to him everything he had ever done in the appallingly wicked life he had lived until then. The old man meditated all night, and the next morning he told Robert what he had to do.

'From now on you must live as a fool who cannot speak. You will live like a dog among dogs, eating and sleeping with them, until the day comes when God will forgive your sins.'

Robert the Devil went back to Rome and did just what the hermit had told him to do. In the streets he behaved like a madman, and let people throw stones at him and mock at him without saying a word. One of the servants of the emperor's household, who found Robert's mad antics very funny, took him into the emperor's banqueting-hall as a sort of clown. The courtiers too thought that the gambollings and caperings of the madman were good entertainment. The emperor himself felt sorry for him, and ordered that he should be given food and drink. Remembering the hermit's instructions, Robert went to drink from the bowls put on the floor for the dogs, and ate the scraps and the meat from the bones thrown down for them to gnaw. And of course that was funny too. The emperor ordered bedding to be set in a corner for him, but he followed the dogs out into the garden and crouched down with them in the kennels. Gradually people became used to seeing him around. And

21

for seven years Robert the Devil lived the life of a madman among the emperor's dogs.

Now the emperor had a very beautiful daughter, but alas, she was dumb. The emperor's steward, a high court official, secretly planned to marry this girl, partly because he was in love with her, but even more because he expected that as the son-in-law of the emperor he could become very powerful. The emperor, however, realized what the steward's intentions were, and he dismissed him from his service.

Swearing that he would be avenged on the emperor, the steward went straight to his enemies, the Saracens, and offered them his services. Before long he arrived back in Italy at the head of a large army, and took up a threatening position on the outskirts of Rome, with the clear intention of capturing the city. The emperor had not expected this attack, and before he could prepare the army and the people of Rome, the enemy were already at the very gates. This might have been the end of Rome had it not been for a miracle.

The day that the battle between the Roman and Saracen forces reached a critical point, Robert the Devil, the emperor's fool, was going through the garden to drink at a spring of water. Suddenly he heard a voice from heaven saying, 'Robert, obey the order God sends you. Take the arms and the armour you will find here, mount the horse that will come to you, and go to the aid of the emperor.' And there Robert saw a white horse, white armour and weapons. He put them on and galloped off at full speed to the Imperial army. Unknown to him, the beautiful dumb princess had seen everything from one of the palace windows.

Meanwhile the Saracens had made such advances that it looked as though nothing could save the Roman empire. Robert arrived in the nick of time. With his sword he lopped off the heads of Saracens as though they had been daisies, he killed as he had killed in the fiercest moments of his brutal life, but this time he was not doing it for the mere pleasure of killing. When the battle was over and the Romans had a clear victory, Robert galloped back to the emperor's palace, hid the arms and armour, and put on his fool's clothes again. And again the emperor's daughter watched from her window.

That evening the emperor held a great banquet to celebrate the victory. Naturally everyone was talking about the unknown knight whose appearance had turned certain defeat into triumph. Nobody except the emperor's daughter knew who he was. She tried with signs to tell her chambermaid to ask her father to take a closer look at his fool. At first the emperor was amused, but as she persisted he grew angry with her for saying things that seemed to him to be stupid. In the end the princess withdrew sadly to her own apartments.

Twice more the same thing happened. The steward was still determined to win the emperor's beautiful daughter, and kept up the siege of Rome. Again the Imperial army was on the point of defeat when Robert appeared in his white armour to save the day. The third time, the emperor commanded some of his knights to follow the unknown warrior and find out who he was. But Robert was quicker than his pursuers. One young knight, however, threw a spear, not aimed to hurt Robert but to stop his horse, and it hit him in the thigh and the tip broke off the lance into the wound it made.

Robert still succeeded in escaping, he put on his fool's dress beside the spring in the garden, and tried to stop the wound bleeding by putting moss on it. It was a deep wound and hurt him very much, and Robert didn't go to the hall where the emperor was celebrating that night, but lay down among the dogs.

The emperor, who wanted above all else to reward the hero who had saved Rome, made a proclamation that if the white knight would come to him wearing his white armour and with the lance-tip that had wounded him, he would give him half the empire, and the hand of his daughter in marriage.

Robert heard nothing of the proclamation. He was lying, with his painful wound, in the dog-kennels. In any case, he would never have told anyone that he was the white knight, for he wanted neither happiness nor power, but only forgiveness for his sins. But the steward heard of it, and it was just the chance he wanted. His love for the princess and his passion for power were as strong as ever. He had lost the battle, and he thought that he had lost what he had hoped and fought for, but now he saw how he could get it. He bought a white horse, white armour and white weapons, and with a broken lance-tip he actually made a wound in his own thigh. Then he appeared before the emperor — and no one in the hall recognized him.

Only the emperor's daughter realized who he was, and she was also the only person who knew who really was the white knight. But however much she wept and tore her clothes in anger, she could not make the emperor understand what was wrong. He had given his word, and there seemed to be nothing she could do to set things right. A few days later the emperor led the unwilling bride to the altar where the false white knight stood waiting for her to become his wife. The service began, and at that moment of utter misery for the poor princess, a miracle happened: suddenly she found she was able to speak. And she cried out, 'This man is a traitor and a liar! Can't you all see that it is the steward who betrayed Rome?' It was as if up to that moment everyone had been blind and now could see.

The traitor ran out of the cathedral to where he had kept a horse in readiness in case something went wrong with his plans. He leapt into the saddle and fled.

The princess led the emperor and the Pope, who had been present in the cathedral, and all the guests into the palace garden, where Robert was lying in great pain. She found the lance-tip under a stone, where from her window she had seen him hide it.

'That is certainly from my lance,' cried the young knight who had caused the wound. Then the princess told them how she had watched the fool.

'He is no fool,' she said. 'He is the white knight you are looking for, and he is the only man I ever want to marry.'

But Robert went on acting as if he were mad, pretending that he couldn't understand anything that was going on.

Suddenly the hermit who had given him the penance came forward.

'My son,' he said, 'you are the man whom men used to call Robert the Devil, but you have suffered enough, and you have saved Rome. God spoke to me in a dream last night, and I know that he has forgiven you.' Robert fell to his knees in thanksgiving.

That same day he married the emperor's daughter, and the celebrations went on for a whole fortnight. Then Robert started back to Normandy with his young bride. He longed to show her to his parents and to tell them of the happiness that was his at last, and that would make them happy too. But when he arrived in Rouen, only his mother could share their joy, for his father had died a few days before their coming.

Only a little time passed before a messenger arrived at Rouen from the emperor. The steward had not yet given up his ambitious hopes and had led another Saracen army to the gates of Rome. Robert raised a force of Normans and hurried to Rome, but before he could get there his father-in-law had been killed by the steward. Robert avenged the emperor's death by challenging the traitor to a duel and splitting his skull with a single blow of his sword. Once their leader was dead, the Saracen army withdrew and never troubled Rome again. Robert returned with his men to Normandy, to his wife and mother, where he ruled successfully for many years.

That is a story about Robert the Devil. The real-life Robert the Devil, whose name appears in history books, was Robert I, Duke of Normandy. Like other dukes of Normandy, this notorious man was renowned for violence, cruelty, cunning and fraud. He did not live such a romantic life as the Robert in the story, but he did go on a pilgrimage as far as Jerusalem, a much more dangerous journey than to Rome in those days.

He married, not an emperor's daughter, but a Danish princess. He had a son, known to us as William the Conqueror, who claimed the throne of England after the death of Edward the Confessor. The English, however, chose one of their own countrymen, Harold, as king. William, furious, invaded England in 1066 and defeated Harold at the famous Battle of Hastings. William the Conqueror was crowned King of England on Christmas Day 1066, and so the real-life Robert the Devil is a distant ancestor of Queen Elizabeth II.

THE PRINCES OF WALES

Everybody knows that the eldest son of the king or queen of England is called the Prince of Wales. But do you know why? The story goes back nearly seven hundred years, to the time when Wales was a country quite separate from England, although its inhabitants were subjects of the kings of England. The Britons called them 'Wealhas', which means 'foreigners', and they spoke a different language, Cymraeg, which is rather like Breton in France, Gaelic in Scotland and Erse in Ireland. The Welsh were divided into clans, and these were often fighting among each other for land and local power, so that they were not much of a threat to the power of the English kings, who were able to control more and more land in the country.

If you look at a map of Wales you will see that some of the regions into which it is now divided have the names of old Welsh kingdoms: Gwynedd and Powys, Dyfed and Gwent. In the twelfth century, King Henry II of England ordered that the native rulers in Wales should stop calling themselves kings and follow the example of the English barons, who were content with the title of lord. But Owain of Gwynedd, who was a strong ruler in his own territory and had conquered part of the neighbouring lands of Powys, said that although he was quite ready to do homage to the English king, he regarded himself as more important than an ordinary baron. So Henry agreed that he and some of the other more powerful Welsh lords should be called prince.

Owain's grandson, Llywelyn I, was an ambitious man and he tried to make the other Welsh lords pay homage to him alone as Prince of Wales, saying that he would do homage to the English king on behalf of them all. He did not succeed in this, but his grandson, Llywelyn II, was more successful. He took advantage of the difficulties that Henry III was having with rebellious English barons to make himself lord over most of north and central Wales. Then he declared that he was the Prince of Wales, and he forced all the Welsh lords, one after the other, to acknowledge him as their lord and to pay taxes to him. In 1267 King Henry of England agreed to sign a treaty recognizing Wales as a principality.

Henry's son and successor, Edward I, was not at all satisfied with this situation, and he determined to destroy what he thought was a serious menace to the western parts of his kingdom. He set about bringing Wales back into his control, and in this he was successful. Llywelyn was killed in a battle, and his brother David was executed. To mark his conquest,

Edward built the magnificent castle at Caernarfon. Edward I wanted to make quite sure that the descendants of Owain Gwynedd would not try to claim the title again, and so he decided to give it to his own son, the future Edward II.

The Welsh people would not admit that they had been defeated, and they longed to get rid of English rule. 'Only a Welsh prince should be Prince of Wales,' they said. King Edward summoned a meeting of the Welsh lords and promised that he would give them a prince who would be all they asked for. They were very suspicious, but all the same they gathered together at Caernarfon, where the king welcomed them in a very friendly way.

'My lords,' he addressed them, 'for too long we have been fighting each other. Too much blood has been shed, and the countryside has been laid waste. We need peace, and we need a new prince.'

'That is true,' answered the nobles. 'But do not try to give us a foreign prince, we would not accept one. It would only mean more warfare.'

'Very well,' said Edward with a smile. 'Will you promise to swear allegiance to a prince who was born in Wales and who does not speak a word of English?' The Welsh were enthusiastic. 'We do promise,' they cried. 'Who is this prince?'

The king signed to a servant, who brought forward his son: he had been born in the castle a few days before! 'Here is your new Prince of Wales,' Edward said. 'Now swear allegiance to him as you promised.' Although they had been cheated, they had given their word, and the Welsh nobles had to swear to be loyal to him. This happened in 1301.

But in the hearts of Welshmen their true prince was Owain Glendower, a descendant of Owain Gwynedd. He too tried to make Wales independent and he too was successful enough for a time to be proclaimed Prince of Wales in 1304. But one day he disappeared mysteriously and no one knows what became of him.

There is a legend that when it seemed that the struggle against the English had failed, he retreated to the mountain of Cader Idris. The mountain swallowed him up, and there in a cavern he awaits the day when he will return to free his people.

THE LUCK OF EDENHALL

For generations fortune favoured the lords of Eden Hall, in Cumbria, and everything they set out to do was successful. They were strong, rich and powerful. Once a fountain-sprite had given a tall crystal goblet to a lord of Eden Hall whom she had loved, and inscribed on it was a prophecy:

'If this glass either break or fall,
Farewell the luck of Eden Hall.'

So the goblet was known as the Luck of Edenhall, and naturally it was looked after with great care by all the succeeding lords. But at last there came into the inheritance a spoilt, proud, haughty young man. One day

he gave a splendid banquet to all the nobles and ladies of the neighbourhood. The food was superb and the wine flowed freely. Pages and servants were kept busy supplying more and more of everything.

The young lord was quite drunk when he suddenly shouted out to the butler — the oldest servant in the castle — 'Bring me the Luck of Edenhall, it's time it was used for drinking!'

The old man turned pale at the idea of taking such a risk as to use the goblet, and he warned his master to think twice about what he was doing. But the young lord was not in a state to think sensibly about anything. He ordered the trumpets to sound while the Luck of Edenhall was taken out of the cupboard in which it had always been kept, unwrapped from the silken cloth which had always protected it, and filled with red wine from Portugal. A purple light shone over everything, beaming from the crystal goblet.

'I drink to the health of my friends in the Luck of Edenhall,' shouted the excited young lord. And he went round the table, touching glasses with each one of his guests. The crystal goblet rang out at first like silver, but as he continued round the table, the noise it produced sounded like a rushing torrent of water, and then like a peal of thunder. All the time the old butler watched in fear and trembling.

'That's what I call a really splendid tradition,' the young lord shouted. 'You have to be a great family for your luck to depend on something as easy to break as a drinking-glass. It has lasted a long time. Let's see how strong it is!'

Once more he crashed the goblet, with all his might, against that of one of the guests. But this was the last time. The goblet shattered to pieces, and at the same time the crash of a thunderbolt shook the night, wild flames arose, the guests scattered.

Then war-cries were heard, and the enemies of the lord of Eden Hall stormed into the banqueting-hall, and soon were in command of the whole castle. When dawn broke, no one was left alive in the smoking ruins save the old butler. He wandered sadly around, looking for the remains of his foolish young master. When at last he found the body, pierced by a sword, a hand was still clutching the stem of the broken goblet. The old man wept for the end of the legendary gift. 'Luck is as fragile as glass,' he muttered to himself, 'and pride is as fragile as luck. Everything man creates will come sooner or later to destruction.'

THE LEGEND OF KYFFHÄUSER

North-east of the Rhön mountains in Germany there lies a high hill called the Kyffhäuser. On its south slope is a cave which is known as the Cave of Barbarossa, and there is a legend which connects it with the Emperor Frederick I, who was called Barbarossa because of his fine red beard.

Also on the hillside is the ruined tower of a castle which once belonged to the emperors. The name Kyffhäuser is said to come from 'Kaiser Friedrich' or Emperor Frederick; but no one knows which Emperor Frederick it was, because Frederick I, Barbarossa, and his grandson Frederick II were both very strong characters and both powerful rulers. Both of them quarrelled with a Pope and were excommunicated, which meant that they had to do without the help of the church or the comforts of religion. Both of them spent much time out of Germany, and indeed Frederick II greatly preferred Italy, his mother's country.

Frederick I was the sort of person about whom legends collect even during their lifetime. He was admired and respected everywhere and is still thought to be the greatest of the medieval emperors. It is not surprising that his own people thought of him as almost superhuman. Barbarossa died in 1190, when he was sixty-five years old, leading the Third Crusade to recapture the Holy Land from the Saracens. He was drowned in the river Salef, in south Turkey, and it was never quite known how he came to die. He had ridden on ahead of his army, perhaps impatient at their slow progress. He may have tried to swim across and found that the current was stronger than he expected. Or he may have ridden into the stream to refresh himself after the weary ride and, his horse slipping, been thrown out of the saddle into the river where his heavy armour dragged him under the water.

As the centuries passed, his exploits and those of his grandson, Frederick II, became confused in people's minds.

One of the legends about Barbarossa tells of the time when the Pope had decreed that the emperor must not go into a church and that no priest should admit him to any service. The Lord of the Holy Roman Empire was, in the eyes of the church, an outlaw. Barbarossa put on a gorgeous oriental robe he had been given as a present, and taking a phial of magic water with him, went for a ride in the forest with a few companions. There, by means of the magic potion, he made himself invisible. But the story may have been about the other Frederick, who was very interested in the possibilities of magic.

The people who could believe that about the emperor could easily believe that the emperor never died. Sometimes, it was said, he could be seen in a river or a lake, his long red beard floating round him and shining in the sun.

The story grew that in the solitary cave on the mountainside Frederick Barbarossa sleeps, his great red beard growing round the table at which he sits. It has twice encircled the table, and when it has grown round it once more, he will awake and fight a mighty battle, and the Day of Judgement will dawn.

Around the high peaks at the top of Kyffhäuser fly many crows. Every hundred years the Emperor wakes up, and he sends a dwarf outside to learn news of the world, and to see if the crows are still there.

'And do the crows still fly above?' he asks.

'Yes, sire, the crows are flying as they have always done,' answers the dwarf.

Then Barbarossa lets his head droop again, and he sleeps for another hundred years. Or perhaps he is only dozing, for many people, especially children and shepherds, say that they have seen Barbarossa in his underground hall.

One day, a shepherd boy was sitting on the ground near the entrance to the cave, watching his flock and playing his flute to keep himself amused. Suddenly he saw an old man was watching him.

'For whom are you playing that tune?' asked the old man.

'For Emperor Frederick, sir.'

'Then follow me.'

And the little shepherd followed the old man into the depths of the mountain. He found everything there gleaming with gold, and many crusaders, knights and counts, wearing swords, stood in a circle, bowing respectfully to the old man. Then the boy knew that this was the emperor himself. He was extremely frightened, but the emperor was very kind. He gave him a golden cup as a present, and then sent him back to his sheep.

The Emperor Frederick has been waiting nearly a thousand years beneath Kyffhäuser, and his beard is still growing.

THE FOUR SONS OF AYMON

Charlemagne was king of France, but he was so powerful and ruled so much land in Germany and Italy and Spain that he was crowned Emperor of the West. He gave a great celebration banquet at his court in Paris to which he invited all the important people in his kingdom: dukes, counts, barons and of course the famous paladins, the twelve knights of his household, together with their ladies. It was a very sumptuous feast, and everyone praised his generosity and magnificence.

Among the guests was Duke Aymon of Dordon, who had performed noble deeds in the service of the emperor. His nephew, Count Hugh of Bourbon, and his cousin, Aymerin of Bourbon, were there also, and during a pause in the entertainments that were provided for the guests, young Hugh of Bourbon went up to the emperor and said to him, 'Sire, you know well that my uncles Aymon of Dordon and Aymerin of Bourbon have served you nobly in the war against the Saracens, and have conquered almost the whole of Spain for your Imperial Majesty. Would you not think it a suitable reward to grant them the lordship of those lands which they have won for you, as a sign of your goodwill towards them?'

Now this was quite a reasonable request in those days, but Charlemagne was not feeling well; perhaps he had eaten too much rich food and had indigestion. He spoke sharply to the young man, who replied none too politely, and suddenly the emperor stood up, drew his sword, and ran it through the young count's body, killing him outright.

Aymon and Aymerin swore to avenge his death. They raised an army and marched against the emperor, and there was a fierce battle. The imperial forces lost a thousand men, Aymon only thirty, but the emperor's army was far larger, and the war dragged on for some time because Aymon would not admit defeat. Much blood was shed before the paladins persuaded the emperor to come to terms with Aymon.

Charlemagne was tired of war, and he made peace with the duke, giving him his own sister, Aya, as his wife. It was a very grand wedding, but the emperor did not go to the feast afterwards, as the custom was, and Aymon felt that he had been insulted again. He was so angry that he swore to take vengeance not only on the emperor, but to kill all the members of his family.

As you will have guessed, Duke Aymon was very easily offended, and he was also very strict and dictatorial in his manner with his own household. Although he loved Aya and she loved him, she was afraid of him too. He was often away from home, fighting in various wars, and only returned for short visits from time to time. So it came about that, as the years went by, Aya bore him four sons, but he did not know and Aya did not tell him about it because she was afraid that he would kill them. They were, after all, Charlemagne's nephews as well as his own sons. She sent them to be brought up secretly by monks, Richard and Guichard in one monastery and Alard and Renaud in another. They all grew up to be strong and noble men, but of them all Renaud, the eldest, was the strongest and cleverest.

Charlemagne's eldest son, Louis, was the same age as Renaud. On his twenty-fifth birthday the emperor decided to make him king of France, and he called his lords and paladins together and announced to them:

'Here is my son, Louis. I am an old man now, and I want you to acknowledge him as king in my place.'

The lords murmured together, and then the Archbishop of Paris, whose name was Turpin, spoke for them all. 'Sire,' he replied to the emperor, 'we accept your right to do as you wish, and we approve your decision. But we cannot have the coronation unless we are all present. Duke Aymon is not here. I know that there is unfortunately enmity between you, but he has also done you greater service than anyone else in the whole empire.'

'That is true,' acknowledged Charlemagne. 'Aymon is brave and just, I admit. He won from the infidels the Crown of Thorns and the Nails from the Cross, and I shall never forget that. Send messengers to his castle at Dordon. I guarantee Aymon a safe conduct.'

When the emperor's messengers arrived, Aya longed for her husband to be friends again with her brother. But Aymon's reply was stern.

'Why should I help to the throne someone who will help himself to my possessions as soon as I am dead?' Then the duchess said to him, 'But if you had had children to succeed you, had you not sworn to kill them?'

Aymon shook his head sadly and said, 'I did once swear to do so, but now I know that if I had any, I would do more for them than any father should do for his children. But what does it matter? We have none, so I shall keep to what I said.'

Then Aya sent for her sons. Duke Aymon was at first unable to believe his eyes, but in the end he had to agree that they must be his own. He embraced them, weeping for joy, and he who a moment before had thought he must be the unluckiest man in the world suddenly found that he was the happiest. Straightaway he made them all knights.

All four of them were fine young men, but Aymon realized that

Renaud was taller, stronger and braver than the others. To lay his sword on Renaud's shoulders in the act of knighting him, he had to stand on a stool. 'Rise, Sir Renaud,' he said, 'and be a courageous and pious knight. I grant you the lands of Pierlamont, Montagne and Montfaucon.'

He gave each of his sons a horse. Renaud patted his on the forehead with his fist, and the horse fell dead — it was not strong enough for him. 'I can see that you are indeed my son!' Aymon exclaimed. 'I have a horse that will do for you. No one can get near it, no one has ever ridden it, but you will be able to tame it. Be careful, though, it is a real devil!'

That was the sort of challenge that the young count liked. He went up to the horse, whose name was Bayard, and as he prepared to seize it, it kicked out and struck him on the head. Renaud fell like a stone. His mother cried out, sure that he was dead, but Aymon told her, 'He's my son, and he will master that brute!'

After a long and hard struggle he did so, and at last Renaud was able to mount his steed. He gripped the horse so tightly with his thighs that Bayard reared up and kicked out with all his might; but the rider would not be thrown off. When the horse finally returned to his stable, covered in sweat, he was as gentle as a lamb. Renaud equipped him with a saddle and harness, and when with his father and three brothers he set for Paris, no knight in the world had a better mount than he. Women would turn to watch him as he rode by, and men murmured, full of admiration, 'That's the strongest and most handsome knight I've ever seen!'

Rumour of this admiration reached the ears of Louis, the son of Charlemagne. He had always believed that he himself was the strongest and most handsome knight in all France, and he was annoyed to hear such praise being given to another. One day he went to Renaud and said to him, 'That is a very fine horse you have there, cousin. Wouldn't you like to make a present of it to your king?'

Renaud answered, with more show of respect than he really felt, 'I wish to serve you as is my duty, cousin. If ever I give my horse away, no one but you shall have him. But I am not going to give him away.'

Louis was very angry, and retorted, 'You are as obstinate as your father. I swear that when I am king and have lands to give my lords, you shall have nothing.'

'That is your affair, sire,' Renaud answered. 'I have enough of my own, I need nothing from you.' And they parted as enemies.

The coronation took place, and the four sons of Aymon bore the canopy over the throne. Archbishop Turpin crowned Louis, and the paladins all swore allegiance to the new king. The four sons of Aymon served at the banquet that followed, as their duty demanded.

King Louis kept his word. He distributed lands to his vassals and to the paladins, but the sons of Aymon received nothing. The Duke, their father, took this as another serious insult, and went to complain to Charlemagne about it. The emperor summoned the four young men, and they knelt respectfully before him. 'You are my nephews,' he said, 'and it is not fitting that you should have fewer possessions than the other lords. You, Richard, shall be marquis of Spain, and you, Alard, of Poland. Guichard shall have land to the west of Paris, and Renaud to the east.'

King Louis was beside himself with rage. 'You have given away half my inheritance,' he complained to his father.

Because he still thought that he was the strongest and most noble person in the kingdom, and wanted to humble the sons of Aymon, Louis ordered that there should be a contest to see who could throw the furthest. However hard they tried, no one could throw further than he could, until he said, 'Let Renaud try. But I think he is readier to talk than to act!' So Renaud took a large stone, and of course he threw it much further than Louis could ever manage. The young king reddened with anger and muttered, 'The Aymon family will pay for this!'

One of Louis's councillors whispered in his ear.

'You can easily take revenge on them, sire,' he said. 'Let it be spread about that Count Alard said that he wants to play chess against you, for the highest prize there is.'

'And what is the highest prize?' Louis asked.

'Whoever wins five games running can cut off the head of the loser.'

'Did he really say that?'

'If you say that he said it, your majesty,' said the councillor, smiling, 'he will not be able to deny it.'

Louis was the best chess-player in the country. After some thought he agreed. 'Summon Alard!' he ordered. When the young count appeared, Louis said to him what the councillor had advised him to say. Alard turned pale.

'That would be wrong and sinful, cousin. How could we play for such a prize as a human head?'

'But that is what you claimed in your boastful talk.'

'Whoever told you that, sire, is a liar.'

'My councillors have said so. Are they liars? I say it too — are you going to call me a liar?'

Alard replied very firmly, 'Whoever says that I said such a thing lies in his throat.'

Louis said no more, but sent for the chess-board. He won the first three games, but then Alard won the next five in a row. 'Your majesty,' he said, 'you will surely agree that I have just won the right to your head. I beg that never again will you be so foolish as to play for such a precious prize.'

Louis felt that he had been humiliated, and he was furiously angry. He picked up the chess-board and hurled it at Alard, cutting open his head so that the blood gushed out. Unwilling to raise his hand against his king, the young count left the room at once. When Renaud heard what had happened, however, his anger knew no bounds.

'That will cost the king his head, I swear it,' he shouted, and no one could calm him down. Taking Alard with him, he stormed into the chamber where Louis was telling his father his version of the incident. Renaud bowed respectfully to the emperor, but he did not bow to Louis. Instead, he took hold of him by the hair, drew his sword, and struck off his head. Then he held it out to his brother, saying, 'Here, take the prize you won at chess.'

The palace was at once in an uproar, and in the confusion that followed the four brothers managed to escape. Charlemagne gave orders that Renaud was to be killed, but by then the Duke Aymon had gathered together his followers, and there was a great and bloody battle outside the city. Most of the Duke's warriors were slain by the superior forces of the emperor's army, and although his four sons were able to get away, Duke Aymon was taken prisoner by Turpin, the warrior Archbishop of Paris.

Charlemagne demanded from Turpin the life of his captive, but Turpin refused. 'Duke Aymon surrendered to me, and I should be unworthy of my calling if I did not consider his life to be of equal value to my own,' he said. Then Charlemagne pronounced sentence of banishment against the sons of Aymon, and threatened that he would burn at the stake the mother of the man who had killed Louis, even though she was his own sister, Aya. The paladins begged Charlemagne not to be so cruel, and finally he agreed.

'Justice shall yield to mercy,' he said. 'If Aymon and Aya swear to give up their sons as soon as they have an opportunity, they may go free.' In deep distress, weeping bitterly, the Duke of Dordon and his wife gave their word to do so.

Knowing nothing of this, the four brothers went to Dordon, where they found their unhappy mother. She embraced them, and then told them they must flee. She gave them gold and precious stones from Aymon's treasury, and adviced them to go south, towards Toulouse, where the Saracen king Begon ruled over the country of Aquitaine.

They did as their mother had suggested, and they were given a friendly welcome by the king, who promised to reward them well if they would serve him. They fought valiantly on his side in three battles against his enemies, but the king failed to give them any reward. When Renaud asked that they should receive some payment for their services, the king only laughed at him. 'What right have you to ask anything from me? You killed your king, your cousin. Those who kill their king are outlaws. Be silent.'

'That is a mean trick,' Renaud replied, with a threat in his voice.

'We have served you as we promised, and you have not kept your word to us. Give us the treasure that is due to us, and we will go.'

When Begon refused again, Renaud drew his sword and cut off the king's head. 'Tie that head to your saddle, brother,' he said to Alard. 'It will serve us as well as treasure.'

They fought their way out of Begon's castle and then rode to Gascony, where Begon's enemy, King Yon, ruled. The head of his enemy was treasure indeed to Yon, who raised an army and set off to attack Aquitaine. With the help of the four sons of Aymon he succeeded in defeating the Saracen forces.

When the war was finally over, Renaud married Clarissa, the sister of Yon. He built a castle on the top of a white cliff, which he called Montauban, and round the castle grew a village, then a town, as people came to live under the protection of the powerful Count Renaud.

Charlemagne heard about all this, and he sent a message to Yon, demanding that he should yield the sons of Aymon and the castle of Montauban to him. Yon refused, and then Charlemagne laid siege to Montauban, a siege that lasted a full year. But he found the castle was too well protected, and in the end the imperial army marched away.

When there was peace in the countryside once more, Renaud and his brothers decided they would go and visit their mother. They had to go in disguise, of course, for fear of being recognized by Charlemagne's men, so they all grew beards and dressed themselves as pilgrims. No one guessed who they were, and when they reached Dordon they had to convince their parents that they were indeed their sons. Quickly Aya hid them away in a remote part of the castle.

But one of Aymon's knights discovered the secret and told Aymon that he must remember the oath that he had sworn to send his sons as prisoners to the emperor. Aymon picked up a club and killed the man, saying, 'This way I can be sure that you will not harm them.' But he realized that he must keep his oath, and he gave orders for his sons to be made prisoners, knowing very well that they would never give themselves up. There was a fight that lasted for two days, at the end of which the four brothers had defeated the knights of Aymon, and their father was at their mercy. Renaud wanted to kill him, but the other sons pleaded for their father. 'We should be cursed for ever if we were to kill our own father!' they exclaimed. 'Let's send him to the emperor in Paris, as the emperor wanted him to send us.' So Aymon was bound and put on a horse, and a squire was ordered to take him to Charlemagne.

'Give our regards to the emperor!' they told him mockingly. So Aymon was taken to Charlemagne's court. 'I tried to keep my promise to you, sire,' he said, 'but my sons prevented me.' It was not easy for Charlemagne to believe that Aymon had really done his best to defeat his sons.

Charlemagne then led his army to attack Aymon's sons at Dordon. The castle there was not so strong as Montauban, and although Renaud managed to escape, his brothers were all captured and taken to Paris, where the emperor declared that they would be publicly executed.

Meanwhile Renaud made his way to Montauban, where he saddled Bayard and set off towards the capital to try to save his brothers. On the way, he took the rest in the middle of a forest, and feeling safe there, he let Bayard wander freely to browse upon the grass and shoots while he himself fell asleep. Bayard strayed some way from his master's side, and a group of peasants who were passing through the forest recognized the famous horse. They were sure that they would receive a good reward for capturing him, so they made a net of willow boughs and caught the horse in it, and took him to Paris, to Charlemagne, who rewarded them as they had hoped. He gave Bayard to Roland, his favourite nephew.

Charlemagne knew that Renaud could not be far away from the place where Bayard had been found, and so he sent troops to search for him. But they returned empty-handed, having seen no trace of Renaud. Meanwhile Renaud had woken up and discovered the loss of his horse and was surprised to find himself addressed by an old man.

'Why do you look so miserable, Renaud?' the old man asked. This was none other than his own cousin, Maugis, who was a sorcerer. When Renaud had told him what had happened to his father, his brothers and his horse, Maugis said, 'Then we will go to Paris and begin by rescuing Bayard. And this will be easy if you do as I tell you.'

Then he changed Renaud's appearance and made him look a sick and weary pilgrim. They reached Paris without any danger of being recognized, and there they took up a position on the bridge over the Seine by which they knew the Emperor must cross the river on his way to a tournament. Roland was to take part in the jousting, riding Bayard.

By his magic arts Maugis then made a golden cup appear, encrusted with diamonds. As Charlemagne went by, his eye fell on this magnificent-looking object, and he stopped to admire it.

'What is that cup you have there?' he asked the two pilgrims.

'Ah, sire,' replied Maugis, 'this is the Holy Grail from which Christ drank at the Last Supper. The Pope in Rome has blessed it, and to whomsoever drinks from this cup, all his sins are forgiven.'

The emperor, quite believing him, dismounted from his horse, knelt down and asked the pilgrims to allow him to drink from it.

'You are welcome to do so, your Majesty,' answered Maugis, 'if you will grant a boon to my sick brother by permitting him to mount Bayard, just for a moment. He is convinced that if he could only sit astride the famous horse he would be well again.'

Charlemagne gave his permission. He drank from the gold cup, and then Maugis led the disguised Renaud to the field where the tournament was to take place, and Roland, not knowing who he was, helped him to mount Bayard.

Once he was in the saddle, Maugis restored his usual appearance, and Bayard, who had had no doubt of his master's identity, galloped off, pursued by many knights. When they had gone a certain distance and a band of the paladins, including Archbishop Turpin and Roland, had outdistanced the rest of his pursuers, Renaud halted, drew his sword and turned to face them. They were astonished to see who it was, and to learn that the other pilgrim had been Maugis. These knights were more prepared to talk with Renaud than to kill him, for many of them were his cousins, other nephews of the emperor. He asked them about his brothers, and they told him that they were imprisoned in a tower and would soon be executed. Then Renaud begged them to do their best to save his brothers' lives by pleading with the emperor, and this they gladly agreed to do.

But Charlemagne was determined to see his nephews hang. There was a furious argument, and finally Turpin said to the emperor, 'You are not acting with justice. The counts of Dordon are the sons of your own sister. They are also our kinsmen, and I know that they have done nothing to deserve such punishment.'

Very angry, the emperor replied, 'Are you trying to oppose me, Turpin? I have said that they must die.'

'And we are determined that they shall not die.'

'I have said that they must pay with their lives.'

'And we have given our word that they shall live.'

Then the emperor, mad with rage, struck the Archbishop. Turpin seized Charlemagne by the throat, and he would have strangled him if the paladins had not intervened.

'Am I not the emperor?' Charlemagne shouted furiously. 'Have I not power to carry out my decisions? Who dares to oppose me?'

'I, sire,' replied the Archbishop. 'I must defend justice.' And he

40

returned to the paladins and said, 'Take your stand beside me, do not abandon me.' And all the paladins lined up with Turpin, facing the angry emperor.

'Are you against me too, then, Roland?' the emperor asked sadly. And the knight replied, 'Forgive me, sire, but it is not right or just for me to fail to defend the lives of my cousins, even if you have decided that they must die.' So, very unwillingly, the emperor granted the lives of the sons of Aymon. That same night, using his magic powers, Maugis helped them to escape from prison and took them back to Montauban.

Charlemagne was still obsessed with the idea of giving what he considered well-deserved punishment to his sister's sons. He was almost equally determined to get hold of Bayard, or of some horse as good as him. He proclaimed that there would be a race to discover which was the swiftest horse in the kingdom, and he had made a splendid golden crown as a prize for the winner.

Maugis heard about the race and said to Renaud, 'That prize is yours for the taking, cousin. Will you enter with Bayard?' Renaud laughed and said, 'I should be recognized at once and flung into prison!' So Maugis changed his cousin's appearance again, and made him look like a very young knight, and he turned Bayard, who was as black as night, into a white horse. Off they went to Paris, where nobody guessed who they were, although both horse and rider were greatly admired. 'If you didn't know that Bayard was a black horse,' people said, 'you'd think that white horse was him!'

Of course Renaud and Bayard easily won the prize, and Charlemagne offered the young knight, in addition to the gold crown, four times the weight of the horse in gold, and any price he wished to ask, if he would sell it to him. Then the count laughed and said, 'Don't you recognize me, your majesty? I am your nephew, Renaud of Dordon, and this is Bayard, and you know that I wouldn't sell him for anything in the world!' Then he rode off as fast as the wind, with Maugis mounted behind him.

Once more Charlemagne was furiously angry. He raised an army and set off to conquer Montauban once and for all. There was a long siege, but the emperor could not make his enemies surrender. In the course of one of the battles, however, Maugis was taken prisoner. The paladins led him before Charlemagne, who had always hated him, thinking he must be some sort of devil because of his magic powers, and he pronounced sentence of death on him.

'Could I just advise you first to make peace with the sons of Aymon, sire?' Maugis said. 'Then they can help you in the war you must fight against the Saracens instead of having to kill your soldiers.' Charlemagne shook his head. 'There is only one person I detest more than you, and that is my nephew Renaud. I should like to see you hang side by side.'

The sorcerer asked for the execution to be postponed until the following day, so that he could have time to prepare himself for death and to repent of all his sins. And he added with a smile, 'I promise you, sire, that I shall not escape unless you yourself come with me.'

Without saying another word, Charlemagne had him put into prison. But during the night Maugis released himself and went unseen to the emperor's bedchamber. The emperor was deeply asleep. 'Get up, your majesty,' said Maugis, 'it is time to go.' Without waking up, Charlemagne was transported to Renaud's castle and laid on a bed there.

When he awoke, to his surprise he saw Renaud and his brothers standing before him. Renaud at once knelt and begged the emperor to forget the past, to accept the loyal service of Duke Aymon and his sons, and to bring peace to the countryside again. When Charlemagne angrily refused to reach any agreement with them, Alard moved forward with drawn sword to kill him, but Renaud stopped him. 'Return to your camp, sire,' he said, 'and answer us as you will. We are ready for your answer, whatever it may be.'

Charlemagne replied by renewing the siege of Montauban, and soon there was no food left in the castle. Renaud said to his wife Clarissa, 'Now we have eaten all the horses except Bayard. It is only fair that I should kill him too, and share the meat out among our men.' But the Duchess and Richard, Renaud's brother, begged him to spare the horse. 'He has served us faithfully and well. We owe our lives to him,' they said. And as if Bayard had understood what was being said, the horse knelt too, and looked at Renaud, with such loyalty and humility that Renaud could not bring himself to kill his horse. Instead he drew blood from him every day, and with that his men were nourished. So Bayard saved his master's life once again.

Meanwhile Archbishop Turpin learnt that the brothers of Aymon had no food left, and he said to Roland and the other paladins that it was shameful to let their cousins die of starvation. Secretly they sent food and drink into the castle, and they told Charlemagne that they thought they would never be able to capture Montauban.

The Duchess Aya journeyed to her brother to beg him to relent and to grant her sons his pardon. She pleaded too on behalf of the mothers whose sons and husbands were fighting in the war, who had to bear the burning of their homes, the ruining of their crops and livestock, all because of the emperor's determination to defeat her sons.

42

At last Charlemagne was moved by her pleading and he agreed that he would end his siege and let peace return to the countryside. But he made two conditions: Renaud must give up Bayard, and go on a pilgrimage to Jerusalem.

Aya went back to her sons and told them what the emperor had said. Alard shook his head and refused to consider for a moment paying such a price for peace. Richard and Guichard agreed with him, but Renaud had the final word. 'If that is the condition on which the emperor is willing to make peace with us,' he said, 'we must agree. It would be wrong to go on fighting if he is prepared to stop.' And so after many years of warfare and hatred, there came peace.

When Bayard was handed over to Charlemagne, he ordered that weights were to be tied to the horse's hooves, and he was to be thrown into the river. But the horse managed to free himself of the stones that had been fastened to make him drown, and he swam to the river bank and stood by his master as though nothing unusual had happened.

Everyone who was present at that scene was amazed. Alard said to Richard, 'We must not allow another attempt to kill such a noble animal in such a cruel way. We should be despised for ever.' But the emperor insisted that the horse must be drowned. The second attempt was equally unsuccessful. The third time, the emperor gave orders for a millstone to be tied around Bayard's neck as well, and again the horse was cast into the river. As he sank beneath the surface of the water, Bayard raised his head and looked at Renaud as one human being looks pleadingly at another. Renaud closed his eyes, he could not bear to watch, and as the valiant horse disappeared beneath the water, everyone wept. He had paid the price of peace.

However according to some people even the third time the horse succeeded in ridding himself of the stones that were dragging him down to the bottom of the river, and again he swam to the shore. But this time he knew that Renaud could not help him, and he galloped away, free, to the forest of Ardennes. And he is still there. On a quiet day, his neighing can be heard in the depths of the forest.

Renaud returned to Montauban and said to Clarissa, 'I shall never ride another horse. Now that I have lost Bayard, I will be a knight no longer.' He gave the lordship of his lands to his sons, Aymonet and Yon, said goodbye to his wife, and started off on the pilgrimage to Jerusalem that was the emperor's second condition for peace. When he got to the Holy Land, he found that the Saracens were besieging Jerusalem, in far greater numbers than those of the Christians who were defending the city. Armed only with his pilgrim's staff, Renaud rallied the Christian forces into an attack, won a great victory and captured the sultan. Then he arranged an honourable peace settlement. As a result, Renaud was asked to be king of Jerusalem, but he refused it, saying, 'Choose someone more worthy than I am to rule and protect the holy city. I have sworn to serve God only with my bare hands, so let me go in peace.'

Renaud sailed back to France, and was soon back at Montauban. To his great sorrow he found that his wife, Clarissa, had died while he had been on pilgrimage. His two sons, however, had grown into fine young men, and they had successfully defended their lands against treacherous enemies who had tried to take advantage of Renaud's absence and their youth. Then he set off as a poor pilgrim again, and this time he made his way on foot to Paris.

News of his great feats in the Holy Land had preceded him, and he was welcomed at court with great honour, where Charlemagne asked him to remain as his courtier and councillor. But Renaud answered, 'I am no longer a knight, your majesty, and I have sworn to serve God in humility and poverty. I have lived long enough to understand that there is no real happiness to be found on earth in power or glory or riches, but only within oneself.'

Once more he returned to Montauban. His quarrel with the emperor was forgotten, his sons were worthy knights, his own fame was widespread. One night, while every one slept, Renaud rose without a sound, and barefoot, dressed in his oldest and poorest clothes, he descended the steps of his castle for the last time.

When he came to the gate, the gate-keeper was surprised to see him preparing to go out into the countryside at that hour of night without his sword, armour or horse. 'Sir,' he warned him, 'you have many enemies. It is dangerous for you to go out unarmed.' Renaud smiled, and told the gate-keeper to pray for him, and he gave him a message for his sons and brothers. 'Tell them to rule my lands as I have ruled them. Tell them I go to save my soul and that they will not see me again. And tell them I bid them farewell.'

Then Renaud noticed that he was still wearing his favourite ring. He took it off and gave it to the gate-keeper saying, 'You have served me long and faithfully. Take this in return for your service.' Then he passed through the gate and disappeared into the night. In the morning the members of his household were very sad when they heard the news the gate-keeper had to tell them. Renaud's sons and brothers searched for him a long time, but in vain. No one could discover what had become of him.

Renaud had gone deep into a forest and there he lived on herbs in a cave as a hermit, and prayed all day and most of the night to be forgiven for all his sins. But after a time he felt that this was not the best use of his time and his strength, and that God would be more ready to forgive him if he did something useful. So he left the forest and travelled wherever his feet took him, without noticing where he was, and one day he found himself at Cologne, where the monastery of St. Peter was being built. This was just the kind of work he had been hoping for. It was something useful he could do well.

He asked the master-mason to give him a trial. 'You look more like a king or a count than a labourer,' the man said. He pointed to a heavy boulder. 'See if you can lift that.' Renaud picked it up as if it had been a piece of paper, and the master-mason agreed that he could join the builders. Renaud was so strong that he did the work of four ordinary men. He mixed mortar, he carried wooden beams, and the heaviest stones were like feathers to him. He would accept no more wages than the bread he needed to keep him going, he drank nothing but water, and he worked while the others rested.

Everyone was full of praise for this exceptional workman — except the other labourers. They were not only jealous of him, they were afraid that they might lose their jobs because of him, for he did so much and asked for so little. So they decided they must get rid of him. Early in the morning, when he was going peacefully towards his work, a gang of them set on him with sticks and hammers. The noble knight who had won so many victories in battle with his sword was killed in the end by a workman's tool. Then they weighted his body with stones and threw it into the river Rhine.

But Renaud had been so saintly in his last years that God granted him a miracle. Thousands of little fishes gathered together, and instead of sinking, his body was carried by them down the river, held up to the surface by their combined efforts, and a great light shone from it.

Crowds of people thronged the banks of the river and the bridges over it, the Archbishop and all the church dignitaries came to witness the miracle, and the workmen who had killed him had to confess to their crime.

Renaud's body was taken from the river and reverently placed on a cart in order to take it to the church for burial. Nobody in Cologne knew that this was the great Renaud of Montauban, but then another miracle took place.

Without being drawn by horses or pushed by men, the cart started moving of its own accord. It went along the road, followed by the Archbishop and the church dignitaries and a crowd of people, all eager to follow the cart until it stopped. It went all the way to Dortmund, and along the route bells rang out without men touching the ropes, the sick were healed, the blind saw and the lame walked. When it came to

Dortmund, where the church of St. Renaud stands today, it stopped, and the bishop there, who had known Renaud as a knight, recognized who lay in the miraculous cart.

It is said that Renaud performed other miracles after his death. One day, when the city of Dortmund was being besieged, the figure of the saint was seen standing on the city wall, stretching out his hand towards the enemy. They took fright and fled, leaving the city unharmed. Since that day, St. Renaud has been the patron saint of Dortmund.

THE REVENGE OF THE MICE

In the old German legend of the mouse tower of Bingen, a stony-hearted bishop met a miserable end, trapped on a rock in the great river Rhine. Austria has a similar tale to tell.

Deep in the forests which line the river Inn lies the lovely, calm little lake of Holtzoester. The people who are drawn to its banks today to drink in its peace and beauty little know the dreadful history of this picturesque spot, which was once the domain of the great Counts of Franking.

The last of that honourable and noble line was a savage and pitiless man. The fate of his subjects meant little to him: he cared for nothing but his own comfort.

'Why should I offer people help or hospitality?' he would say. 'Loving my neighbour won't do me much good.'

His tastes were quite different. He was not even content with shutting passing merchants in his dungeons and demanding ransoms, but would lock away beggars and tramps and any unsuspecting stranger who unknowingly set foot on his land, leaving them to die a lingering death on their diet of bread and water. Anyone unlucky enough to get in his way, to glance at him once too often, to dare to answer back or even simply to displease him was condemned to end his days in the dungeon. It was a sentence of death passed solely by this evil man, without judge or witnesses, without law or mercy.

Yet this did not prevent the Count from throwing sumptuous banquets, with tables piled high with delicacies and the choicest wines flowing like water. On great occasions the master of the house would lead his guests to the dungeons, have the trapdoor opened and say playfully, 'Listen! What can you hear?'

Overcome with horror, the fine ladies and splendid lords could hear, through the stink from the dungeons, the shrieks and groans of the wretched, innocent victims. But the Count would roar with laughter, and say, 'That's the mice from my attics. Isn't it fun to hear them squeak?'

Some of the Count's guests were themselves hard, cruel men, uncaring of others and full of contempt for the human race. Even so, every one of them felt his blood run cold. As the years went by, visitors became rarer and rarer, until at last the Count was left all alone in his great hall, taking his meals in gloomy solitude.

Even the menservants and maids left him one by one, not simply because they could endure his maltreatment no longer, but because they would sooner die than serve such an evil master. Only a single old, greying valet remainded faithful to him. And since the Count no longer had anyone to impose his will on, he took out his anger on his dogs, beat his horses and laid into his cats.

The end was not far off. Over the years real mice and rats had invaded his castle. First in the cellars and then in the attics they spread and multiplied, making ever more daring raids on his pantries, storerooms and granaries.

The Count sent his cats to hunt them down, but they were too frightened to touch the voracious rodents. He sent in his dogs, but that too was in vain: they soon fled yelping, their tails between their legs. Whenever night fell there was an infernal noise. An army of mice and rats would dance on his tables and benches, devour his corn and meat and cheese, gnaw at his carpets, his books and even the sheets on his bed. Some of the braver ones would even take a fancy to the end of his nose or his toes and begin to nibble at them. Sleep was impossible. Fear filled him night and day, and he grew thinner and thinner.

Then, in the nick of time, he had an ingenious idea. He would built a little castle on the island in his lake — that lovely, calm little lake.

'Rodents hate water,' he thought. 'They'll never venture there.'

No sooner said than done! He engaged an army of workmen at fabulous wages, and they hurried to erect his new retreat. The moment it was ready the Count had his one faithful old retainer row him over to the island, where he fell at once into the deep, refreshing slumber he had so sorely missed.

But the next morning, when he looked out of his window to savour his new-found peace and quiet, he trembled at the sight that met his eyes.

A legion of mice was advancing on the island. With them came the rats: tough water rats, easy-going house rats. The procession of rodents was endless. They were rowing over to him on planks and boards, in cases and boxes, in pots and pans. Uttering little cries and squeaks, they showed their menacing teeth, a strange light shining in their eyes.

When the old servant saw the procession of vengeful animals, even he took fright. Forgetting his master in his panic, he jumped into the only boat and rowed frantically to the far bank, never to return.

Beside himself with terror, the Count had no choice but to lock himself in his bedroom. It was to no avail. The sharp teeth of the rodents gnawed a way at the wooden door, and soon they were upon him. This time it was his shrieks that were to be ignored. Before long they had devoured him, to the very last lock of his hair.

The ancestral stronghold was soon a ruin. The little castle on the

48

island gradually crumbled away to dust, and in the end the little island itself was swallowed up into the depths of the lake. The evil deeds of that one man had brought about the end of an illustrious line, and the revenge of the mice was complete.

THE GODS WITH ANIMAL HEADS

From the dawn of time the people of Egypt felt close to nature, even seeing their gods as natural forces. For nothing will thrive in a desert, and in Egypt the crops cannot grow unless the great River Nile brings them water. So Egyptians pray every year that the Nile will overflow its banks and fertilize their fields.

In ancient Egypt people thought animals had souls, just as men did. Even the trees, plants and boulders were seen as living beings, with friendly or hostile moods. Some animals were actually sacred. Hares, jackals, vultures, baboons and more besides were thought to be gods in animal form, and able to protect people. So many of the Egyptian gods were shown with animal heads.

The moon god Thoth wore the head of a baboon or the sacred ibis bird. Amon, greatest of the gods of Thebes, had a ram or goat's head.

The falcon circling in the blue skies of ancient Egypt was seen as a special protector of kings and men. In the desert at Memphis, where many of the ancient pharaohs are buried in a great necropolis, a statue of a falcon stands in the sand, watching over the mummies of the dead and keeping their bodies intact to ensure they are immortal. The god Sokaris there has a falcon's head. At Edfu in Upper Egypt the priests built a huge statue of a falcon before the temple of the sky god Horus; and at Giza, near Cairo, another falcon representing Horus stands in the temple of the dead of the second pyramid, receiving symbols of life and joy from the local god, who appears as a standing wolf.

When the young sun god was born, Thoueris attended in the form of a female hippopotamus with woman's arms. The god Khnum, who created humans on his potter's wheel, has a ram's head, and the goddess Hekat who helps him wears the head of a frog. In the Egyptians' eyes even live-stock and wild animals had supernatural powers.

The cow was a particularly sacred animal. A hundred years ago the penalty for killing a cow in Egypt was still death, and even today cows are sacred in India. The ancient Egyptians believed the cows were the gods' companions even before the world was made. In those times beyond memory, they said, the sacred cow Ahet carried the young sun god between her horns.

Gods would often turn into a cow or bull as a sign of their invincible strength. The god Horus sometimes wore a bull's head instead of appearing as a falcon. The priests and the people worshipped statues of bulls in temples, seeing them as the souls of the gods. Isis, mother of

51

Horus the sky god, might wear a cow's horns. Isis sided with Horus when he fought his father's murderer, the god Set, who took the form of a hippopotamus.

The greatest cow goddess went back to prehistoric times. Hathor, lady of the west, appeared, they say, on the west bank of the Nile near Thebes, and fed on clumps of grass and swamp papyrus. Sometimes she had a woman's face and a cow's ears, and often she wore a cow's horns with the disc of the sun held between them.

One story says that she went to meet a dead pharaoh in the guise of a goddess of death, to bid him welcome to the world of shadows. When the pharaoh Rameses II ruled some 3300 years ago, the sacred cow Hathor was his divine protectress and fed him with her milk. She ruled all the gods and was mistress of the sky.

One day, the legends say, when a queen was governing Egypt, Hathor went to her.

'Beloved daughter,' she said to the queen. 'I am your mother, and your beauty is my doing. It was I who put you on the throne of Horus.'

She went up to the throne and licked the queen's hand, as a mother animal does to her young.

'I lick your arm, my darling daughter, and your body. You shall live and be happy for ever. You have fed on my milk, and my wisdom is in you. I will protect you from evil, as is the will of your father Ra.'

The bull god, who was standing behind the cow, now came up to the queen.

'I have come to protect you, beloved daughter,' he said. 'I give you the herds of cattle which graze in the marshes of the Nile delta. I will make your herds multiply, and I will create a sacred cow, Hesat, so that you live forever and the famine spares your people. Hesat will live in Upper Egypt.'

That is how the capital of the province of Messer in Upper Egypt came to be called Tep-Jehn, capital of the sacred cow. Hesat lived there in a temple in the care of the most important priests. If the king came to the town, he would bring the animal a pitcher of milk as a sacrifice.

Hesat was immortal. When one sacred cow died, the priests would choose another so that there was always a Hesat there, filled with the spirit of the gods.

Ancient Egyptian writings tell us that in 310 BC, when the king Ptolemy I Soter was on the throne, the sacred cow of the time was fourteen years old. One morning one of the stable boys found her stretched out dead on the ground. In great distress he called the priest, who confirmed that Hesat was dead.

'Her majesty Hesat has been struck down,' he announced to the High

Priest and the guardians of the temple, in a voice trembling with emotion.

The gods and their servants bowed in homage, and before the assembled priests the scribe in charge of the holy book made the solemn declaration that was laid down in the scriptures:

'At the third hour of this day, the soul of her majesty Isis Hesat rose to the ocean in the sky, to become one with Ra, the sun.'

The priests murmured magic words. Then they carried the sacred cow's tail across the temple to drive out evil spirits. Finally the servants of the gods marched in procession to Hesat's stable with four embalmers. The statues of the gods and sacred animals bowed to Hesat's body, and the High Priest paid tribute to her.

Soon the sad news spread throughout the capital and the province. Memorial ceremonies took place far and wide in honour of the noble animal. Hesat was embalmed and then buried with much pomp and circumstance.

A new sacred cow was chosen at once. She was given the name of Melet-veret, the great cow of the ocean in the sky. This time it was a joyful procession that went to the stable in the temple, as the priests and the faithful accompanied her to her quarters.

In the second month of the rising of the Nile, on the seventh day, the priests erected a monument to Hesat. To this day you can see it in Cairo, in the Egyptian Museum. There, Hesat lies on a pedestal, while four falcon wings carry the sun disc. To left and right there are sceptres decorated with jackal heads. A statue of the sun god in the guise of a falcon watches over Hesat. There is also a scorpion, the sacred animal of the goddess of life, so often menaced by the scorpion's deadly sting. The priest of the dead and King Ptolemy approach the goddess with respect, to pray and bring her their offerings.

For in times past people did not think themselves masters of nature, with the right to change or destroy it as the fancy took them. Instead they sought to be at one with nature, and this is why the Egyptians held animals sacred.

TALES ABOUT AN ISLAND

Off the north-west coast of Germany, just where Denmark begins to jut out towards Norway and Sweden, lies a long, thin island called Sylt. Those who live there, and indeed the people who live on the whole string of islands that continues down along the German coast and the coast of Holland too, are Friesians, and the islands, many of them favourite places for seaside holidays, are known as the Friesian Islands. From these islands came the ancestors of the black-and-white cows that are so familiar in our fields; and the language that the Friesian people speak is more like English than any other. The people of Sylt have always been sailors and fishermen and whalers, and the name of their island comes from the Danish word for herring. For their coat of arms they have a silver herring on a blue and white background. It's not surprising that they thought of their island as a ship, and that, long ago, they even thought of the world as a huge vessel, the Mannigfual.

There is now a seven-mile dam with a railway running along it, which joins the island to the mainland, and in summertime tens of thousands of holiday-makers lie in the sun on the sandy beaches. But when the holidays are over, the island is a different place, lonely and sad, with pelting rain lashing the place as though it was trying to destroy it, and howling winds drowning the mournful cry of the seagulls.

The people of Sylt say that these winds and the raging stormy waves they bring are all the fault of a Danish king from long ago. This king had promised to marry an English queen, but he broke his promise and jilted her. In those far-off times, it is said, there was a mountain range, the Hoveden, joining England to France and so protecting the North Sea. Garhoven, the English queen, gave orders that a passage should be made in the mountain wall, so that the waters of the Atlantic ocean could pour into the North Sea and flood the coast of Denmark. The breach was made, and the Atlantic waters raced up the channel towards the north. Hundreds of thousands of people were drowned along the Friesian and Danish coasts, and the name of the faithless Danish king disappeared too, for the few survivors were forbidden ever to mention him. So Garhoven had her revenge.

There was in fact a terrible high tidal wave which hit those coasts in about the year 600. The Friesian land was broken up into four parts, and the coast to this day looks as though it had been torn up, very untidily.

When the dangerous breakers arrive from the north-west, the islanders say that it is because of Pitje of Scotland. He is the lord of the winds, who lives in the mountains of Scotland, and from there, as his fancy takes him, he sends misfortune of one kind or another — like terrible storms, high tides and ship wrecks. Dykes are breached, harvests are bad, and there is disease and death. For the islanders, Pitje is the devil himself.

Sylt was still joined to the mainland by a narrow strip of land until another terrible high tide in 1634, and the fear that there may be more flooding must always haunt the islanders.

The lagoons between the island and the mainland are shallow, and were once the haunt of sorcerers, gnomes and good and bad spirits. Some people say they still lurk among the sand-dunes, and you can sometimes hear their mocking laughter as they bustle about among the shoals and on the sandy heathlands of Sylt. All over the island there are little mounds, called Hoogs, and these are really tombs which were made long ago, probably in the Bronze Age. But people used to think that they were underground castles, and that the stone axes and flint spearheads that were found near them had been made by the gnomes in their underground workshops.

There were giants, too, on Sylt. These were fierce, dangerous giants, five or six metres high. They had a watch-tower and three forts on the island, and one of them, the castle of Tinnum, is still standing. The largest of the giants' tombs is near the Kampen lighthouse. There lies Brons, the king of the giants, killed in battle against the gnomes. He was buried in his war-chariot of solid gold, but if anyone ever dared to break into Bronshoog, a mysterious unseen hand gave him a terrible beating. When this became known, no one ever went looking for treasure there again.

There is another legend about one of these hoogs, the Klowenhoog. It is called after another king who was Klow, king of the seas. He is believed to be buried in it in a golden galley. Klow had great power over the sea. Like Pitje of Scotland, he could make the waves grow into towering breakers whenever he wanted. He could raise storms and squalls, and he could cause death and misery whenever he pleased. The waters around Sylt are very dangerous indeed. There is a cemetery called the Graveyard of the Homeless, full of the graves of strangers without a name, sailors whose bodies the sea has washed up on shore.

Very sinister and suspicious things happen when Klow, king of the seas, has his way with the wind, they say. On Christmas night 1713, there was a terrible storm, and a ship from one of the ports on the island was wrecked on the shoals south of Westerland, on its west coast. All the crew were drowned except for the pilot, Manne Tetten, who managed to reach the shore by clinging to a wooden chest.

Although it was Christmas night, there were robbers on the lookout for victims, and they killed the unfortunate pilot as he scrambled ashore, shivering and exhausted. Then they buried him in a hollow among the dunes near the old jetty. Well, they tried to bury him! They could not conceal the body completely because one of the dead man's arms raised itself, with the fist clenched threateningly, above the surface of the sand. For several hours the murderers tried to bury the arm and its clenched fist below the ground, but it was useless, they found that they just could not do it and the arm was bound to give them away. Then they were filled with panic and one of the robbers took an axe and chopped off the forearm. But the bloody stump of arm again thrust itself through the sand, terrifying the slayers. Leaving the chest, which they had found to be full of silver, they fled away as fast as they could. The next day a fisherman passing that way found the chest and the arm. Since then the ghost of Manne Tetten haunts that part of the jetty on stormy nights. The local people call it the Dikjendeelmann, the Jetty Devil-man.

The best-known name in the history of the island is that of Pidder Lung — Long Peter. He lived in Sylt around 1500, and in the eyes not only of the inhabitants of that island, but for all the Friesian islanders, he was a bold, daring hero and a champion of freedom.

In those days the district was governed for the king by a magistrate who lived in the mainland town of Tonder. Henning Pogwisch was a cruel and tyrannical man whose only concern was to get as much money as he possibly could from the people over whom he had been given power. His helpers in this despicable work were his own sons. One day he sent his eldest son and a troop of soldiers to collect taxes from the unwilling fishermen, who could do little about it, since the magistrate had power and they had none.

At midday, Pidder Lung was sitting down to dinner with his parents and brothers and sisters when young Pogwisch and the soldiers burst in, uninvited and without so much as a by-your-leave. The islanders were eating a dish of green cabbage, which was all that they could afford to eat in the middle of the day. Pogwisch sniffed and made a face and said contemptuously, 'That stuff stinks, is it for the pigs?' No one answered. Then Pogwisch put on an important air and said, 'I've come to collect your taxes. Are you going to need help to find the money, or will you do it willingly?'

Pidder Lung was then about twenty-eight years old, a real giant of a man. He looked the young tyrant up and down scornfully, with half-closed eyes, and answered, very slowly, 'The islanders of Sylt are free men. No one has the right to claim taxes from us.' Pogwisch laughed. 'You free men!' he sneered. 'You're fishermen, you don't count for anything. Don't make me laugh!' And he spat right into the middle of the dish of cabbage.

Then Pidder got up, his eyes blazing. When Pogwisch saw his size, and the expression on his face, he turned pale, and drew back in fear. But Pidder got hold of him by the scruff of his neck and pushed his face into the pot of hot cabbage and held it there, saying, 'He who spits into cabbage must eat it!' So Pogwisch was smothered to death in the cabbage, as every Frieslander knows. Then Pidder Lung attacked the soldiers, repaying with a blow every penny that the soldiers had taken. Bruised and battered, they returned to Tonder with their dead leader.

However, the magistrate had a representative on the island, Erk Mannis, and to escape punishment for his bold action, Pidder had to flee from his home. He collected around him a band of desperadoes, for many rebels, and pirates, and sailors who had deserted from their ships, joined him, and soon Pidder Lung's pirate fleet was feared up and down the coast. From his masthead flew a flag, not with a skull and crossbones, but with a gallows painted on it, and the motto *Better dead than a slave*.

Pidder and his gang mostly attacked rich merchant ships, and they raided wealthy towns. He boasted of being 'the scourge of the Danes, the bane of Bremen, the crusher of Hamburg, the terror and oppressor of the Dutch'.

For many years Pidder Lung harried the coasts and sea-routes of the North Sea and the Baltic. But when he eventually returned to visit Sylt, in 1518, Erk Mannis was still waiting for him. He was arrested, and hanged on the gallows near Keiten.

THE TREASURE OF SOEST

North-west of the Rhön mountains in Germany is the city of Soest, an old city which still has its medieval walls and gates and many fine buildings which were put up in the Middle Ages. So old is the town that some of the houses have been lived in for over a thousand years, and in an ancient cemetery there are tombs in which were found jewellery, coins and cooking pots from long ago. That is perhaps one reason why the local people have believed that somewhere near the city a fabulous treasure lies waiting to be discovered — and a beautiful girl waits to be released from enchantment. The treasure is believed to be buried in the ruins of a castle — or perhaps, some say, in an old tumbledown cowshed, or, according to others, on the site where a house once stood. Nobody is very sure, no one living knows exactly where it is nor ever knew anyone who did know. The treasure, they all say, is locked up in an iron chest and is guarded by an enchanted princess and a black dog.

In the distant past many knights went to Soest, hoping to rescue the princess. According to the legend, the rescuer had to be a young nobleman who had never been suckled by a woman. First of all he had to find the treasure, then free the princess, and then open the chest with a fiery key. If he did this he would inherit a kingdom and become enormously rich.

As the centuries passed, treasure-seekers of all kinds made their way to Soest in large numbers: tramps, noble lords, poor students, greedy idlers and simple-minded peasants. But no one ever found the princess, or happiness either, for the place where they looked seemed sinister and haunted, and they were quite glad to get away from it still alive.

One day a little girl from a village near Soest was looking after her goats. As they grazed, the goats kept moving further and further away from the village. The little girl followed them, and without noticing what was happening, she found herself at the sinister place where the treasure was supposed to be hidden. Suddenly a beautiful young lady, whom she had never seen before, appeared.

'What are you doing here?' asked the unknown lady.

'Forgive me, lady, if I am doing wrong, but I was just looking for food for my goats, and a few berries for myself, because I am hungry.'

The lady pointed to a basket full of cherries, and said, 'Help yourself, child, and then go. You must never come here again, and you must never speak to anyone of what you have seen here, or you will have great misfortune in your life.'

The little girl thanked the young lady, and went off with her goats. But when she tried to eat the cherries, she saw that they were made of pure gold. She ran home quickly to show them to her brothers, and of course they wanted to know at once where she had got them from. But the little girl never dared to tell them, so afraid was she of how the lady might punish her if she disobeyed her command.

According to the legend, the princess and her dog still guard the treasure of Soest, and she still awaits the man never suckled by a woman who will come and free her from enchantment.

THE RABBI AND THE SORCERER

Long ago in Poland there was a Jewish rabbi whose name was Baal-Chem. He was travelling homewards, to a place called Miedzyborze, with some of his students after a visit to Berlin. One evening, as dusk fell, he entered a Jewish inn. He found the inn-keeper in a very worried state, not at all willing to let strangers into the house, which is unusual in an inn-keeper. There were many candles burning, and Baal-Chem asked the man, 'What's happening? Why are there so many candles, why are you so anxious and why don't you want to let anyone into your inn?'

'Because tomorrow my baby son is going to be circumcised,' answered the inn-keeper. The rabbi was very surprised. 'But that is an occasion for feasting and laughter, not for tears,' he said.

'Not for me, rabbi,' the man answered. 'I have had five sons, and each one of them has died at midnight on the night before his circumcision, in mysterious circumstances and without any sign of illness. This time I am going to spend the night by my son's bed in the hope of preventing such a thing happening again.'

Baal-Chem thought that there must be something magic involved, and he said to the inn-keeper, 'I will see if I can help you.' He ordered his students to hold a sack open beside the baby's bed.

'When midnight strikes, you will see or hear something fall into the sack,' he told them. 'When that happens, pull the strings quickly to shut the sack, and wake me up at once.'

At midnight a storm broke, the candles blew out, and all of a sudden a cat, from nowhere at all, fell into the sack. The men pulled the cord to close it up, and then woke the rabbi. 'Now get some sticks and give the sack a good beating,' he ordered. The students found some sticks and started to hit the sack. When the rabbi thought that they had done enough, he told them to untie the sack and throw it out into the street.

The baby survived the excitements of the night and was duly circumcised next day, lying on the rabbi's lap. The inn-keeper was very relieved and greatful, and he begged the rabbi to stay for the party.

'All I have to do now,' he said, 'is to take some gingerbread as a present to the lord of the castle, since he had said that he wants some.' As he said this, the man started trembling all over.

'What are you afraid of?' asked the rabbi.

'The lord is a bad man, Baal-Chem. All us Jews are afraid of him.'

'Go without fear, my friend. God will protect you,' said the rabbi. The lord of the castle was not in the castle courtyard, where he usually met the inn-keeper, but he was in bed, ill. Very humbly and fearfully the inn-keeper went to his bedchamber, and offered him the gingerbread.

'Who have you got staying with you?' the lord cried. 'Who is that man?'

'He is a noble Jew from Miedzyborze, sir, a learned rabbi. He has saved my son's life.'

'Tell him to come and see me.'

The inn-keeper ran home and said to Baal-Chem, 'Go, go now, rabbi, don't stay a moment longer! The lord of the castle says he wants to see you, and that is a very bad sign.'

'I am not afraid of him,' said the rabbi, and he set off for the castle.

The lord looked at him intently, with more curiosity than hostility. 'You attacked and ill-treated me,' he said.

Baal-Chem agreed. 'You are a sorcerer, and you took on the form of a cat to suffocate the inn-keeper's innocent baby, as you have killed many others before. With God's help, I was stronger than your magic.'

The lord of the castle looked at him now with hatred. 'I was taken by surprise. Will you agree to have a duel with me, to see which of us is the greater magician?'

The rabbi said that he was quite willing, and they decided that the encounter would take place in a certain field, in the presence of their respective supporters. The lord summoned other sorcerers, Baal-Chem collected together his students and other travelling-companions. He drew a circle around them, and another round himself.

'Watch my face,' he told his disciples. 'As soon as you see my face change so that I begin to look a different person, you must start at once to pray to God that He will come to my aid. That's all.'

The lord of the castle also drew a circle around his supporters and one around himself. Then he sent a cat to attack the rabbi. But as soon as the cat reached the circle, it vanished into thin air, leaving no trace. The lord gave a wicked smile. Then he sent a dog, a wolf, and finally a bear to attack the rabbi, but the power of Baal-Chem made them all disappear one after the other. The lord summoned up all manner of other animals, ordering them to attack the rabbi and destroy him, but none of them had any power against him.

Finally there came a herd of wild boar, breathing fire, and they rushed upon Baal-Chem and broke through his circle. Then the rabbi's face began to change. He looked upwards and his features gradually became unearthly. As he had ordered them, his students called upon God and prayed fervently that the rabbi would be granted greater strength.

62

When the boars came to the second circle there was a sudden cloud of smoke, and the animals disappeared into it. This all happened twice more. Then the sorcerer came out of his circle and said to Baal-Chem, 'I acknowledge that you are stronger than I am. My strength is fading away. Let me take leave of the world before you kill me with the force of your gaze.'

The rabbi answered, 'If I had wanted to kill you, you would not be talking to me now. I only wanted to prove to you the existence of God, and that I can do more with His help than you can with your magic. Look upwards.'

When the lord of the castle raised his eyes, two stags came running across the field towards him, and they drove the points of their antlers into his eyes. He was blinded, and so he was never able to make use of his magic powers again.

WHEN THE FIRE CAME DOWN FROM HEAVEN

Near the foot of Mont Blanc lies the Mer de Glace, the Sea of Ice, green, sparkling, and very cold. The people who live above Chamonix say that once, where the ice now lies deep, there were flowery green meadows and flourishing farm lands. The tender grass fed healthy herds of cows, and when winter came the barns were full to the roof with hay and grain. Nature was very generous here.

But the peasants who lived on this fertile plateau were very mean and hard-hearted. God watched them for a long time, hoping to see some sign of their selfishness changing to kindness, but He watched in vain. Everyone knows that it is easier to find a needle in a hay-stack than to find a spark of pity or generosity in a heart where avarice has taken root.

All the same, God thought He would give them one more chance to show that they were capable of changing their ways, before condemning them forever. So He sent an angel down to earth, disguised as a bent old man, and he went from door to door, begging for bread or help of some kind. But all that he received was curses, insults and many ways of saying no, which were no use for eating. Finally the angel visited the last house on the high plateau. A fat, red-cheeked peasant came to the door, and when the angel asked him for some bread, he just scowled without saying a word. 'It is so cold, sir. Will you let an old man sleep in your straw this chilly night?'

'Go away, you old beggar!'

'For the love of God...'

'Quick, before I get a stick to you.' And the door slammed in the angel's face.

Now this peasant had a daughter, about eight or nine years old. She was a sweet-natured little thing, and she had been watching the poor old man dragging himself from house to house in vain. She stole a crust of bread from the kitchen, ran after the stranger and offered it to him.

Then a miraculous thing happened. Before the little girl's eyes, and seen only by her, the old bent beggar changed into a shining angel. The little girl's mouth opened wide in surprise. The angel said to her, 'Don't be afraid, little girl. Go quickly, and get whatever is dearest to you in the world, and then run away to safety. God is going to destroy this place and everything in it.'

The little girl was very sad and bewildered, and at first she wanted to do nothing but cry. But she was also sensible, and so instead she ran back into the house to look for her spinning-wheel. The angel told her to take the path that led down into the valley, and then she ran away to safety as fast as her little legs would carry her.

The sky turned black as night as great storm-clouds gathered, and a fearful tempest broke out. Dozens of flashes of lightning zigzagged down the sky, and thunder shook the very mountains. When the little girl stopped to look back, she saw that all the houses on the high plateau were a mass of flames. The earth opened up, and nothing living survived the punishment sent by God.

Now the little girl did indeed cry. She had nothing left in the world, only her life and her spinning-wheel. Nobody knows where she found a new home. Where there had been alpine pastures was now a thick sheet of ice. Never again would a flower grow there, or a cow graze, or a house arise. God had turned the high plateau into a desert of ice.

MOOR AND POPPENRODE

The Rhön mountains in Germany lie north-east of Frankfurt. It is very rugged and beautiful country, but life for the country-people there is still very difficult, working the stony soil. Although there is a new road through the mountains, which brings money into the area, there are many people living there who do not have enough to live on with any comfort.

Near the top of the highest mountain, where the wind always blows around the bare peaks, two villages once stood: Poppenrode, with a red marsh around it, and Moor, in the black marsh. According to legend, both these villages were destroyed because the people living in them were fonder of gambling and dancing, of filling their bellies with food and whetting their whistles with drink, than they were of doing good deeds and thinking about God. No doubt their poverty made them want to enjoy whatever they could find to cheer them up before doing anything else.

There is only a stone bridge left where Poppenrode once stood, and of Moor only the village tree remained, beneath which they all used to sit, young and old, on summer days.

This region is now supposed to be haunted by spirits — the souls of the girls who used to live in these villages, who disappeared with them, and who cannot find peace. On misty days they drift through the air, dressed in long white robes. And when there is a fair in the nearby village of Wüstensachsen, they mingle with the villagers, singing and dancing, and all the young men fall in love with them, for they are very beautiful. But at midnight, a white dove calls to them, and they go away into the mountains, singing, and you can hear them for a long while, until they disappear into the marshes. Whoever follows them will die as the marsh will swallow them up.

The Rhön mountains are also said to be a haunt of the devil. Close to the castle at Milseburg is the Devil's Wall — a sheer and imposing cliff of columns of basalt, twenty or thirty metres high. There are a number of nooks and crannies pierced into the steep face of the cliff which have names like the Devil's Chair and the Devil's Granny's Milk-can. It is very awe-inspiring place.

This must be where the devil stays when he pays a visit to the Rhön mountains. A little further on, there was a place called the Devil's Mill — a water-mill on a stream in a deep ravine. There the devil used to grind up rocks to make sand, and they say that he meant to keep the mill

working until the whole of the Rhön mountains had been ground away. That has not happened yet.

The people who live in the Rhön mountains say that on stormy nights, a huge dark man, dressed all in black, leaps over the rocks and prowls around the mill, making sure that there are enough stones to keep the grindstone busy. Could this be the devil?

WILMA AND THE GIANT

Once, when there were still giants about the world, a king of Denmark was killed in battle. His queen, Helga, was broken-hearted, but she had a little daughter called Wilma, and a little son who was even younger, who did their best to make her happy again.

As she grew up Wilma became more and more beautiful, and everyone loved her dearly. One day, when her brother the prince was still quite small, Wilma went down to the shore to watch the ships out at sea. The hour came when she should have come home, but there was no sign of her, and the queen was very worried. She sent servants to look for her, but they could not discover what had become of her.

Queen Helga could not forget her daughter, and she mourned her constantly. The prince had been so young when Wilma disappeared that he could hardly remember her himself, and one day he said to his mother, 'You never talk about anything but Wilma, you never do anything but cry about her. Let me go in search of her.'

At first the queen would not hear of such a thing, as she was afraid of losing her son as well. But at last she agreed and gave the prince her blessing, saying, 'I cannot die until I have seen Wilma again. Go, then, and bring back your sister.' The young prince went looking for her from village to village, from town to town, and then he bought a boat and set sail for Sweden. There he sailed from bay to bay, from port to port, still looking for his sister.

Once, when he had dropped anchor for the night on a lonely coast, he saw a beautiful fair-haired girl doing some washing down by the sea.

'Who are you, pretty maiden?' the prince asked her.

'Who are you, stranger?' replied the girl. 'You're the one who has just arrived here, you must say who you are first.'

'I come from Denmark,' the prince told her. 'I am the son of Queen Helga, and I am searching everywhere for my sister Wilma.'

The girl threw her arms round his neck. 'I am Wilma,' she said, weeping for joy and sorrow. 'The horrible giant Rosen kidnapped me and brought me here to be his wife. Come with me and I'll hide you, otherwise he'll kill you for sure.'

The prince shook his head. 'Let's run away now,' he said. 'The wind is in our favour and will take us to Denmark very quickly.'

'No,' said Wilma, 'because Rosen will see the boat and he'll soon chase after us and catch us. Wait for night-fall. Perhaps we can manage to escape when it's dark.'

Wilma led her brother to the giant's castle beneath the ground, and hid him away in a dark corner.

When the giant came back from his work he sniffed the air and said, 'I can smell human blood.' 'There's no one here but ourselves,' Wilma told him.

'But just now a crow flew over the mountain with human flesh in its beak. Three drops of blood fell from it, and I'm busy clearing up the mess.'

The giant Rosen went into his castle inside the mountain. Again he sniffed the air and muttered, 'I can still smell human blood.'

So then Wilma changed her mind, and she put on a very affectionate, sweet, coaxing manner and said, 'My little brother has come from Denmark to pay us a visit. You must be very nice and kind to him, and not frighten him.'

At first the giant was prepared to be angry at such an unexpected visit, but then he relented and he grunted, 'Well, if my brother-in-law has come from your country to see us, I must be friendly. He shall take your mother a chestful of gold as a present. So go and fill the chest.'

But instead of putting gold in the chest, Wilma hid inside it herself. The giant took hold of the chest and tucked it under his left arm, and then he took up the prince under his right arm. With his seven-league strides he was soon at the sea-shore, where he put everything into the boat. The prince hoisted the sails and set off westwards through the night, while Rosen went back to his underground castle. But when he could not find Wilma there, he howled and moaned with rage. He knew he would never be able to bring her back, because it was he himself, without knowing it, who had carried her away.

RÜBEZAHL AND EMMA

Rübezahl was a mountain spirit who used to live in the Harz mountains in Germany. When that part of the country became too full of people, he moved away to the Giant Mountains in Bohemia and there are many stories about him. He particularly liked being in mountains where there were mines, and the miners who worked in them became used to seeing him around. Sometimes he would steal their dinners from their lunch-boxes, putting a lizard or a toad in them instead. But he never forgot to put in a gold coin or a precious stone as well.

In fact Rübezahl liked helping simple people, and people who most needed help. A rich man had to be particularly good and especially nice for Rübezahl to take any notice of him. And although he liked being useful, he also liked to have fun. He used to begin by scaring people a little, or leading them along the wrong road, before giving them one of his presents or the help they needed. Anyone who tried to tease or mock him generally paid for it.

This is the story about how he got his funny name, which, when translated, means Count-the-turnips.

Rübezahl only fell in love once in his whole life. The young lady's name was Emma, and she was a king's daughter. Rübezahl, who at that time was only an ordinary mountain spirit without a proper name of his own, saw her for the first time sitting by a spring in the forest with a group of her friends. It would have been useless to ask her father for her hand in marriage. A mountain spirit has shaggy hair and knobbly bones and a rather wild air, and he would not stand any chance at all with an ordinary king, looking like that. So he had to use magic.

First of all he changed the spring of water into a beautiful marble pool surrounded by flowers. When Emma went back to the spot one day and saw the pool, she took off her clothes and went into the pool to bathe — and immediately disappeared, going straight to the bottom. Her best friend leapt into the water to help her, but she could find nothing there at all, only the marble.

Rübezahl welcomed Emma to his underground kingdom, where he had a palace with many splendid rooms and halls with magnificent furniture and marvellous gardens full of lovely flowers. He turned himself into a handsome young man. Emma looked at him, and quite liked what she saw, and she let him show her over his palace. That night she slept in a bed with a silken canopy, and the next day she made a tour of the gardens on horseback, accompanied by the young man who was really Rübezahl. But gradually Emma began to feel homesick, and she longed to go back and see her father and her friends. And she began, too, to think about her fiancé, the Count of Ratibor, whom she was soon to marry.

Rübezahl could not bear to see his beloved unhappy and even cry a little, and he found what he thought was a remedy. He brought her a basket of turnips and a magic wand with which she could change the turnips into all the people she liked best and wanted to have with her. So Emma changed the turnips into her friends, even into her cat and her dog, and for several days she was quite happy. But one morning she found her friends and her cat and dog all shrivelled up, because the turnips had dried and wrinkled. Then Emma realized that they had not been real, that it had all been a trick.

Rübezahl brought her more basketfuls of turnips, but each time Emma became sadder. There was nothing that he could do to make things better, even though he could produce there, under the ground, a whole field of turnips, when above the ground there were no turnips at all because it was winter. Emma now had only one idea in her head and that was to escape.

In her unhappiness the idea suddenly came to her that she could change turnips into people not just to keep herself amused but to help her get away. So she turned one into a magpie, and she gave it a letter to take to her fiancé, Count Ratibor. In the letter she asked him to come to the fountain in the forest in three days' time, with knights and horses, and to wait for her there.

When she thought the right moment had come, she said to Rübezahl, 'I think it would be nice to change all the turnips in the field into bridesmaids and guests for our wedding. Please go and count how many there are, so that I know how many people to expect.' And she sent him out into the field.

The mountain spirit set out at once to do as his beloved had bid him. While he was gone, Emma changed one of the turnips into a horse, saddled and bridled, and she mounted the horse and rode off to the fountain where the Count was waiting for her. And that's how Rübezahl got his name Count-the-turnips.

Other people who made fun of him, or who tried to get the better of him did not get off as lightly as Emma, whom he loved. For instance, there was a shepherd who once said that people who believed in mountain spirits were donkeys, and Rübezahl made bulls' horns sprout from the shepherd's head.

He made the nose of one peasant grow so long that he had to stretch

his arm out in front of him as far as it would go in order to blow his nose.

Once there was a goose-girl who wandered with her geese along the edge of the forest singing a little song which made fun of him. Rübezahl made himself look like a shepherd and went to meet her. He cuddled her, stroked her chin with his hand — and made a little billy-goat's beard grow there, which the poor girl had to keep for the rest of her life!

WHY THE STARS ARE IN THE SKY

To the Eskimos the stars are not just put in the sky to give light or guide the wandering traveller. They are living things, sent by some twist of fate to roam the heavens forever, never swerving from their paths.

One of these creatures who left the earth and went to live in the sky was Nanuk the bear. One day Nanuk was waylaid by a pack of the fierce Eskimo hunting dogs. Nanuk knew only too well that Eskimo dogs are not to be trifled with, and he tried to give them the slip. Faster and faster he ran over the ice, but the dogs were still at his heels. For hours the chase went on, yet he could not shake them off. In the fury and terror of the hunt, they had come very close to the edge of the world, but neither Nanuk nor his pursuers noticed. When at last they reached it, they plunged straight over into the sky and turned into stars. To Europeans they are the Pleiades, in the constellation of Taurus the bull. But to this day Eskimos see them as Nanuk the bear, with the pack of savage dogs out for his blood.

Up in the sky directly overhead the Eskimos see a giant caribou, though we call it the Great Bear. Over on the other side of the sky, they can make out some stars in the shape of an oil lamp. (We say it is the constellation of Cassiopeia.) On the horizon between the lamp and the caribou the Eskimos see stars like three steps carved out of the snow. They call it the stairway from Earth to the sky, but we talk of Orion the Hunter.

Sometimes, on the darkest nights, the Eskimos' dead ancestors come out and dance. The stars are the lights round their dance floor. Then Gulla glows across the sky: the shimmering pattern of the Aurora Borealis, or Northern Lights. To the Norsemen it was Bifrost, the bridge from our world to Asgard, home of the gods.

But to the people of the Far North, the loveliest and most wonderful star of all is the sun. They see her as a young girl of dazzling beauty. In their brief Arctic summer she is there night and day, for this is the season of the midnight sun, when her brother Aningan, the moon, chases her round and round the North Pole so she cannot escape over the horizon.

Aningan the moon is a great hunter, and he chases animals as well as his sister the sun. He has a faithful pack of hunting dogs to help him. Sometimes his hounds are carried away by the joy of the hunt, and they jump over the edge of the sky and run down the stairway in Orion to Earth. That is why there are shooting stars.

After hunting Aningan rests in his igloo, which he shares with his cousin Irdlirvirissong. His cousin loves jokes and games, and sometimes she comes out and dances in the sky. She is so funny that if the Eskimos see her they roar with laughter. But first they make sure none of their sorcerers or their other leaders are nearby, for if Irdlirvirissong knows that people are laughing at her she will be angry, and her punishments are terrible. She kills people who make fun of her, and eats them up.

The sorcerers are powerful, and ordinary Eskimos tremble before them, particularly Angakog, the mightiest sorcerer of all. Yet even Angakog's magic arts are powerless against the planet Jupiter. For Jupiter is mother to the sun and the moon, and a constant peril to all sorcerers. They have to be very, very careful, or old mother Jupiter will open them up and devour their livers. Angakog trembles in fear of her, even as the ordinary folk tremble in fear of him.

MOTHER EAGLE AND THE HUNTER

Once upon a time there was an Indian who was the most famous hunter for hundreds of miles around. This was because he had magic powers which enabled him to lure any wild animal into his clutches.

'The grass is sweeter here,' he would call to a stag. And the stag would trust him and come, so that the hunter could put an arrow in its ribs.

He even dared to lure down the fierce eagles who circled over the forests looking for prey.

'There's some tender meat for you here,' he would call up to an eagle. 'Come down and get it!' And when the eagle flew down to seize the meat in its talons, the hunter would come out of hiding and send an arrow straight to its heart.

It was a dangerous game. 'Take care,' people warned him. 'Beware of the mother eagle's revenge.' But the hunter just laughed.

One day he saw the mother eagle circling high up in the sky. She was the biggest and strongest of all the eagles. The hunter waved up to her.

'Come down, mother eagle,' he shouted. 'There's meat here for you and your little ones.'·

The mother eagle glided slowly down. Suddenly she dived at the hunter, ready to sink her talons in his body. Terrified, he fled and hid in a hollow tree. But the mother eagle followed him, dragged him from his hiding place and carried him off into the skies. Far through the air she flew, to her eyrie on a rock which no man could climb. Then she put the hunter down and flew off to seek other prey.

The eaglets flapped their wings in excitement and began to peck the hunter with their curved beaks. The hunter dodged, and gave them a morsel of dried meat that he carried in his bag. Then he cut up the leather strap of the bag and tied the strips round the eaglets' beaks.

When the mother eagle came back and saw what he had done, she was beside herself.

'Take those things off my children's beaks!' she screeched.

'Gladly,' answered the hunter, 'but only if you first promise to take me back to the ground.'

'Never!' cried the mother eagle.

For two days she tried to feed her little ones, but in vain. She perched on the edge of the eyrie wondering what to do. Her little ones were so weak now that they could hardly stand.

'You'll die for this!' said the mother eagle to the hunter.

'Then your little ones will starve to death,' answered the hunter. 'But if you promise to take me back to the ground, I'll take off the straps.'

For a long time they argued. At last the mother eagle said: 'If you promise to seek the consent of the spirits before you ever again kill an eagle or deer, I'll carry you back to the ground.'

The hunter agreed. He untied the eaglets' beaks, and the mother eagle bore him back to the ground.

The hunter kept his word, and so did his sons and grandsons, for they too felt bound by his promise. Now, when hunters kill deer, the eagles have the right to take what humans cannot eat, and no man may attack them.

'Come!' call the Indians to the eagles. 'Come and get your share.' And so it will be for ever.

THE ROLLING HEAD

Once upon a time, an American Indian legend says, there were two brothers. One day a beautiful young woman came to see them.

'May I come and live with you?' she asked. 'I'd like to keep house for you. I'll see you won't regret it.'

The two brothers talked the idea over in private.

'Very well,' said the Older Brother at last. 'You can be the Younger Brother's wife.'

And so she married the Younger Brother, and they all lived happily together.

One day the two brothers were out fishing when an immense fish swam up to the surface. The men looked at each other.

'How on earth can we catch that?' asked the Younger Brother.

'The best way,' said the Older Borther, 'is for you to tie a rope of hickory fibre round your waist and wade in after the fish. When you've caught it, I'll haul you in.'

And that is what they tried. But the fish was much too big. He just swallowed the Younger Brother and cut the rope with his teeth. The Older Brother watched in horror from the bank, then ran for help.

'Help! We must catch this huge fish!' he cried, but not a single animal came forward to help him. They were all terrified. He ran up and down calling till at last the oystercatcher heard him.

'I'll help, Older Brother,' it called.

The oystercatcher dived onto the fish again and again, raining blows with its pointed beak till the fish was dead. The Older Brother dragged the fish to the bank and opened it up. Too late! The Younger Brother's body had already been digested, and only his head remained. The Older Brother began to weep.

Then the strangest thing happened. The Younger Brother's head opened its mouth and began to speak.

'You can help me, Older Brother. Wash me carefully and put me on a tree trunk. Tomorrow morning I'll come home, and then I'll sing a magic song.'

The Older Brother did as the head had asked. Then he went home and told everything to the Younger Brother's wife.

'He's not a man any longer,' he said to the woman, 'he's nothing but a head. You're my wife now.'

Next day the Younger Brother's head came flying through the air. It perched on the roof and sang a magic song:

Back to my home I am come now to rest.
Here I grew up, and here's all I love best.
Day is now passing, and I will not roam.
Listener, stay with me here in my home.

The Older Brother and the young woman shivered. Without leaving their house they called to the head, 'What do you want, head of Younger Brother?'

'I want my wife,' replied the head.

'But she's my wife now,' said the Older Brother. He had no intention of giving up his wife.

'I see,' said the head, and thought at once of revenge. 'But I'm hungry. Won't you at least pick me some fruit from that tree?'

The woman was frightened. 'Don't go out,' she begged the Older Brother. 'He's going to kill us.'

But the Older Brother felt he could not refuse the head, as it could not pick the fruit itself. The couple came out of the shelter of the house and set to work. Suddenly the head flew over, bit into the fruit and spat the skin into the woman's face. She gave a piercing cry, and the Older Brother went to climb the tree and chase the head away.

'Don't do it, Older Brother,' warned a crow, 'or you'll be killed. Run away with your wife while there's time.'

So the Older Brother seized his wife by the hand and they ran away as fast as they could. But the head chased them, sometimes rolling along the ground and sometimes flying through the air.

'Give me my wife!' it kept crying. 'Give me my wife!'

In their distress the Older Brother and his wife took refuge in the clay house of a wild wasp. Inside, the woman lay trembling on the ground. Outside, the head was still wailing, 'Give me my wife!'

'She isn't here,' called out the wasp.

'You're lying,' replied the Younger Brother's head. 'Older Brother and my wife have hidden in your house. I can see their footprints in the clay.'

But the wasp turned the woman into a man. Now the Older Brother and the New Man could leave the house.

'Give me my wife! Give me my wife!' yelled the head again when it saw them.

'She's not here,' said the wasp. 'Can't you see the Older Brother came with a man?'

But the head did not believe her. 'You've hidden her, wasp,' it shouted, and forced its way into her house. It soon saw there was no one there, but it was still suspicious.

'You've dressed her as a man, wasp,' it said.

'Of course I haven't,' said the wasp, 'and what's more I can prove it. We'll have an archery contest between Older Brother and the man you think is your wife.'

The Younger Brother's head agreed, and the wasp set up a row of four clay pots as targets. The New Man hit all four, the Older Brother only one.

'Do you still believe this is your wife?' asked the wasp.

'I suppose not,' admitted the head, 'but let's see if he's a good hunter.'

And it set off with the New Man to go hunting. Soon their way was barred by a muddy river.

'Show me you can swim!' demanded the head. 'Let's see who can reach the other bank.'

In they jumped, but under the water the New Man sang the magic song:

> Back to my home I am come now to rest.
> Here I grew up, and here's all I love best.
> Day is now passing, and I will not roam.
> Listener, stay with me here in my home.

And when the head heard this song, it became forever a captive of the water.

The New Man regained her true shape and went on. For some time she had been pregnant, and after a while she had three babies. She hid them in the hollow of a bamboo, and she wandered on.

One day she came to the house of a tribal chief. She was so beautiful that the chief married her. He even made her his chief wife, something which made the other wives very angry.

'This won't do,' said the women to each other. 'We must show our husband she's no good. Let's suggest a competition.'

They went to the New Wife and said, 'Let's see who can roast the most maize.'

The New Wife agreed, and went to her friend the wasp.

'Help me,' she begged. 'The chief's other wives want to get rid of me.'

So the wasp sent the oystercatcher to help her. It flew round the villages gathering roast maize, and soon brought so much that the New Wife won the competition easily.

The other wives were very vexed. Soon they had another idea.

'You're a beautiful woman,' they said to the New Wife slyly. 'Let's see which of us has the shiniest hair. Our husband can decide.'

This time a bird with glossy, shimmering plumage flew to the New Wife's aid. He rubbed his breast on her hair, which then took on his

84

marvellous colours. When the woman appeared with her rivals before the chief, her hair shone in the sun with a wonderful silky sheen, and she won the contest outright. Furious, the other wives withdrew.

'She must go,' they whispered to each other. 'The chief only has eyes for her. He takes practically no notice of us now.'

They agreed to invite the New Wife to play ball. They would kill her with a bat, making it look like an accident.

Now the wasp itself flew to the New Wife's aid and gave her some advice. The game began. In the middle of it, before the other wives could set their plan in motion, the New Wife brought out her children from the hollow bamboo where she had hidden them.

They were powerful creatures: the wind, the thunder and the lightning. The wind blew up a storm, stirring up the dust and throwing the women to the ground. The thunder roared, and the lightning struck them dead.

When it was all over, the woman and her children left that place and went towards the west. As she journeyed, she sent her children and grandchildren in all directions. That is how the Earth came to be colonized, for the woman's descendants founded villages wherever they went. They were the first men and the first women of the American Indians.

THE OTTER'S SKIN AND DRAGON'S BLOOD

In the beginning there were gods and giants in the world as well as people, the Norse legends say. The gods were worshipped in Northern Europe, and some gave their names to our weekdays. Wednesday comes from Woden, who was Wotan to the Germans and Odin the All Wise to the Norsemen.

One day Odin went walking to the coast of Norway with two of the other gods, Hoenir and sly Loki.

When at last the gods came in sight of the sea, they saw a waterfall cascading from the top of a rocky outcrop into the waters of the fiord. Suddenly Odin stopped.

'Look!' he cried, pointing. There on a cliff beside the waterfall was a splendid glossy otter, gnawing a fat salmon with its fine sharp teeth.

Loki laughed slyly, picked up a rock, and threw it at the otter, killing it outright. Then, pleased with himself, he hung its glossy skin round his shoulders.

The three gods went on. All day they walked until, just as the sun was setting behind the sea, they came to the palace of Hreidmar the giant. Hreidmar, a great magician, came out to greet them.

'Welcome, gods,' he said in a friendly tone, and Odin returned his greeting.

'We've been walking for hours, Hreidmar,' he said.

'Will you let us rest in your home?'

The giant agreed readily, led the gods into his hall and had food placed before them. But his sons, the dwarfs Fafnir and Regnir, watched the smiling gods suspiciously. After supper, the gods retired to their rooms.

Just then Hreidmar called his sons out of the palace, to where Loki had dropped the otter's skin. It was already beginning to freeze, and the frost made the otter's silky coat even shinier.

'Look at this,' said Hreidmar mournfully. The dwarfs' eyes narrowed.

'I've seen those eyes before,' said Regnir, filled with foreboding.

'Where's our brother Otr?' asked Fafnir, with mounting fury. 'He hasn't come back from hunting on the coast.'

'And Otr,' added Hreidmar's muted voice, 'loves salmon, and often turns into an otter to catch them. The gods have killed your brother.'

The giant and his sons vowed to avenge Otr's death. They slipped back into the palace, hurled themselves on the three gods and tied them up. Odin and his companions, caught by surprise, had no chance to defend themselves. What could Odin the All Wise do now?

'I am desolate, Hreidmar,' he appealed to the giant. 'We didn't know the otter was your son. What can we do to make amends?'

Hreidmar thought long and hard. 'You gods are mighty,' he said at last. 'Stuff this skin with gold till it stands upright. Then pour gold over it till not a hair of its fur is to be seen.'

'Not even a god can do that,' protested Odin.

'A mass of gold like that?' gasped Hoenir. 'Where on earth could we find it?'

The giant's sons grinned from ear to ear. But the god Loki, who was famous for his cunning and malice, was smiling too.

'Don't worry,' he said calmly to his fellow gods. 'Leave it to me. If you set me free, Hreidmar, I'll fetch your gold.'

'Very well, Loki,' agreed the giant cautiously. 'But mind you keep your word, or Odin and Hoenir will die.'

'Gods always keep their word,' answered Loki sulkily. And the dwarfs sulked too, but their father undid Loki's bonds, and soon he was hurrying away.

It was the Nibelung dwarfs that Loki sought, in the dark misty land of Nibelheim as far north as it is possible to go on Earth. Deep in its snow-covered mountains the Nibelung king Andwari and his dwarfs were watching over priceless treasures. Andwari frowned when he saw sly Loki, for the god's malice was feared by everyone.

'What do you want?' he asked warily.

'Your gold,' answered Loki straight out. 'All your treasure!'

The Nibelung king gnashed his teeth in anger. But what hope had a dwarf against a god? Already Loki had managed to get into his cave, which was heaped to the roof with gold and dazzling jewels: gleaming gold bracelets, necklaces and rings, goblets and vases of gold, swords set with precious stones, shining gold buckles like boar's heads and eagles and dragons.

Loki threw down a sack.

'Fill that!' he commanded, in a voice which brooked no argument. The dwarfs knew they had to obey. Hands trembling, they gathered the priceless things together. But the sack seemed to have a hole in it, and no matter how hard the poor dwarfs tried it was never full. In the end the cave was completely empty. Looking round for more, Loki caught the gleam of a ring on the dwarf king's finger.

'Give me that ring!' he ordered Andwari.

'No, Loki!' This time the Nibelung king refused. 'You go too far.'

But the god grabbed the dwarf by the beard and tore the ring from his finger.

'That ring will bring bad luck, Loki,' warned Andwari, goaded beyond endurance, and he uttered a terrible curse. 'He who wears it will be miserably killed, and the Nibelungs' treasure will bring good to no one.'

Loki laughed in his face. He picked up the sack and hurried back to Hreidmar's palace. There he threw the sack of gold down in front of the giant.

'Take what you want, old man,' he said grumpily.

The eyes of the giant and his sons gleamed with greed. Busily they filled the otter's skin almost to bursting, then heaped up jewels of every possible kind around it and over it, until not a hair of its fur was to be seen.

'Well, Hreidmar, are you satisfied?' said Loki triumphantly. 'Now set Odin and Hoenir free!'

But Regnir was still examining the heap of treasure, and at that moment he sneered. 'There's still one hair gleaming here,' he gloated. 'That's a fine big ring you're wearing, Loki. You can use it to hide this hair!'

The god was forced to obey. Now everything Hreidmar wanted had been done. He set Odin and Hoenir free, and the three gods hurried away.

Hreidmar took the Nibelung treasure and locked it in a huge chest. His sons looked on in surprise.

'What are you doing, father?' cried Fafnir, suddenly wary. 'Don't we all get our fair share?'

The giant shook his head. 'You're lazy good-for-nothing dwarfs. I still have to feed you. It's my treasure.' And he went off to bed.

Angry, the two dwarfs wondered what to do. 'What a miser!' said Fafnir. 'And what a pig-headed old man,' added Regnir. 'We're his sons. We shouldn't have to wait till he dies and we're old and grey before we get any treasure. I want my share now!'

He flung himself on his sleeping father and battered him savagely with a great hammer till he was dead. Already the Nibelung's curse had found a victim.

'Now we'll split the treasure, Fafnir,' he told his brother. 'Half and half.'

'But you killed our father, Regnir. I didn't,' sneered Fafnir spitefully, 'and so the treasure's all mine. And if you stay here any longer I'll make sure you die for your crime.'

90

Regnir fled, screaming vengeance and swearing to kill his brother. Fearing his brother's anger, Fafnir remembered the magic powers he had inherited from his father and changed into a dragon. He gathered up the treasure of the Nibelungs and escaped to Hungary. There he lurked in a cave, hiding his treasure under his great belly and spitting fire and poison. No one dared come near.

Regnir had trailed Fafnir secretly, but he was powerless against the monster. To kill the dragon, a warrior would have to be invincible.

Where could Regnir find such a warrior? Far and wide he searched, but at last he heard of Siegfried, son of King Siegmund and Queen Sieglinde of the Voelsungs, who were directly descended from Odin the All Wise.

At that time Siegfried was at the royal court of Xanten, close to the great River Rhine and near what is now the border between Germany and Holland. Regnir went to Xanten and persuaded the king to make him his armourer. Then he forged a magic sword for Siegfried and urged him to kill the dragon Fafnir.

Young Siegfried was eager for glory. He mounted his valiant charger Grane and rode to Hungary. Again and again he attacked the dragon and was driven back by its poisonous flames, but at last Siegfried laid the dragon low. Mortally wounded, Fafnir still had time to pass on the curse of the Nibelung king: 'You too will die, Siegfried, now you have the treasure of the Nibelungs.'

The son of the gods just laughed. Fafnir vanished in a burst of flame like an erupting volcano.

Cautiously, Regnir walked up to the victor.

'You are a great hero, Siegfried,' he said, flattering the young man. 'Now give me the treasure. It's mine.'

'Was it you that killed the dragon?'

'Don't let's quarrel. But you see, Fafnir was my brother. The treasure was left to me by our father, and he stole it. Look, I want to eat his heart in revenge. Cook it for me in the dragon's flames.'

And indeed flames were still shooting from the dragon's mouth. Siegfried agreed, and Regnir tore the heart out of the dragon and speared it on the end of his sword. Siegfried held the heart over the flames. When he thought the meat was cooked, he felt it with the tip of his finger, and burnt himself. Instinctively he put his finger to his mouth to still the pain, and some of Fafnir's blood went on his teeth. The blood possessed the magic powers of Hreidmar, Fafnir's magician father, and all at once Siegfried could understand the birds. What had been just squawks and trills and whistles suddenly took on meaning. He shut his eyes and concentrated.

Above his head some tits were perched in the branches of a lime tree, singing gaily.

'Just look over there,' twittered a blue-tit. 'There's Regnir himself, desperately muttering away to trying to work out how he can defeat Siegfried.'

'Yes,' said a coal-tit. 'Siegfried is cooking Fafnir's heart instead of bathing in the dragon's blood and making himself invulnerable. How careless! That may cost him his life.'

And a long-tailed tit began to warble in a clear little voice: 'If he has any sense, he'll beat the dwarf to it, and get rid of Regnir before Regnir surprises and kills him.'

Siegfried opened his eyes. He thanked the birds for saving his life, and stabbed the treacherous Regnir to death. Then he ate the dragon's heart, which gave him supernatural strength, and bathed all over in Fafnir's blood. Now he was invulnerable, except for a small spot on his shoulder where a lime leaf had clung, so that Fafnir's blood could not touch it.

Now the victorious Siegfried returned to the River Rhine, this time to Worms, capital of the powerful King of Burgundy. The king's daughter was enchantingly beautiful, and her father adored her. But one day, as she stood at the window of her chamber, the sky became dazzlingly bright, and a fire dragon, borne on powerful wings, flew down, seized the princess in his claws and carried her away through the air to the castle of a terrible giant, Wolfgrambaer. The giant, a magician, had fallen in love with the king's lovely daughter, and had enlisted the help of the dragon. Having carried the princess off and delivered her to his master, the dragon returned to his cave on the Drachenfels (Dragon Rock), a mountain overlooking the banks of the Rhine.

People remembered an ancient prophecy which said that a hero, and only a hero, could save the captive princess. The messengers of Fate had chosen Siegfried for this noble task, but no one knew the way to the castle of Wolfgrambaer the giant.

One day, when Siegfried was out hunting, his faithful bloodhound disappeared into the bushes. Siegfried rode his horse into the under-growth. Nose to the ground, the dog had found the track of something very strange. Siegfried had never seen anything like it: immense marks of pads and talons which had sunk deep into the ground. They must belong to a monster of incredible size.

For four days Siegfried followed his dog through a hostile forest. He had to kill bears and chase away wolves. His brave horse, Grane, nearly broke its leg in a fox's earth. Still the dog stuck to the trail, trotting along with its tongue hanging out, going they knew not where.

Suddenly, deep in one of the great forests which then stretched away on both sides of the River Rhine, they met a battalion of elves. At their head rode their king Egwardus, on a horse with trappings black as ebony.

'Welcome to my realm,' he greeted Siegfried courteously. 'Where have you come from, and where are you going?'

'I'm looking for Dragon Rock,' answered the young hero. 'Can you tell me where it is?'

The king of the elves went pale, and avoided the question. 'Why are you going there?' he asked. 'No one should dare go near Dragon Rock.'

Siegfried laughed scornfully. 'Just show me the way, little king. I'll do the rest myself.'

'Never!' said Egwardus reprovingly.

But Siegfried took him briskly by the throat, lifted him off his horse and gave him a good shaking. 'Show me the way, little midget,' he ordered, 'or you'll regret it!'

Reluctantly the little king gave in. 'Fate will punish me if I give away the secret,' he groaned. 'For Wolfgrambaer is my master, and he ordered the dragon to carry off the King of Burgundy's daughter.'

'But I'm going to slay the dreadful giant,' replied Siegfried, 'and then you'll be free forever.'

The elf king saw the sense of this, and instead of making for Dragon Rock he led the young hero straight to the foot of Wolfgrambaer's mountain. Siegfried cupped his hands and shouted up to the castle on the mountain top.

'Hey, you monster!' he yelled, 'are you going to give back the king's daughter?'

'Cheeky boy!' thundered the giant, and he uprooted a thick oak tree and went to club Siegfried with it. But the hero jumped nimbly aside, and the tree shattered like a stick of glass. The fight went on and on. Sooner or later Siegfried would surely have died, but Egwardus, with great presence of mind, came to the rescue.

'Take this helmet!' whispered the elf king. 'It will make you invisible. Then you can hide and kill the giant.'

Siegfried followed his advice, and had no trouble in bringing the huge giant to his knees. Wild with anger, Wolfgrambaer was forced to let the king's daughter out of her prison.

But no sooner was she free than there was a roll of thunder. The dragon and his nine sons had flown over the mountains to the aid of their master the giant.

Siegfried brandished his enchanted sword, and at once the young dragons panicked and fled. Their father was made of sterner stuff, and ready to fight the hero to the death, but soon a great swish of Siegfried's sword cut the dragon in two, and the Rhine Valley was safe from the evil monster at last.

Siegfried took the king's daughter safely back to Worms. Her father was overjoyed, and gave his sister Kriemhilde to Siegfried in marriage as a reward. For a time they lived happily together there, on the banks of the Rhine, but their peace was not to last.

One night Princess Kriemhilde had a bad dream, which left her very frightened. Next morning she went to tell her mother, Queen Ute.

'Mother, I dreamt I was training a fine hawk to hunt. It was loyal to me, and I was very fond of it. But two other hawks fell on it, and they clawed and pecked it to death. What does the dream mean, mother?'

'Alas, my daughter,' answered the Queen. 'The hawk is a man, a noble one, someone you dearly love. Two other nobles, cowardly men, are going to kill him.'

Before long the king's friend Hagen, who had always hated Siegfried, ambushed him and sank his javelin in his shoulder, just where the lime leaf had clung when Siegfried bathed in the dragon's blood. So the princess's dream came true, and so did the curse of the little Nibelung king Andwari.

THE STORY OF THESEUS

Back in the time of the ancient Greeks the gods ruled the world. The Greeks believed that their dreams and visions were wishes of the gods and acted upon them. They also believed in oracles. An oracle was a priest or priestess who by mysterious means was able to predict the mood of the gods and give advice. But the oracles were not always clear and often the questioner would go away only to act upon a misunderstanding. Theseus, Oedipus and Aeneas were heroes who had many exciting and daring adventures as a result of what they were told in dreams or through an oracle.

Now it happened once that a group of Athenians had wickedly killed the son of Minos, King of Crete. Minos was furious and looked for immediate revenge. He sent a powerful army to attack the Athenians, who were already suffering from plague and famine as punishment from the gods. Desperate, they approached the oracle for advice. The oracle declared that only human sacrifice would satisfy Minos and the gods, and so it came to be that every nine years the people of Athens had to choose seven young boys and seven young girls by drawing lots. These unfortunate children were then sent to Crete as the Minotaur's victims. The Minotaur, half man and half bull, fed upon human flesh and lived in the labyrinth of King Minos. The parents who did not lose a son or daughter were naturally relieved and thankful, but the people as a whole were fraught with misery. Yet they knew that if their king, Aegeus, did not send a boatload of victims to Crete, their peace would be shattered.

The time for the third sacrifice came and men gathered in taverns around the harbour. Among them sat the pilot of the ship which took the children across the sea to their doom, a ship with immense sinister black sails.

'Why doesn't Aegeus send Theseus?' one of the men demanded. 'Why should Theseus get away with not going while all the rest have to submit to their cruel fate?'

'Well, it seems that he is really Aegeus's own son,' the inn-keeper suggested. 'The King sent him to Troezen to be brought up by his grandfather.'

'But Theseus hasn't been in Athens very long, he wasn't even born here,' butted in a man who was slightly drunk. 'Anyway Aegeus wants him to succeed him as king when he himself dies.'

'Some say that Theseus is not Aegeus's son, but the son of the god

Poseidon,' the inn-keeper commented. There was a loud guffaw from the drunken man, who continued: 'And I've heard it said that he killed Periphrates, the bandit who murdered travellers with a cudgel, and Sinis too. It was Sinis who used to pull down the higher branches of two pine trees, such was his strength, then tie up a traveller, an arm roped to each tree, and then let the trees spring upward, wrenching the man's body in half.'

Quietly sitting in a corner, a stranger listened in on their animated conversation. When he heard this story he eagerly joined in: 'That's right — I saw the remains of Sinis's dead body. Theseus is an exceptional man: he's only sixteen, strong as an ox, and very brave. He even killed Procrustes.'

'Was that the one they called "The Stretcher?"' a voice intervened.

The gathering grew interested and drew towards the stranger. 'Have a drink,' urged the pilot, 'tell us about Procrustes.'

'Procrustes had two beds,' the stranger began, 'and when a weary traveller arrived asking for shelter at the end of a day's long journey, Procrustes would offer him a bed. If the innocent traveller was short then he would be given a large bed, whereupon Procrustes had his arms and legs stretched to fit the size of the bed: the traveller paid with his life. If a tall man turned up, the evil Procrustes would provide him with a smaller bed and later on viciously hack off his limbs until his body fitted it. Nobody survived, of course.

The sailor downed his drink and shuddered. 'And what did Theseus do?' he inquired. The stranger smiled. 'He forced the huge brute into taking the little bed and in due course gave him the same treatment,' he replied. 'Thanks to Theseus our roads are now safe for travellers.'

'It sounds as though Theseus is taking after his famous cousin Hercules,' commented one of the listeners. 'He's trying to look after our people and stamp out evil with his heroic deeds. He's obviously not idle.'

While they were talking about Theseus in the tavern, the people of Athens were crowding into the market-place, anxiously waiting to draw lots to decide which children to sacrifice. Theseus himself was there, and as he moved amongst the throngs of people he sensed all the intense resentment that they felt against him, a newcomer to the city. Full of vigour he stood up and, facing them all, made a fiery speech: 'I will go to Crete as one of the fourteen sacrifices,' he cried. 'I will find a way to destroy the Minotaur, and save those who sail with me from a gruesome death. We shall no longer have to sacrifice the youth of Athens. We shall hoist the white sails, father,' he shouted to Aegeus, 'not the black ones as before, for this time we will return.'

But King Aegeus had only just been reunited with his son after long years of absence and pleaded with him not to go. The crowds however cheered their approval, filled with renewed hope.

At this Theseus knew that he had won the hearts of the people. Accompanied by his fellow travellers he went to the temple of Apollo to implore his aid and pray for success. He made an offering to Apollo, and also, on the advice of the oracle at Delphi, to Aphrodite, the goddess of love, although at the time the offering to Aphrodite puzzled him.

Theseus arrived in Crete and only when in the presence of King Minos did he realize the reason for making an offering to Aphrodite: the daughter of Minos, Ariadne, had clearly fallen in love with him. The two lovers met in secret and one day Ariadne gave Theseus a ball of magic thread. 'The Minotaur lives inside a maze,' she whispered. 'It was built for my father by the inventor Daedalus. Take this and guard it safely, for without it you will never return. Be sure to fasten one end of the thread to the entrance of the labyrinth, then carefully unwind it as you enter. When you have killed the monster, gently rewind the thread into a ball again and in so doing retrace your steps to freedom.' Ariadne also gave him a magic sword to help kill the Minotaur. The following morning, together with the chosen children, Theseus was flung into the fearful labyrinth.

There was a fierce and gory fight, and after an heroic struggle Theseus at last killed the Minotaur. His clothes drenched with blood and splattered with the monster's saliva, he left the wounded beast to die. Exhausted, he made his way to the shaken group of children and with them cautiously began to follow the magic thread, soon emerging at the entrance safely. They lay low until night time and then crept towards the Cretan ships to drill them full of holes. When they had done this they set sail for Athens, taking Ariadne with them.

On the way home they stopped at the island of Naxos, and there the god Bacchus appeared to Theseus in a dream. 'I wish to have Ariadne as my wife,' he declared. 'You must sail back to Athens and leave her here. If you disobey, my anger will follow you wherever you go.' Tortured with misery Theseus submitted to the god's wish, partly out of fear and partly respect. Unable to disobey Bacchus, he abandoned the lovely Ariadne on the lonely island as she lay asleep. When she woke and found that Theseus had deserted her she wept bitterly and long. 'Cruel Theseus,' she sobbed. 'Is this how much you loved me? Is this my reward for all the help I've given you to escape? Oh come back, please please come back!'

Her cries of anguish were carried along with the sea breeze, and Theseus heard her torments and their faint echoes as his ship sailed out into the waters. Overcome by grief he ordered the black sails to be hoisted, completely forgetting his promise to use the white ones.

As the ship approached Athens, Aegeus caught sight of the black sails. Agonized by the thought that his son was dead he hurled himself from a high cliff into the sea. Theseus landed only to be met by the tragic story of his father's death.

Theseus then became the king of Athens. He dedicated the ship in

which he sailed to Crete to Apollo, and for many years afterwards it was left on display for visitors from other countries to flock round. The young king realized the weaknesses of the country: people lived scattered in small communities, each village warring against the others, and of course brigands and robbers took advantage of this. Theseus decided that a strong country must have a chief city which would protect the surrounding countryside, and with this idea in mind he travelled for many days, from village to village, trying to persuade the Athenians to put an end to their quarrelling and fighting and to unite in a single state. 'Your rights and laws will be preserved,' he told them. 'I will protect your freedom, and if war comes I will be your commander-in-chief. Those who are guilty of crimes will be duly punished. I will do all I can to safeguard your happiness. Athens will be your state and you will all have a say in how it is run.' As a king Theseus showed that not only was he strong and courageous but that he could also rule peacefully and govern his kingdom wisely. In this he excelled, perhaps even more so than Hercules himself.

The Athenians were willing and happy to accept Theseus's rule, but there were a few rich and influential men who believed that ordinary folk would be given too much say. Theseus was impetuous, however, and soon made the changes he believed to be right. He encouraged the people to work hard, respect the gods and feel directly responsible for their country; Athens became a commonwealth with a council of nobles and an assembly of the people to decide how the state should be governed; the city was dedicated to the goddess Athene. The state grew and flourished under his rule and it became renowned worldwide for its prosperity.

Now at this stage in his life Theseus was lacking in one thing, a wife. For a companion he kidnapped a beautiful Amazon called Hippolyta and married her. Although Hippolyta herself was happy, the Amazons, a ferocious war-loving race of women, were clearly enraged. They decided on revenge. Athens once again faced a bitter and bloodthirsty war.

The Amazons surprised them by unexpectedly arriving in the harbour of Athens, and all too quickly the city was surrounded. They charged into the city on horseback, brandishing their javelins, unrelenting in their attack. Theseus, with his warrior-wife beside him, led the Athenians, only to be driven back. Finally, after much bloodshed, a javelin whistled unseen through the air and struck down the fair Hippolyta. Now that Hippolyta was dead, the Amazons declared peace with Athens and retreated. Athens prospered after the bloody war and Theseus was acclaimed as a wise and just ruler.

But here the gods took a hold on events and put a stop to his good fortune. After reigning happily and successfully for many years, during which his son Hippolytus grew up to be a man, Theseus married again, his choice falling on Phaedra, the youngest sister of his old love Ariadne.

Phaedra was as lovely as her sister. However, she immediately became attracted to Hippolytus. Although she resolved to drive this passion from her heart, Phaedra continued to yearn for him, and one day when Theseus was away she confessed her love to the prince. Hippolytus, aghast at her confession, rejected the pleas of his stepmother. Phaedra reacted violently, sinking into such deep despair that she committed suicide by hanging herself. To punish Hippolytus she left a letter in which she laid the blame on him, making it appear that he had tried to make her run away with him. It read: 'I would rather die than be seduced by Hippolytus and be unfaithful to my dear husband.' Theseus was enraged when he found the letter and banished the innocent Hippolytus from the country.

On the very same day Hippolytus was found fatally wounded on the wayside of a road which skirted the seashore. His horses, as though bewitched, had suddenly bolted and dragged Hippolytus along the ground entangled by his reins. His injuries were so severe that he was barely recognizable. Although he was rescued and carried to the king by servants, it was too late and he died soon after. Hippolytus's innocence was then revealed to the king by one of the maids whom Phaedra had used to deliver love letters to Hippolytus, and Theseus in his grief gave orders for his wife and son to be given a special burial.

Theseus had by now put the city to rights, and deeply saddened by these tragedies he left the city accompanied by his friend Pirithous. They were attracted by Helen, the daughter of Zeus and Leda, and the most beautiful lady of their time, who lived in Sparta. Theseus and Pirithous plotted to kidnap her, draw lots for her, and after that seize another of Zeus's daughters for the loser. Theseus won Helen and sent her to his mother while he and Pirithous descended into the underworld to carry off Persephone, the wife of the King of Hades. The deed was not accomplished, and instead the two travellers found themselves nailed to a rock by Hades. There they had to stay until Hercules came to the land of the dead and released them.

Meanwhile trouble had been brewing back in Athens. Helen's brothers, Castor and Pollux, had raised an army and invaded Athens in an attempt to retrieve their sister. Athens defeated, they rescued Helen with the aid of Menestheus, who was man-in-charge in Theseus's absence.

Menestheus had treacherously betrayed Theseus and stirred up the vicious resentment which the few rich and powerful men felt for the king. He succeeded in winning their support and when Theseus returned Athens was divided again into rival parties. Angry, dismayed and full of remorse at having left his people for an unworthy cause, he tried to put things to rights once more. He struggled without success, for weakened by tragedy and hardship he no longer had the strength. He decided to retire and made plans to spend the rest of his life peacefully on the island of Skiros, where he owned land. Even this was denied him, as Lycomedes, the king of the island, believed the lands to be his, and to remove the threat of Theseus he mercilessly pushed him from a high cliff where he met a cruel death on the rocks below.

Athens soon forgot about Theseus and all his good work. Several centuries later, however, he was remembered. When Cimon of Athens captured Skiros he took the advice of an oracle and transported the bones of the great Theseus back to Athens. At first he had not known where to look, but one day he had noticed an eagle tearing huge clods from the earth. He interpreted this unusual occurrence as a sign from the gods and, after the eagle had flown to a safe distance, started digging. Many feet below he found a highly ornate coffin, and inside it the skeleton of a very tall man, together with a lance, a sword and other weapons. And so Theseus, his remains returned to Athens, was at last honoured by the people as the founder of the first democracy.

THE STORY OF SAINT MEINRAD

Meinrad was the son of a count who lived by Lake Constance, in Switzerland, in the days of Charlemagne. When he was quite young he entered the monastery of Reichenau, on an island in the lake, as a monk. But he was so shy, and so much preferred to be alone, that one day he left the monastery and built a little hut on a mountain in a lonely, out-of-the-way place, where he spent all his time in prayer and fasting. But very soon the news of this hermit who, it was said, could even work miracles, spread far and wide, and people began to come to see him, to ask him to pray for them, to beg him to cure them, in ever-increasing numbers. Seven years after he had started living on his own, his remote hermitage had become a place of pilgrimage.

But Meinrad wanted to dedicate his life to prayer and solitude, and so he withdrew again, this time deep within a forest. With the help of a carpenter from a village on the edge of the forest, he built a little chapel to house a statue of the Virgin Mary that he had been given by the abbess of Zurich. Food was scarce in those parts, but he was supplied with all he needed for life by a pair of ravens, and as a pastime he trained them to speak. He preferred talking to them to talking to other human beings.

One day, in the year 861, when Meinrad had been living there for many years, two criminals who were fleeing from justice came to hide in the lonely forest, and they discovered the hermitage. Imagining that the hermit might have some hidden treasure, they decided to kill him. So they went to his cell, made a show of being very respectful, and greeted him with the words 'Glory be to Our Lord Jesus Christ'. 'For ever and ever, amen,' replied Meinrad. 'I can see that you are hungry, do sit down. I have very little to offer you, but you are welcome to it.' Then the two robbers went towards the hermit, ready to murder him, but the ravens flew up into the air, beating their wings against the bandits' faces, and stabbing at them with their beaks.

Meinrad had been warned by God that these men would kill him, and so he told the birds to stop attacking them, for he did not want to act against God's will. He let himself be set upon and stabbed to death by the two wretched criminals, and as he died he murmured, 'Let there be light, O God!'

At once a bright light, far stronger than the midday sun in summer, filled the forest, and the two murderers were dazzled by it, and fled in fear. But the ravens flew with them, croaking, 'Murderers! Murderers!' As they came near to the village, they passed the carpenter who had helped Meinrad to build his chapel. He recognized the ravens, and he had a feeling that something horrible had just happened. He went back to his cottage and asked his brother to chase after the two men, while he ran to the forest. There he found the body of the holy man, with candles burning at his head and his feet. It was said that they had been put there by angels.

Meinrad's slayers were soon captured, for the ravens went on shrieking round their heads, and they did not leave them until the men were on the gallows.

Meinrad was buried on the site of the hermitage, and a hundred years later the Benedictine monks built a monastery where Meinrad was buried. The monastery of Einsiedeln — which means Hermitage — is a very famous one.

In 946 the Bishop of Constance came to consecrate the new monastery, and just as the service was about to begin, a voice was heard crying out three times, 'Brother, stop! God Himself has consecrated this building.'

THE DEVIL'S HUNTSMAN

Even today the devil's huntsman haunts the forests of Europe, although there is not much forest left in Belgium, which is where his story began. On stormy nights his horse's hooves can be heard crashing through the undergrowth, and he howls like a dog, screeches like a bird of prey and grunts like a bear or a stag.

On the edge of the forest of Wynendael, which belonged to the Count of Flanders, there lived a peasant. He had a son, but the son had no interest whatsoever in working in the fields like his father. He did nothing but hunt, he thought of nothing but hunting. He left his old parents to labour and sweat to produce food for their livelihood while he roamed through the forest, hunting game of all kinds: deer and wild boar, bears and hares, pheasants and partridges. 'He will come to a bad end,' his father worried. But nothing could alter his passion for hunting.

One day the old peasant fell ill, and when he realized that he had not long to live, he sent a neighbour to find his son. 'Tell him to come and see me,' he begged, 'so that I can say farewell to him, and try once more to persuade him to change his ways. He is a peasant, and his place is in the fields.'

The son was harnessing his horse. He heard his father call, with sorrow in his voice: 'Come to me, son! May God help you to know where your duty lies.' But according to the young man, his place was not in the fields but following the tracks of wild creatures to kill them, and he was not interested in his duty. He took his gun, mounted his horse, and whistled up his dog. He paid no heed to the pleading and tears of the dying man.

Then his father lifted up his arms to heaven and cursed him. 'Hunt, then, if that is all you want to do! Hunt on and on, without rest, for ever!' And so saying, he died.

From that day on, his son was a lost man. He never left the forest, and ever since then he has been galloping, galloping, spurred on by his passion for hunting, but even more by his bad conscience. His phantom haunts all places where there is plenty of game, and he will have no rest until the world comes to an end.

FAIR MELUSINE AND THE
TREASURE OF KING HELMAS

A long time ago in France there was a count of Poitiers who, while out hunting one day, met a beautiful lady named Melusine in the forest. He immediately fell in love with her. To his surprise, for he had never met her before, she called him by his name, Raymond, and she seemed to know all about him. 'I will marry you,' she said, 'but you must never try to see me on Saturdays, and you must never ask what I do on that day.' He promised, and they had a very grand wedding, and they lived happily for many years. Melusine appeared to be very rich, and she built many towns and castles in Count Raymond's lands, some of which still exist, the chief of which was Lusignan.

They had ten sons, and although they were all strong and nobly-formed, each one had something odd about his face. The eldest was Urian, who had one red eye and one blue, the second was Eudes, and one of his ears was as big as a fan. The third was Guy, and he had one eye higher than the other, and the fourth was Reynold, who had a mark like a lion's pad on his cheek; and then came Antony, who had only one eye, but he could see twenty leagues with it. When they grew up, these five older sons went adventuring in the world, and they all married princesses, so that Urian became king of Cyprus, Eudes earl of March, Guy king of Armenia, Antony duke of Luxemburg, and Reynold king of Bohemia. A successful family, you might say. The strongest and bravest of them all, however, was Geoffrey, the sixth son, who had a tooth which stuck an inch out of his mouth like a boar's tusk, so he was known as Geoffrey Long-tooth.

One Saturday, the Earl of Forestz, who was Count Raymond's brother, paid an unexpected visit. He was surprised not to see Melusine, and asked his brother where she was. When Raymond answered that he did not know, the earl teased him about what she might be doing without his knowing, and Raymond, forgetting all about the promise he had made to her so many years before, went to her private apartments. He found that one of the doors was locked, and, his curiosity aroused, he made a hole in the door with the point of his sword and looked through it. What he saw filled him with horror. He saw Melusine in her bath, and although from the waist up she was the wife he knew and loved, from the waist down she had a great serpent's tail, striped blue and silver. He quickly stopped up the hole with wax, went back to his brother angrily, and told him he must go at once. Raymond was very sorry indeed that he had broken his word, and feared that he would lose Melusine. But she was as sweet and loving as ever, and seemed not to know that she had been spied on.

At the time that this happened, Geoffrey Long-tooth was away from home, dealing with a seventeen-foot giant that had been terrorizing the countryside around the Garonne river. He had a terrific fight with him, and managed to kill him with his great strength and sharp sword, by cutting off the giant's arms, one by one, and then cutting through his legs, and finally splitting his head in two with a single blow. News of this feat reached Northumberland, where the giant's brother lived, being as much of a plague to the people there. So they sent messengers to Geoffrey Long-tooth, asking for his help.

But before he went off to deal with this new menace, Geoffrey returned home to Lusignan. There he learnt that his brother Froment, the seventh son, had decided that he did not want to be a knight like his brothers, but to become a monk, and with his parents' consent he had entered a nearby abbey. When Geoffrey heard this, he was so disgusted at the idea of his brother as a monk that he rode at once to the abbey and set fire to it, burning all the monks inside, including Froment. When he came to his senses he was of course sorry for what he had done, but by then it was too late. Although he swore to rebuild the abbey, there was no way he could bring the monks back to life.

When the news of this awful crime reached his father, Count Raymond was enraged with Geoffrey and also full of grief for the death of Froment. When Melusine tried to comfort him, Raymond lost control of himself, and he accused her of being the cause of the disaster.

'Ah, false serpent!' he cried. 'How could any good come of my having married you? None of our children is an ordinary human, and now one of your sons has killed the best of his brothers!' No sooner were the words out of his mouth than he repented. But when Melusine heard them, she looked at him with eyes full of love and of sorrow.

'Alas,' she said, 'I could forgive you the first time because you said nothing. But now I must leave you forever.' They kissed lovingly, while all the lords and ladies of the court wept at the thought of losing Melusine. In front of them all, she leapt to the window and turned into a winged serpent. Three times she flew around the castle, making pitiful sounds of lament, and then she disappeared.

Geoffrey meanwhile was on his way to Northumberland. He was greeted with great joy when he arrived, because everyone expected that he would free them from the giant Grimold that was causing them so much trouble. He was led to the mountain of Brombelyo, where they

108

said he would find the giant, and Geoffrey started up the mountainside alone.

When the giant Grimold saw him coming, he laughed at the idea that a single knight should be so bold as to come to fight him. He picked up a great club, and with a fierce roar he demanded to know his name. Without answering him, Geoffrey rushed forward with a spear, and he was so strong that he knocked the giant clean over. But Grimold leapt up again quickly, and repeated his question. This time Geoffrey told him. When he heard that his enemy was the son of Count Raymond of Poitiers, he was scared, because he knew that he was doomed to die at his hands. But he lifted up his club and aimed a blow at Geoffrey, who dodged to one side, so that the club struck the ground and buried itself a foot deep. He pulled it out and tried again, and this time when Geoffrey side-stepped, the club went three feet into the earth. While Grimold was pulling it out, Geoffrey hit his leg with his sharp sword with all his might. The giant gave a howl, and disappeared into a hole in the mountainside. Geoffrey rushed after him, but when he looked inside the hole it was as dark as night and he could see nothing. So he went back down the mountain, meaning to go back next day to finish the job.

The people were all astonished to see him come back alive, and even more surprised when he went back the following day. 'Whatever happens,' he said, 'I will find out what is inside that hole.' So he set off into the darkness, using his spear to feel the way in front of him. At last he came to a chamber under the ground, carved out of the rock and lined with gold. In the middle of it he saw a noble tomb, set on six pillars of gold, with the statue of a king on it. Beside the tomb was the marble statue of a queen, and in her hands there was a tablet on which was written a strange inscription.

'I am the fairy Presina,' he read. 'Here lies my husband, the noble King Helmas of Albany. When we married he promised that when I had a baby he would not come to see me until I had recovered. But I gave birth to three fair daughters at one time, and he broke his word, so I had to leave him. When my daughters were fifteen years old, I told them how I had left their father, and they were so angry that they enticed him here and imprisoned him in this mountain until he died. To punish them, I decreed that Melusine should be turned into a serpent every Saturday, that Melior should live with a sparrowhawk in a castle in Armenia and never marry until the end of the world, and that Platina should guard her father's treasure within Mount Coinqs in Aragon, accompanied by dragons and monsters, until a descendant of King Helmas should come to claim it.'

When Geoffrey read this he realized that his mother was the daughter of Helmas of Albany and the fairy Presina. But he still had to deal with Grimold the giant. There was another passage leading from the tomb chamber, and he went along it until he found him. Grimold rushed at him and struck him on the helmet with a mallet and although Geoffrey was dazed by the blow he managed to thrust his sword into the giant's body up to the hilt. The giant cried out, 'I am dead, I am dead,' and fell headlong, lifeless.

Geoffrey was greatly praised and thanked by the people of Northumberland, but he refused to take any reward. He hurried back to Lusignan to tell his father what he had learned about his mother's ancestry, but he found the Count very unhappy about the loss of his dear wife. The Count told Geoffrey how it had all come about, and Geoffrey was so enraged with his uncle, the Earl of Forestz, for having caused his father to discover Melusine's secret, that he leapt on his horse and at once rode to the Earl's castle. Seeing his nephew approach with drawn sword, the Earl took fright, and fled up the stairs of a tower to escape his anger. When he reached the top, however, he slipped, and he fell to the ground far below, dying instantly.

Sadly, Geoffrey rode home and told his father the story. Count Raymond decided that he had lived long enough in the world, and that he would leave his lands to his sons and become a hermit. He went to the monastery of Montserrat, near Barcelona, and spent the rest of his life there in penance. He left the lands of Lusignan to Geoffrey, and his other two sons, Raymond and Thierry, became the lords of Parthenay and Forestz. Every year they paid a visit to their father, and when they set off for their visit in the year that Raymond died, a serpent appeared, moaning, on one of the towers of the castle of Lusignan. It was Melusine, warning them that they would find their father dead.

Many men went in search of the treasure of King Helmas, but none returned. One of them was an English knight from the court of King Arthur, who was determined to bring the treasure back with him from Aragon. He set off, accompanied by a single page, and travelled until they came to the foot of the mountain of Coinqs. There he left the page and started up the long narrow path which led to the top. Almost at once he came across a hideous dragon, which ran towards him with its mouth wide open and flames coming out of it, ready to cook and devour him at one and the same time. The knight drew his sword and cut through its neck at a blow, and the dragon fell dead.

The knight could not rest at all, for there was no place to sit down without sitting on a snake. He went on, and soon he saw a huge bear snarling at him. The bear tore away the knight's shield and clawed at his shoulder, but he slashed with his sword at the bear's snout, cutting it so

that the beast could not bite. Then the bear reared up and tried to hug him, but they fell down together, and the knight managed to plunge his dagger into its throat. On he went, slaying many other dragons and beasts until he came to the iron door of the cave in which lay the treasure. Within the mountain lived a hideous monster which had only one ear, no nostrils and one eye, which was a yard wide. Its breath came out of its ear, and when it snored everything for miles around was deafened.

It was an evil hour for the knight when he entered the cave. He was a brave man, but he was not descended from King Helmas. All the

dragons he had vanquished so far were like kittens compared with this monster, and it attacked him at once. He struck it with his sword, but it just bit the blade in half, and then it gobbled the knight down as if he had been a bun. And so the English knight died, which was a great pity.

The knight's page waited at the foot of the mountain for three days and then he returned alone to England. On his way there from Aragon he passed through Lusignan, and he told Geoffrey Long-tooth where and how the knight had perished. Geoffrey thought that he ought to go and destroy such a monster, and he asked his brother Thierry, the lord of Parthenay, to take charge of his lands while he was away. But just as all his preparations for the journey had been made, Geoffrey fell ill and died. He was buried in the abbey he had rebuilt after he had burned down the old one with the monks inside.

The treasure of King Helmas remains undiscovered to this day. But everyone in Poitiers, Lusignan and Parthenay will tell you the tale of Melusine.

MELIOR AND THE SPARROWHAWK

The curse of the fairy Presina on her second daughter, Melior, was perhaps a crueller one than she laid on Melusine, the youngest, who after all had a loving husband and a flourishing family, except for the unfortunate Froment.

The castle to which Melior was sent to live was in Armenia. Within the castle, day and night Melior watched the sparrowhawk, which sat on a perch beside her, until some knight or other came to try his luck at the adventure he had heard about. For a whole week (or some say for three days) he had to keep the hawk awake, with no companion, no sleep, no food to help him. At the end of that time Melior would come to him and offer him whatever on earth he wanted, because he had performed his task well.

Many people came to try to achieve this. Once there came the king of Armenia, and he watched the sparrowhawk successfully. When Melior asked him what his wish was, he said that he wished for Melior herself. Now that was the one thing he could not have.

'You are foolish,' she said, 'and that is not a wise wish, for I am not an earthly creature but a spirit.'

'But I am rich, and powerful, and I have everything that I want, except only you,' replied the king.

'You could and should have asked for peace, for yourself, your people and your successors,' said Melior. 'Instead, as a just reward, there will be war and no peace in your kingdom, until the ninth generation from now, and you will lose all your power and your riches.'

And so it happened. The kings of Armenia never knew peace again, and all his family became poor and needy.

After that there came a knight of the Order of the Templars. He too watched the sparrowhawk for seven days, and when he was asked his wish, he said that he would like his purse always to be full of gold. Melior granted his request, but she warned him that it was wrong to take pride in riches and to put his trust in his purse, and that his brother knights of the Order should beware of such failings.

Another time a humble man's son came to the castle of the sparrowhawk. He too endured the trial of watchfulness, and was offered a wish by Melior.

'What I want,' he said, 'is very simple. I want to be wealthy and successful in trade. That is what I was born to do, and what I want to do better than anyone else.'

Melior granted his request, and he became the richest merchant in the land. He could not count even one thousandth part of his wealth.

But woe to those who came to watch the hawk and fell asleep! They were lost for ever, and never were seen again in the world of men.

THE STORY OF OEDIPUS

The Greek oracle at Delphi once gave King Laius of Thebes a fearful warning: one day, as punishment for a crime he had committed, he would be killed by his own child. So when his wife Jocasta gave birth to their first-born son, King Laius stole the baby, roped its feet together and hammered a nail through them. On the king's orders the infant was then taken away by a slave to be abandoned on Mount Citheron. The slave was a kind-hearted man and naturally felt sorry for the child. Unable to see him left to the mercy of hungry wolves, he gave him to a shepherd who looked after the flocks of King Polybus of Corinth. As a result of the nail-wound, King Laius's son grew up with deformed feet, and he was named Oedipus or 'Swell-foot'.

Now as King Polybus and his wife Merope had no children of their own they took a fancy to the young Oedipus and decided to bring him up as their own child. Oedipus lived in ignorance of his adoption until his late teens. His foster-parents had considered it best to hide the truth from him, as they loved him dearly and wanted him to succeed Polybus to the throne. If he had known he was not really their child there was always the danger that he might have left them. One day, quite by chance, Oedipus overheard some people talking about him and saying that he had been found on a mountainside by a shepherd. Oedipus, deeply disturbed and upset by this information, went in immediate search of the oracle at Delphi in the hope of finding out who his parents really were. The oracle only added to his unease and disturbed him further: 'You will kill your father and marry your mother!' Oedipus was told. This strange utterance had the impact of a thunderbolt: Oedipus, not believing the rumours about his parentage, still thought of Polybus and Merope as his parents, and he was aghast at the thought of causing them harm. His whole body quivering with horror and fright at what he had been told, he set off immediately on a long journey which would take him to a remote part of Greece.

After some days of travelling, Oedipus arrived at a narrow pass between Delphi and his destination. At this point a chariot came rushing towards him, forcing him to jump to safety at a second's notice. Enraged, he thrashed out at the driver with his stick. At this an old man seated next to the driver seized a spear and leapt out to defend him. Oedipus fought well, and in the struggle that followed he killed the old man and all his servants, with the exception of one who managed to flee in terror.

Oedipus considered himself to be in the right, as he had, after all, only acted in self-defence. What he did not know was that the old man he had killed was in fact King Laius, his real father: the first part of the oracle's prophecy had come true. King Laius had been on his way to ask the oracle at Delphi how he could rid Thebes of the Sphinx, a hideous monster with a woman's head, a lion's body, wings like an eagle and the tail of a serpent. As with many other monsters in Greece, the Sphinx was the offspring of two other formidable creatures: Typhon, a giant with a hundred heads, and Echidne, who was half woman and half speckled serpent and ate men alive. The Sphinx also gorged itself on human flesh, and recently it had begun to prey on the people of Thebes. It asked every visitor to the city a riddle, and those who could not answer were throttled and then eaten alive. One of its latest victims had been the son of Queen Jocasta's brother Creon. When the news of Laius's death reached Thebes, Creon was made Regent, and he proclaimed that whoever could free the city of the deadly Sphinx could marry Jocasta and become King of Thebes.

Oedipus found the challenge of this announcement exciting. He had no wish to return to Corinth for fear of fulfilling the oracle's evil predictions and killing King Polybus. At the same time, the oracle's prophecies had made him fearless of his own death. When he arrived at the foot of the Sphinx, it leered down at him, gloating at the prospect of its next meal. With total confidence, it barked out its most difficult riddle: 'What is it that moves on four feet in the morning, two in the middle of the day and three in the evening, and is at its weakest when it uses most feet?' Oedipus's mind raced. 'Well?' snapped the Sphinx, hovering over him impatiently. Oedipus defied the monster's impatience and made a long pause before replying: 'It is man. In the morning of life, when he is a baby, he crawls on all fours, and it is then that he is weakest. In the sunny afternoon of manhood he walks erect on his strong legs, but in the cooler evening of life the old man uses a stick as a third leg, to help him walk.' The Sphinx howled with rage at having its most difficult riddle solved, swished its serpent's tail violently and leapt from the mountain to die shattered to pieces in the valley below.

Thus Oedipus laid claim to the crown of Thebes, and he married the widow of the dead king, his own mother. The second part of the oracle's prophecy had come true. As a ruler the people found him fair in his decisions, and the state became wealthy and secure. He and Jocasta had twin sons, Polynices and Eteocles, and two daughters, Antigone and Ismene. Oedipus had no idea that his children were also his brothers and sisters, and Jocasta certainly did not realize that her children were also her grandchildren.

Many happy and peaceful years passed until one day a dreadful plague began to spread through the entire country of Thebes. Many families died of the sickness, but the gods remained strangely silent and no prayers were answered. The people deduced that it must be some sort of punishment from heaven, and they implored Oedipus to help them, as they thought the gods favoured him. Oedipus could only reassure them by saying: 'Each of you suffers for himself, but none suffers more than I do, because I suffer for you all. Wait until my brother-in-law Creon returns from Delphi. He has gone to find out from the oracle what is the will of the gods.' When Creon returned, he reported that the oracle had said: 'The murder of King Laius weighs like a curse upon the whole country. The killer must be punished before the gods will forgive.'

Still in complete ignorance of the fact that he himself was the assassin, Oedipus issued requests to the people telling them to come forward and speak out if they knew anything about the circumstances of the King's death. For this information he offered a handsome reward. Anyone who withheld information would be doomed to spend the rest of his life in loneliness, not being allowed to speak to anyone or take part in any religious ceremonies. As for the murderer, he would be cursed and banished from human society to live in misery, branded with shame, for the rest of his life.

Anxious to explore every possible source of information, Oedipus sent for Tiresias, a blind soothsayer. On hearing the King's questions, Tiresias turned pale and refused to answer. 'O King, forgive me. The answer is a terrible one, and will bring great unhappiness to you. Allow me to keep my secret, and you keep your own.'

But Oedipus, still unaware that he had anything to hide, threatened to punish Tiresias for his silence and accused him of being in league with the murderer. The soothsayer finally gave in, and with much reluctance replied slowly: 'All the punishments to which you have sentenced the guilty man you must carry out yourself. For it was you who killed King Laius!'

Oedipus was thunderstruck. Furious at the suggestion, he accused Tiresias of being an evil trouble-maker. But the soothsayer stood firm and fearlessly repeated his assertion that Oedipus had killed Laius, his own father, and had then married his own mother, Jocasta. 'O King, I pity you,' were his parting words. 'Shame and scorn will follow you wherever you go.'

The people of Thebes were horrified and in their confusion did not know what to think. Oedipus and Jocasta refused to believe Tiresias, but Creon began to have an awful suspicion of the truth.

'It's all superstitious folly,' said Jocasta. 'These oracles really don't know anything, it's all trickery, they just invent these awful stories to cause a stir. They have nothing better to do. An oracle once prophesied that Laius would die at the hands of his own son. So we of course took the most dreadful of precautions: when our son was born we had him tied up and abandoned on a wild mountainside. I wept for many long hours, cried myself to sleep, and took a long time to recover. But you see the oracle was wrong — Laius was killed by a band of brigands, where three roads meet.'

Oedipus started at her last sentence. Jocasta had unwittingly triggered off some distant memory. He made her recount all she knew about Laius's death. When she had finished, Oedipus turned away and buried his face in his hands. A cloak of shame and deepest remorse enveloped him. 'Tiresias was not blind,' he said, his voice unsteady and choked. After a long silence, he continued: 'He is the only one who could see clearly.' He sat transfixed in horror, his eyes rigid in an unnatural gaze. Jocasta was disturbed by his sudden strange behaviour and begged him repeatedly not to take any notice of the oracle.

After a while Oedipus began to come to himself, and he issued a court order to find the servant who had witnessed the murder of King Laius and who had subsequently fled in terror. It was discovered that he had committed suicide when the man whom he knew to be his master's murderer had succeeded to the throne. At that moment a messenger arrived from Corinth. King Polybus had died, and the people of Corinth were clamouring for Oedipus to succeed him. 'There you are!' cried Jocasta. 'See how reliable the oracles are! They had you believing you would kill your father, and now we find that he has died peacefully in bed.'

But Oedipus was beginning to understand the truth of his terrible story, and he became taken over by an obsession to know every detail of the murder, however frightening. It turned out that the messenger from Corinth was in fact the shepherd who had looked after the abandoned baby and taken it to King Polybus. This same man was also able to identify the slave who had been ordered by Laius to leave the baby in the mountains. By this time, Oedipus was certain of his crime: he, Oedipus, was the killer, and Jocasta was his own mother. On the point of madness, Oedipus rushed through the palace in search of Jocasta. When he reached her chamber, he saw her body hanging from a rope in the centre of the room. Unable to bear the truth, she had hanged herself. As Oedipus laid her body on the ground, he wrenched her golden brooch from her dress and thrust it into both his eyes, blinding himself.

Grimacing with pain, Oedipus slowly groped his way to the door of the palace. Standing before the noisy crowds of people, he confessed to the crimes he had committed, unknowingly and unwillingly. As he stood before them, bowed with shame, the crowds felt a wave of pity for him. It was true that they had loved him, respected him as a just ruler, but now they were confused, because he had brought them great misfortune. They realized that fate was being cruel to him, and many of them wept. Creon went up to Oedipus and, taking him firmly by the hand, led him away from the people to his own children.

Even though Oedipus had suspected Creon of bribing Tiresias to make his accusation, he now humbly begged him to bury the poor queen and to rule as regent until his sons were old enough to be kings, and to be a father and guardian to his daughters. As for his own punishment, he asked that he should be eternally banished. He quietly and sadly gave his blessing to his children, asked Creon's forgiveness and finally implored the gods to protect the people, who would suffer so much on account of his crimes. Now poor Oedipus wished only to die. Life could only offer misery, so why continue?

However, the days and the months passed and gradually Oedipus came to feel that Jocasta's death and his own blindness had been sufficient punishment. He was after all still king, or so he thought, and so he returned to Thebes and asked Creon to be allowed to stay there. Creon's pity had turned to hardness, however, and even Oedipus's own sons tried to drive him away, as they were more interested in coming to power themselves. Only his daughters remained faithful and loving. Ismene stayed at home and tried to make her brothers feel more sympathy for their father. Antigone, the elder of the two, chose to accompany her father in his wanderings. So the people gathered to greet their king were met only by a blind beggar accompanied by a sad, beautiful girl. The two passed through the crowds and, descending the hillside, gradually disappeared into the distance and finally passed beyond the frontiers of Thebes.

These two figures wandered helplessly for many years, abandoning themselves to poverty and extremes of climate, from scorching sun to torrential rain. They got by on the charity of those who took pity on them, and they were happy with their small lot. They honoured the gods and one day an oracle promised them an end to their suffering. But unfortunately the oracle was vague and only told them that after many travels, Oedipus would come to a country where the Eumenides, known as the Kindly Ones, would give him peace. But what was Oedipus to make of that? The Eumenides were also known as the Furies, the avenging goddesses. He was puzzled, but he thought it best to trust the oracle to speak the will of the gods, and he had long ago decided that whatever destiny they may choose, he must bear it.

On their travels Antigone and Oedipus came to a village called Colonus, just outside Athens. As they rested by the wayside, a passer-by told them that they were sitting on holy ground, consecrated to the Furies. Oedipus breathed a long sight of quiet relief — at last the words of the oracle were going to come true.

At that time Athens was ruled by Theseus. Oedipus persuaded the stranger to take a message to Theseus, entreating him to come to the sacred grove. On his way to the king the stranger could not hold his tongue and talked excitedly to the people he met in the streets.

Gradually a crowd began to gather, and suddenly Antigone saw a face she recognized: it was her own sister Ismene. They embraced in great excitement at seeing each other again, and Ismene told Antigone everything that had happened. Polynices, the first-born of the twins, had

become king, and he had suggested to Eteocles that they should reign in alternate years. But Eteocles wanted to rule alone, and he drove Polynices away. 'Polynices went to Argos,' continued Ismene. 'He has married the daughter of King Admetus, and with his father-in-law's help he is determined to win back Thebes for himself.'

Oedipus was distraught at the news. 'Will the gods never have mercy on me?' he asked. 'The oracle has spoken of you again,' Ismene continued. 'It says that your sons will never gain power without their father. So in order to have power, they must find you, dead or alive. Creon has been informed of the oracle's predictions, and he is journeying here to persuade you to go back to Thebes with him. He reckons that if need be he will take you there by force.'

'And when I die, will they bury me in Thebes?' Oedipus asked.

'No, that they can't do, because you murdered your father.'

In despair, Oedipus raised his arms to heaven and said: 'They are no sons of mine, if all they can think about is their obsession to rule, instead of taking care of their father and loving their people. Eteocles will not continue to be king, and Polynices will never see his country again, for I will never go back to Thebes.'

King Theseus then came to the sacred grove and welcomed Oedipus most warmly to his country. Oedipus begged to be buried in Athens. 'Please at least let me leave my body with you, and it may bring you good fortune.' Theseus promised that his army would protect Oedipus, and when Creon arrived and tried to force the blind man to return to Thebes with him, Theseus and the people of Athens refused to allow him to be taken away.

Then came the day when Oedipus knew that his life was coming to an end. There were storms, with flashes of lightning and peals of thunder, and everyone took these to be signs from the gods. Oedipus asked Theseus to accompany him along the road, and Antigone and Ismene supported him as he walked. At a certain point, he stopped, bade them a last farewell, and asked to be allowed to walk on by himself into the mountains. No one knew or saw how Oedipus died. When Theseus, Antigone and Ismene had walked a little way, they looked back, but Oedipus was not to be seen. The gods had forgiven him and he was at last at peace.

BREAD FOR THE POOR

One year during the reign of King Casimir III of Poland there was a terrible famine. There had been no rain for several years, and nothing could grow but weeds. The corn withered on the stalk, the cattle died of thirst in their stalls, and the only things to be found in plenty were poverty and wretchedness.

The king was loved by his people for his justice and goodness, and so it was not surprising that he ordered the royal granaries to be opened and their contents given to the poor, and that he sent money to the more distant corners of his kingdom so that the peasants could buy grain from other countries. In spite of all he could do, thousands of people died of hunger, and then disease struck the survivors.

A few hours' journey from Gdansk there lived a rich man whose barns were filled to bursting with corn. But he kept their doors tight shut, and if he sold any at all, he asked an extremely high price for it. He was absolutely stony-hearted, and even when little ragged children begged a crust of bread at his door, he would drive them away with a whip. He himself had everything he wanted, and he wanted everything he had for himself alone. But still he wanted more.

One day he dressed up in ragged clothes and went to the monastery at Oliva. At the door, he moaned and groaned and said, 'I am a poor man, I'm dying of hunger. Help me, for God's sake!' And the monks gave him a loaf of bread.

The rich man hid the bread under his ragged jacket. On his way home, he met an old woman who was carrying a child, dying of starvation. 'Have pity, sir,' she begged him. 'My little granddaughter had had nothing to eat for days, and she will surely die unless you have something to give her.'

'Go to the monastery at Oliva,' the rich man said, angrily. 'They will give you something there.'

'But I'm too weak to go so far, sir. You have just come from there.'

'Why do you call me "sir"? I'm only a poor man, just look at my rags.'

'Underneath your rags you are carrying a loaf of bread,' the woman said. 'For the love of Christ, give me just a little of it for this child.'

'You are quite mistaken, woman,' the heartless man answered. 'I am carrying a stone under my rags, not bread. I need it to build a bridge, and we don't have many stones where I come from. Let me go, I'm in a hurry. I have no time to waste like this.'

Then the old woman said, 'You are lying. Since you are so unfeeling, I hope that the bread turns to stone!'

At once the rich man felt the bread become heavy, very heavy. It had turned to stone. This miracle changed his heart, and as soon as he got home he opened his granaries for the poor people to help themselves to what they needed.

The stone which had been bread was kept for a long time in the monastery at Oliva, as evidence of the miracle.

DENGHI THE SNAKE GOD

Long, long ago, before white people set foot in Fiji, spirits and gods ruled the islands and their people. Sometimes they took human form, sometimes they appeared as fish, birds or snakes. Always they were worshipped and feared by the people of Fiji.

Greatest and most powerful of all was the Snake God Denghi. He it was, the legends say, who made all the islands in the Pacific Ocean between Australia and America. To this day, countless tales of Denghi are passed down from one chief to the next, as King Taliaitupu, of the Fijian isle of Naiau, confirms.

The legends date from a distant age, before the islanders of Fiji knew how to make boats, and before the Bau tribe came to rule the most powerful kingdom in the islands. At that time — the time when the world was still good — each tribe lived in isolation, for people could not go from island to island as we can now. They lived on fruit, which grew in abundance, and fish which they caught in the shallows of the sea. They led a simple and modest life, happy and contented. They had what they needed. Why should they ask for more?

True, the people of Fiji in those remote times did want to cross the sea. They often stood on the shore and gazed at the vastness of the ocean. On the horizon, rising from the morning mist, they could see other islands. Did people live there too? They would have loved to know, but they had no way of finding out.

Of course they could only see the little islands nearby. They had no idea that Vanua Levu was much larger than Naiau, or that Viti Levu was larger still. They could not know that there were hundreds of islands all around, or that Fiji was only a grain of dust in the immensity of the South Seas — one of countless grains of dust in the Pacific Ocean. But their hearts leapt when they saw the huge herons which nested on the island rising into the air and vanish into the azure sky.

'Oh to have wings and fly away,' they cried. 'Or fins, so we could swim through the sea like sharks. Or if only we could float on the water for miles like the tree trunks which the high tides leave on the beach.'

Now the tribes of Fiji have a sacred mountain, Mount Nakauvandra, whose summit is often hidden in the clouds. High up there lived the Snake God Denghi, who knew of the islanders' longings. His cave was guarded by a curtain of live snakes, hanging down from the rock with their fangs at the ready. The islanders were afraid of the mountain, for they dreaded the mighty serpent as much as they adored him.

And well they might, for he was very powerful. When the Snake God lay down in his cave in the evening and closed his eyes, night would fall on all the islands. When he turned over in his slumber, the islands would tremble, and people would say it was an earthquake. And when Denghi woke up in the morning and opened his eyes, dawn would break over all the islands.

One day Denghi laid two eggs. From one came his eldest child, his son Rokola, and from the other his daughter Uto. Then he had three more sons: Rokomutu, Kausambaria the woodworker and Nagai, the messenger of the gods.

Denghi fed his children on bananas and a root called the yam. He taught them how to make fire, and everything that gods need to know.

At that time not all the islands were there. Some were just coral reefs under the sea. So one day Denghi said to his son Rokomutu:

'There's not enough land for the people to live on, Rokomutu. Go out and make them some islands.'

So the Snake God's son went down into the sea, scraped up some sand and piled it up on the coral reefs to make land. But wherever Rokomutu's cloak trailed on the ground, it became rocky.

Many stories are told of Denghi. One night he was woken by the noise of surf breaking on the coast of Raki-raki. Pushing aside his curtain of live snakes, he called to his son Nagai, the messenger of the gods.

'Go and tell the reef to be quiet, Nagai,' he ordered. 'I can't sleep!'

And since that time the surf breaking on the coast of Raki-raki cannot be heard.

Another time Denghi was disturbed by bats, and he sent Nagai to chase them away. The god's son cut down a great nokono tree and, wielding it like a huge club, chased the noisy bats out of their trees. But then the tree flew out of Nagai's hand, curved through the air in a great arc and fell far away in the water near Raki-raki. Nagai ran to retrieve his club. He had no trouble finding it, and being a giant, he pulled it out on to dry land as if it were light as a feather.

One of the gods of the Vuya tribe was watching, and he was so amazed by Nagai's might that he called his chief. The men had never seen anything like it. They found it terrifying, and decided to kill the giant. They would lure him into a house and then surprise him. So they offered him food and drink and were very friendly, so as not to give their plan away. But Nagai saw through them.

'Build a big pig-sty,' he ordered.

The Vuyas obeyed. When the sty was ready, Nagai opened his wristband, took out a hundred pigs and placed them in the pen.

'That's to thank you for your welcome,' he said.

127

The Vuyas were even more amazed. But something stranger still was to come. Hanging from Nagai's ear was a tiny scrap of masi, the splendid cloth made from mulberry bark which the Fijians wear at feasts. Nagai now pulled the scrap of cloth, and in no time he had rolls and rolls of the costly stuff.

'This is for you,' he told the Vuyas, 'to thank you for having me as your guest.'

But the miracle made the Vuyas even more afraid of Nagai. Trembling, they invited the stranger to spend the night with them. Secretly they planned to attack him in his sleep, for his powers filled them with terror.

But how much greater was their fear and misery next morning, when they awoke to find not just that they had slept through the night and missed their chance to kill him, but that Nagai had gone, while the king of the Vuyas lay dead in his house.

Fearing the strange god's vengeance, they stole away and settled elsewhere. To this day still, the members of the Vuya tribe remember the old story, and it is said that when they have to go to Raki-raki, they never linger long.

Another time Denghi remembered the islanders' longing to cross the sea, and he called his eldest son Rokola and the woodworker Kausambaria.

'I am going to show you something, my sons,' he told them. 'This will make you masters of all the islands of Fiji.'

And he taught the two brothers a new art: how to build outrigger canoes, which could carry many people.

'Now you can go from island to island,' said Denghi. 'In times to come they will call you the great boatbuilders. Your tribe will be greater than all the others, and you will rule a mighty empire.'

And so it was. Rokola, chief of the tribe of boatbuilders, became king of the Fiji islands. The boatbuilders became a mighty people, more powerful than the people of Bau came to be later, for at that time, when the world was still good, no one else knew how to build boats.

Rokola and his people became very proud. On the mountain opposite Mount Nakauvandra they built a great city called Nantavea, so strong that their enemies were powerless against them.

Denghi the Snake God often visited the city of Nantavea, and taught Rokola and his people many useful things. So they became cleverer than the other Fiji islanders, and were rich and lived in plenty.

In the end they began to oppress the other tribes, and made them pay more and more taxes. Little by little they grew lazy. Why should they make any effort? There was no shortage of strangers come to the city to

128

find work. What's more, there were slaves. For the boatbuilders would sail away to pillage other islands and bring back prisoners, who then slaved away as servants and labourers. The boatbuilders, masters of all, lived in comfort and became arrogant.

Now Denghi had a beautiful black turtle-dove, Turukawa. When the Snake God lay down to sleep, Turukawa would roost in the fig-tree at the entrance to his cave. At daybreak, she would puff herself up:

'Kru-kru-kruuu!' she would coo, and Denghi would wake up and come out, and his great voice would thunder over the valley to the boatbuilders' city.

'Dawn has broken! Get up and go to work!'

By this time the boatbuilders were finding it harder and harder to wake up. Often they feasted late into the night, so dawn found them still stretched out under the palm trees, deep in slumber. Slaves and power had poisoned their hearts, and they cursed the god when he disturbed their rest.

'You are cruel, great Snake,' they grumbled and groaned. 'Why do you torture us with work, when that's the last thing we want?'

'If you don't work, you will perish,' warned Denghi. 'Why do you think I taught you to make boats? Why, so that you can go fishing, and visit the other islands to keep peace in your empire.'

'Giving orders is quite enough,' retorted King Rokola, the eldest son, to his father. 'We shouldn't have to do the work as well. What's the use of power and slaves if we have to do the work as well?'

In vain the Snake God tried to convince the boatbuilders. Rokola and his people just laughed. Instead of going to Mount Nakauvandra to sacrifice to Denghi, they sprawled all day in the shade of the palm. The Snake God began to lose patience.

'I didn't make you the masters of Fiji so that you could fritter away your days like this!' he scolded.

But they took no notice at all. In fact King Rokola and Kausambaria the woodworker had had enough of their father. Rokola fretted:

'It's all the fault of that cursed turtle-dove Turukawa.'

'The turtle-dove?' Astonished, Kausambaria stared at his brother.

'Who else?' said Rokola irritably. 'If she didn't wake the god every morning with her horrible "kru-kru-kruuu", he'd leave us in peace. Just imagine: if Turukawa doesn't wake up Denghi, he goes on sleeping, and we don't have to get up and work. Life will be heaven.'

'I suppose so,' said Kausambaria. 'But so what? How are you going to stop the dove from waking Denghi?'

'With this, brother,' laughed Rokola, and he took an arrow from the quiver on his back.

A shiver went up Kausambaria's spine.

'No, Rokola, we can't do that. Denghi will punish us if we kill Turukawa.'

But Rokola swept aside his protests with an irritated wave of his hand. 'What can the god do to us? We're strong and powerful. We can defend ourselves.'

'But our brothers and the other giants will help him.'

'We're stronger.'

'He's our father.'

'And a tyrant.'

'He's the god we must obey.'

But proud Rokola drew himself up to his full height: 'And I, I am the King of the boatbuilders, to whom all the islands owe allegiance. We are a great people, and bold one. Put your trust in me.'

Rokola ordered his tribe to prepare secretly so that they could defend the city against Denghi. He had spears made, and bows and arrows, and strong walls. Thousands of slaves were set to work.

Denghi saw all these preparations, but said nothing. He loved his sons, but he no longer trusted them, and his heart was heavy.

'Father,' said Rokomutu to the god. 'Rokola and Kausambaria are planning a revolt against you!'

Denghi smiled.

'Do something! Stop them!' begged his daughter Uto.

Denghi said nothing.

'The boatbuilders are cruel tyrants, great god,' Nagai, the messenger of the gods, told his father. 'The people are restive, the women are weeping, the slaves are dying, and our brothers want to rise up against you. It's time to remind them you are Denghi the All-Powerful.'

The Snake God turned away. He still hoped that Rokola and Kausambaria would come to their senses and decide to obey him again.

But while he slept, his two sons came to his mountain Nakauvandra. They tiptoed up to the fig-tree on which Turukawa was roosting. Rokola put an arrow to his bow, took aim, and shot the dove through the heart. She fell dead to the ground. The two brothers hurried back to their city, called all the soldiers to arms, and goaded the slaves on to finish building the walls.

Next day Denghi overslept. When at last he opened his eyes, he had a feeling he had slept longer than usual. He had not heard Turukawa's morning call.

'Why didn't you wake me, Turukawa?' called the god, puzzled, expecting to hear her 'kru-kru-kruuu' in reply. But all was still.

130

Denghi got up, pushed aside his curtain of snakes, and came out. There, lying dead under her fig-tree, was the beautiful black turtle-dove. Her feathers, usually so bright, had turned dull, and in her breast there was an arrow — the arrow of Rokola.

Denghi bent and smoothed down the ruffled plumage. He wept, for he loved both the turtle-dove and his sons, who had caused him so much pain. His heart was full of sorrow, and his head full of rage.

'Rokola!' the god's voice roared across the valley like a thunderclap.

Behind the half-built walls of Nantavea, where the boatbuilders were hurrying the slaves, Denghi's eldest son stood up straight.

'Yes, father,' he answered. 'What do you want?'

'You have killed my turtle-dove.'

Rokola laughed. 'It's only a turtle-dove, father, nothing more. It's nothing to get excited about.'

'But I loved her.'

'And what about us?' retorted Rokola, spitting out all the venom that had built up through years of resentful obedience. 'We're your children. Yet you torture us.'

'You too I have loved. To you, above all the people of Fiji, I have given knowledge and power. Riches and joy I have heaped upon you. And yet you rise up against me. How can you be so ungrateful?'

'Because we've had enough of bowing down to you!' said Kausambaria.

'Fie on you!' hissed Denghi. 'Fie on you, Rokola, and all your people! You have taken my Turukawa. I shall take your empire and give Fiji to the Bau tribe and your brothers. From now on you boatbuilders will be the slaves of other tribes, and will be scattered far and wide across the islands!'

'Just you try it, god!' scoffed Rokola. 'There are too many of us. You may be a god, but you can't hurt us. But you're welcome to try if you dare. You can't scare us!'

Denghi smiled: 'You're a fool, Rokola. You are building walls, I see. Do you think they will save you?'

'Yes, we're safe behind them.'

'Ah, Rokola, my son, is there no end to your madness? Build on, then! Build your walls as thick and high as you like. Build them to the sky! But don't forget your enemy is a god.'

The boatbuilders just yelled abuse and went on building the walls. At last the slaves had finished, and Rokola climbed to the top of the fortifications.

'Hey, big snake,' he shouted over the valley. 'Come out of your hole!'

Denghi appeared on Mount Nakauvandra.

'Have you finished the wall?' he asked.

'We have,' answered Rokola, 'and no people in the world has ever built a stronger one.'

Denghi smiled a bitter smile.

'What do you know of the world? Do you really think this island, or the islands you can reach with your boats, are the world? And what do you want?'

'I want you to fight. I want to prove we are stronger than you. I want our children one day to say: "Once upon a time on Mount Nakauvandra there was a terrible Snake God called Denghi, but our ancestors killed him and freed our people from his tyranny."'

Now Denghi was wild with fury. His eyes glowed. He tore a great tree out of the ground and threw it into the sky, rending the clouds. And it began to rain.

Day and night it rained. The waves began to flow higher and higher up the beaches, and soon the swollen sea had flooded the land. Higher and higher the water rose up the walls of Nantavea. At last the waves dashed the walls to pieces, flooded the city, and buried Rokola and most of his men.

Only a couple of thousand of the boatbuilders were able to find boats, rafts or tree-trunks and escape. Many were swept away by the sea. Some drowned, some landed on islands far away. And when the waters had subsided and the survivors felt firm ground under their feet at last the spots where they landed sprouted vesi trees, which were then held sacred by the people of Fiji.

So the boatbuilders were scattered far and wide across the Fiji islands. They became slaves to the chiefs of strange tribes, and had to build boats for the people they once ruled. Some of them managed to settle on the islands of Bau and Kandavu, but most made their homes on the banks of the river Rewa, on Fiji's main island of Viti Levu. And to this day this is the boatbuilding centre of Fiji.

Strangely enough, the flood that swept away Rokola's city made another part of Fiji fit to live in. At that time the island of Vatulele was just a coral reef where nothing would grow. But the fig-tree in which Turukawa the turtle-dove had perched outside Denghi's cave when the world was still good was torn up by the great waves of the flood, and was swept away to the reef of Vatulele with earth still clinging to its roots. The earth covered the beds of coral, and so the island was born. Then the Fijians sailed to it, built huts and began to fish, and people have lived on Vatulele ever since.

And on Mount Nakauvandra the king of the Bau tribe, the new rulers of Fiji, built a temple to Denghi, the great Snake God who had lived in the cave.

THE CALL OF THE OWL

Long ago in the Red Indian tribe of the Cherokees there was a widow who had a very beautiful daughter. When the girl was old enough to marry, her mother took her aside.

'It's time, my child, to find yourself a husband,' she said. 'Your father was a famous hunter. Only another man like him is good enough for you.'

Her daughter agreed, but she was a difficult, temperamental girl, and none of the young men of the tribe pleased her. One was too small, another too ugly, a third too poor and a fourth too simple. But one day a very handsome young man appeared at the widow's wigwam. She had never seen him before.

'I am U-gu-ku,' he said. 'I would like to marry your daughter. I've always wanted a wife as beautiful as her.'

'My daughter,' replied the woman, 'must marry a good hunter, so she never goes hungry. My husband was a famous hunter, and we always had plenty of meat.'

'I'm a very good hunter,' answered U-gu-ku.

He was a pleasant young man, and so the widow called her daughter.

'This is U-gu-ku,' she told her. 'He wants to marry you.'

The girl liked the look of the young man, and so the marriage took place.

Next day the widow went to her new son-in-law.

'There's no more meat in the house,' she said.

'Don't worry, mother of my wife,' replied U-gu-ku. 'I'll go hunting.' And off he went. But when he came back, all he had were three paltry little fish.

'I'm sorry,' said U-gu-ku. 'I had no luck hunting today, so I decided to go fishing. I've brought you three fish. No doubt I'll have better luck tomorrow.'

Their supper that evening was not very lavish. But worse was to come, for next day all that U-gu-ku brought back from the hunt were three lizards.

'It's as if there's a curse on me,' said U-gu-ku sadly. 'But don't worry. Tomorrow you'll have meat.'

On the third day U-gu-ku returned very tired from the hunt, and handed the widow three scrawny little bits of meat that the other hunters had left behind. His wife and mother-in-law could not understand it. They began to wonder if U-gu-ku could be trusted.

'He told me he was a good hunter,' said the widow, 'but he has hardly killed a thing. Don't you think you should follow him secretly and see what he's doing?'

The girl agreed, and on the fourth day of her marriage she followed her husband into the forest, hiding behind the trees. When they came to the river, to her surprise and horror, U-gu-ku turned into an owl.

'U-gu-ku — oooooo — oooooo — oooo,' he cried, flying up into the air and out over the river. Then, suddenly, he swooped down to the water and seized a little crayfish.

The young woman was horrified to think she had an owl as a husband. She ran back home as fast as she could, weeping as if her heart would break.

That evening, when U-gu-ku returned, the crayfish was all he had.

'Is that all you caught?' asked his wife.

'An owl stole the rest from me,' he replied.

'But you're the owl!' cried the young woman furiously. 'You've lied to me, you've tricked me, and what's more you're a dreadfully bad hunter!'

'No, I'm not,' protested U-gu-ku. 'I may be a bad hunter for a man, but for an owl I'm a very good one.'

'Get out of my sight!' shouted his wife. 'I never want to see you again.'

So the owl flew away into the forest, crying and hooting dolefully. He was terribly unhappy, for he loved his wife with all his heart.

'U-gu-ku — oooo — oooooo — oooooo,' went the sorrowful voice, as U-gu-ku mourned his loss. And every night since then, the owl's lament has been heard, as he sings of his lost love.

THE DAWN OF THE NORSE GODS

Once upon a time, say the Germanic legends of northern Europe, there was no world, just a vast and lonely void. There was no land or sea, and no people. The stars had not found their places in the sky, and the sun wandered aimlessly, not knowing that there was a course for it to follow.

Far in the north lay Niflheim, the frozen land of mist and darkness. Deep in the south was Muspelheim, the land of flames, ruled by Surtur the Fire Giant. Between the two yawned the lonely void, the great abyss of Ginnungagap. Rivers of salty ice poured out of Niflheim into its lonely depths, there to be melted by warm winds from the south. Hvergelmir, the Well of Life, was at the bottom of the abyss, and life began when Ymir the Ice Giant sprang from the well.

Ymir lived on the milk of the magic cow Audhumla. Not a blade of grass grew in that desolate place, and so the cow licked the ice. It tasted very good, and the cow rubbed her rough tongue on it again and again. After a while the hair of a man appeared. Audhumla licked and licked until his hair came free, and then his head, and at last his whole body. This was Buri, the father of Borr, who in turn fathered three mighty sons: the gods Vili, Ve and Odin, whom some call Woden or Wotan.

In time, Borr's sons slew the great giant Ymir, and from his body they made the world we know. They called it Midgard, the middle world, for it lay between Niflheim and Muspelheim. Ymir's flesh became the land, with his bones for mountains and his teeth for rock. His hair became the trees and grass, while his blood flowed round the world to become the seas and rivers. The sky was Ymir's skull, held in place by the branches of a mighty ash tree, called Yggdrasil, the World Tree.

Odin and his fellow gods — the Aesir — lived in the land of Asgard in the branches of Yggdrasil. Asgard had many regions, many halls. One was Gladsheim, the palace where Odin lived with his wife Frigga. Odin was the Allfather or All Wise, king of the Germanic gods (or the Norse gods, as they are often called). He watched over Midgard from Lidskialf, his seat above Asgard. Two tame ravens called Hugin and Munin perched on his shoulders, or flew about gathering news for their master. Odin often visited Midgard, the land of men, or rode across the sky on the valiant Sleipnir, an eight-legged horse who could outpace the wind. Frigga too would travel forth, in a heavenly chariot drawn by cats, which were the animals she loved best.

Yggdrasil, the World Tree, bound together heaven, earth and hell:

Asgard, Midgard and Niflheim. Its three roots ran to Midgard and Niflheim and into Jotunheim, the land of giants. The gods could descend to Midgard by the Rainbow Bridge, Bifrost, guarded by the god Heimdall.

Many wondrous animals lived in the roots and branches of the World Tree. Four deer leapt from branch to branch, and at the top roosted a wise eagle, a goshawk and Widofnir the golden cockerel. There were two more cockerels: the brown cock of Hell, and Fialar, red as fire, who watched for Ragnarok, the Day of Destruction which would end the world. Ratatoskr the squirrel ran up and down the tree all the time, carrying news between the eagle and Nidhoggr the dragon, who lurked in Niflheim gnawing at one of the World Tree's roots.

Among the roots, too, was the Well of Urd, home of the Norns, three sisters who knew all the past, present and future. Nearby was Niflheim, the shadowy hell where the goddess Hela ruled the souls of the dead. The only mortals who escaped going to Hell were warriors who died in battle: their souls went instead to Asgard, to feast in Valhalla and wait for Ragnarok, when they would fight on the side of the gods. The way to Hell was watched by Garm, the fearful 'hound of the bloody chest'.

Hela's father was the wicked and crafty Loki, half god and half giant. He often behaved as if he was the gods' friend, but really he was their enemy and would lead the forces of darkness against them when the world died. Loki also had two sons, Fenris and Jormungand. Jormungand was the World Serpent, symbol of evil, who lay in a circle round Midgard like a band of wickedness. Fenris was a cunning and vicious wolf. The god Tyr had managed to chain him, but only at the cost of losing his hand. Both of Loki's sons were waiting for Ragnarok, the day when all bonds would be broken and they could rise up against the gods. On that last day of the world, the Day of Destruction which the Germans call the Twilight of the Gods, the forces of good and evil would meet and destroy each other.

Many long years after Midgard was created, Odin's beloved son, Baldur the beautiful, was killed by his blind brother Hodur through Loki's trickery. The whole world mourned for him. The gods wept, and so did their bitter enemies the giants. Humans and animals wept, and the trees and other plants, and even the rocks and stones shed bitter tears. Only the heartless Loki did not weep for his crime.

Odin the Allfather was deeply troubled. He sensed that the Day of Destruction would not be long in coming, as the gods measured time. He went to Haid, a mortal woman with the gift of prophecy, and questioned her.

'There shall come a day,' Haid answered, 'when Fialar the crimson cockerel sees the twilight of the gods in the distance. He will give the alarm, and his brown brother in Hell will answer him. Garm the Hound of Hell will slobber and bay to his mistress to release him. On the Rainbow Bridge Heimdall will blow his horn to herald the end of the world. Fear and horror will seize the human race. Brother will fight brother and children will rise up against their parents. Their bodies will drift down the rivers and seas, down through the roots of Yggdrasil to Hell, and the dragon Nidhoggr will devour them.

'Skoll the wolf will swallow the sun and moon, and the wolf Fenris will burst his bonds. Jormungand the World Serpent will uncoil and rise, sending tidal waves to lay waste the coasts. Then, with his brother Fenris and Garm the Hell-hound, he will advance on Asgard. Surtur the Fire Giant will lead his warriors of flame from Muspelheim against the fortress of the gods.

'You, Odin the Allfather, will blow your horn to muster the gods and warriors of Valhalla for the last fight. Then the two armies will meet with such force that the rocks will shatter, and the land will be swallowed up by the sea.

'Garm will attack the God Tyr, and each will slay the other. Thor the Thunder God will smash Jormungand's skull with his great hammer and then perish, poisoned by the great serpent's deadly breath. Loki and Heimdall too will meet and fall in combat. Even you, Odin the Allfather, will be devoured by the foul Fenris, but your son Vidar will avenge you: Vidar will tear off the wolf's jaw and kill it. Then all the world will be engulfed by the flames of Surtur the Fire Giant, and every one in it shall perish.

'But do not despair. A new world will rise from the sea, covered in green meadows and fields of swaying corn, thick forests and smiling countryside. Sparkling waterfalls will plunge into the valleys with a froth of silvery foam. Eagles will wheel in the blue sky, and the song of birds will fill the air.

'Of the gods only your sons Vali and Vidar will survive, and Thor's sons Magno and Modi. Baldur will return from the dead with his brother and slayer, Hodur. One man and one woman also will survive, and they will people the world anew.'

WHY THE WORLD IS HOW IT IS

In the beginning of time Fidi-Mukullu created the world, and then the people and animals. In those far distant times, longer ago than anyone can imagine, Fidi-Mukullu lived in a village far to the East, but no one knew where.

Animals and people lived in peace in the forest, sleeping and eating together without fear. But they lived in darkness, for the world was shrouded in an endless night.

One day all the folk of the forest — people and animals — gathered to discuss what they could do about the darkness.

'Surely there's daylight somewhere,' they said. 'Dawn must be hiding, that's all. We must go out and find it.'

'I'll find the dawn,' offered the antelope, and off she trotted. The others listened as the sound of her hooves died away in the forest. Then they sat silent for a long, long time — no one could say just how long, for there were no days to measure time by. They felt strangely alone, even though there were so many of them.

At last they heard a sound. Soon it grew into a rustling in the undergrowth, and the antelope was with them again. For a while she was too exhausted by her long and arduous journey to speak. When at last she spoke, they knew from her sad voice that her news must be bad.

'I made my way towards the West. Long, long have I travelled, but I found no light. My friends, the darkness is everywhere.'

When they had got over their disappointment, the forest-dwellers discussed who next to send in search of daylight. At last they decided on the buffalo, and off he went. When he returned, he too had no hope to offer them.

'I set out towards the North. Far, far have I travelled, but I found no dawn. My friends, the shadow is all around.'

'Let me try,' said the elephant. 'I'm big and strong. If anyone can find the dawn, I can.'

But his luck was no better. When he returned, he said:

'I marched to the South. Hard, hard have I travelled, but I found no day. My friends, the night is endless.'

The folk of the forest did not know what to do. They trembled fearfully in the night and yearned for daylight. But then Muboa, the dog, stood up.

'I'll look for the sun,' he barked. 'The antelope has speed, the buffalo stamina and the elephant great strength. The antelope has a keen eye, the buffalo has a sensitive tongue and the elephant has a sharp ear. But I have a good nose. Perhaps the dawn is hidden under the earth. I'll sniff here and sniff there and when I've found it, I'll dig it up.'

His friends wished him luck, and some birds, who did not dare sing in the dark, set off with him.

'We'll come too,' they twittered. 'If the dawn isn't hidden underground, it may be up in the sky, where only we can find it.'

'Head for the East,' the others advised. 'There wasn't any sign of light anywhere else, so perhaps that's where the dawn will be.'

So the dog and the birds set off towards the East. Muboa had swift legs and a strong heart. On and on he ran, with the birds behind him. Everywhere they went, the world was in darkness. After a long, long time they glimpsed a village hidden in the forest. The birds scouted on ahead. Soon they were back, all aflutter with excitement.

'Beyond the village there's a faint redness in the sky,' reported a cockerel. 'What do you think it could be?'

Then Muboa too made out this bewitching gleam, which gave a golden sheen to the roofs of the huts.

'Wait for me here in the forest,' he said to the birds. 'The cock and I will go to the village to find out the meaning of this rosy glimmering. Maybe it's the dawn.'

When the pair reached the village, dawn was breaking. It was Fidi-Mukullu's village. Muboa laughed and said to the cock:

'Look! We've found the dawn at last. Isn't it lovely? Tell the other birds.'

The cock crew. The others answered him with a singing and squawking and cheeping and twittering fit to wake the dead, for they had found their hearts' desire — daylight.

Once, twice, three times crew the cock: 'Cock-a-doodle-doo!'

Far away the humans heard. 'The dawn has come!' they burst out.

Then the sun rose and flooded the world with light. Man and beast alike were filled with joy.

'Hooray for Muboa!' they cried. 'You've brought us the dawn, Muboa. You shall be our first chief!'

And so it was. Muboa the dog ruled over the folk of the forest, both animal and human.

But when Fidi-Mukullu saw this, he frowned. 'There they are, all happy together in the forest,' he muttered to himself, shaking his head. 'Peacefully living on nuts, roots and insects. I'll soon put a stop to that.' And he went to the humans.

'Leave the forest and build a village,' he commanded. 'Obey me and I shall give you fire.'

142

And so the humans went off to build a village and receive the gift of fire, while the animals stayed in the forest.

'Dig in the ground and you will find iron,' said Fidi-Mukullu next. 'Melt it in the fire, and make heads for your arrows.'

And he showed them how. The humans were quick to learn. They made bows and arrows and learnt how to use them. The animals crept up in secret to see what their old friends were doing.

'Now go and hunt!' ordered Fidi-Mukullu at last. 'Kill the animals and roast them.'

And the humans obeyed. The animals fled and hid in the forest, knowing they could not live in peace with humans any more. But the hunters chased them and many were killed. The animals tried to defend themselves. If an elephant found itself faced with a man, it would seize him in its trunk and dash him against a tree till all his bones were shattered. If a gorilla saw a man walking down a forest path, it would not always vanish, but might chase the man and kill him. Sometimes the animals would flee, sometimes they would attack. But the humans were more cunning. Little by little the animals were forced back further and further into the depths of the forest, though the humans still had as much meat as they could eat.

'Meat is delicious,' they said to Fidi-Mukullu after a while, 'but it gets monotonous after s while.'

So Fidi-Mukullu taught them to sow. They reaped millet, maize and cassava-root, and lived in plenty. It was a happy life.

But there came a time when no rain fell and famine swept the land. People prayed for rain, but none came. The stocks of food ran out, and no more grew in the fields: there was nothing to eat at all. Desperate, the people went to their chief.

'We must have rain,' they pleaded. 'Can't you make it rain?'

The chief decided to turn to Tombo-Mukullu. The road to him was a long one, for he lived many, many miles away, while Fidi-Mukullu now lived up in the sky. Tombo-Mukullu could be whatever he chose: man, woman or child. On one day he might be an old crone, the next he might be a little child, all covered with down. Tombo-Mukullu knew much powerful magic.

The men picked up their clubs, bows and spears. The women carried their wretched children, cheeks sunken and eyes feverish from the famine. The bones showed through the children's scaly skin. They were in utter misery.

Everyone set out to appeal to Tombo-Mukullu. It was a long, silent and grief-stricken procession that Tombo-Mukullu saw making its weary way to the door of his hut.

143

'What's happening outside?' asked his wife. 'I felt a shiver — like a premonition.'

'There are some people coming.'

'Do they want to kill you?'

'Well, it hasn't rained for a long time.'

Not a word was said as the people gathered outside the house. Soon it was an enormous throng, yet still it grew. Many could hardly stand from weakness. Many too had collapsed from fatigue or despair, and lay helpless on the road from the village.

Then the chief stepped forward. His head was hung with ornaments and he held his spear firmly in his hand.

'Tombo-Mukullu!' he shouted.

Tombo-Mukullu came out of the house, huge and powerful.

'What do you want?' he demanded.

'We are hungry,' the chief replied. 'Send us some rain to make the plants grow. We are starving.'

Tombo-Mukullu examined them. The men were scarcely more than skeletons, and famine had carved lines in their skin. The women lowered their eyes. Their breasts were shrivelled, and they held their children out to Tombo-Mukullu.

'They are dying, Tombo-Mukullu,' they pleaded, weeping. 'We just can't feed them anymore. See how hungry they are. Help us!'

'Wait!' ordered Tombo-Mukullu. He told his wife to bring two bowls of porridge out to the people huddled in front of his hut.

'Eat!' he said to the many starving people, all of them close to death.

'There are only two bowls,' said the chief. 'Who is to eat first?'

'You will all eat!' commanded Tombo-Mukullu.

And so they did. Everyone had two helpings and yet the bowls stayed full. The children wolfed down their porridge, and smiled for the first time in weeks. The grown-ups gulped the food down ravenously too, murmuring their pleasure as they filled their bellies. When all had eaten their fill, they rolled on the ground, licking their lips and patting their bellies.

'You are naked,' observed Tombo-Mukullu.

'We've always been naked,' answered the chief. 'So have the animals. That's how Fidi-Mukullu created us.'

'But the animals have hides to protect them,' pointed out Tombo-Mukullu. He picked up a scrap of material and said:

'Clothe yourselves with that!'

'With that scrap?' asked the chief. 'It will hardly cover one of us.'

'Take it and put it on!' ordered Tombo-Mukullu.

The chief picked up the scrap and wrapped himself in it. Then he

144

looked at the ground: the scrap was still lying there. First the men clad themselves, then the women, and still the scrap remained. They cut off piece after piece, and there was plenty for everyone. Then Tombo-Mukullu picked up a short length of cord and said:

'Make yourself belts!'

They cut belt after belt from the cord and still there was enough for everyone. Once more the chief spoke to Tombo-Mukullu:

'You feed us and clothe us, Tombo-Mukullu. You are like a father to us. But can you make it rain for us?'

'I shall make it rain,' replied Tombo-Mukullu. And he sent the wind to fetch the rain. The wind blew away through the trees. Everyone surrounded Tombo-Mukullu, pushing and jostling. They all wanted rain for themselves.

'Make it rain on my land,' cried some. 'No, on mine,' yelled the others. They shoved and shouted and started to fight. Tombo-Mukullu lifted his hand angrily.

'You are all my children. If it rains for one, it will rain for all. Now go home and wait.'

The people set off for their village. They were still on the road when the rain started to fall. Soon they were soaked. But at least they had clothes now. They sang and danced and stuck out their tongues to catch the raindrops as they fell. It was a day for rejoicing, a day to remember. The rain poured down on everyone, rich and poor, young and old. The millet, maize and cassava grew again, and the grass was green and fresh once more. They remembered that day as long as they lived.

From his home in the sky Fidi-Mukullu ruled and watched over the world he had made. There was such misery in it. If people grew old, they died. If they were bitten by a viper, they died. An evil spirit might possess them and make them die. Fear was always with them. Life was hard, and death was harder. Hundreds of men died in wars, and the victors would kill the old folk and carry off the women and children. People wept at the cruelty of life. Their sorcerers would weave spells to ward off sickness and death, but often they did not work.

Once there was an old couple who had stayed together through a long hard life. They had helped each other through many troubles. Finally the old man had to watch helplessly as his wife died. No one could save her, or tell him why death had taken her from him.

'It is the will of Fidi-Mukullu,' was all the magician could say.

The will of Fidi-Mukullu! Angrily the old man made himself a big wooden drum and marched off into the forest. There he found the great hollow tree which reaches up to Fidi-Mukullu's village in the sky. He placed his drum in the middle of the hollow trunk and began to beat it.

All night long he beat his drum and sang this song:

Great god, all-powerful as you are,
by your leave only are we here.
Yours was the mind that made the world,
and yours the spirit that gave us life.

You make the day give way to night,
because for you that seems the best.
But as for me, once day has fled
I sing to you a song of woe.

Why in the flush of your success
did you go on and invent time?
Time, which makes our sweet youth fly
and man grow old and sad, and die?

Why, tell me why, is death our fate,
oh god the mighty, god the great?

Every night the old man sang his lament, and the hollow tree carried
the sound up to the sky. The jungle trembled with the rumble of the
drum. 'Oh, Fidi-Mukullu,' cried the old man. 'Why must we die?' And
Fidi-Mukullu heard. 'What's that?' he said. 'Why is that man calling
me?' But no one could tell him. The mournful song and the beating of the
drum continued night after night, until Fidi-Mukullu could stand it no
longer.

'Where is that man?' he said at last. 'Find him! Bring him to me!'

His servants went to look for the old man, but they found no trace of
him. The following night the lament went on as before. Fear began to
spread in the sky and on the earth. Meanwhile Fidi-Mukullu's fury was
reaching boiling point. He summoned the red forest-ant before him and
ordered:

'Lufumbe, find me this man with his drum and his miserable
wailing!'

Lufumbe set out, eating as she went. She chewed herself a path down
through the forest to the hollow tree, and found the man.

'Come with me!' she ordered. 'Fidi-Mukullu wants you.'

The man followed the trail she had made until he came to
Fidi-Mukullu. The god's face was furious. His voice was like thunder:

'Who on earth do you think you are? You sing that I'm a god and that
I've made a good world to live in. But at the same time you complain
about death. Am I not a god?'

146

'You are a god,' the man replied.

'And so I can do what I like?'

'Of course, since you are a god.'

'So why are you complaining?'

'Because I'm human. You will live forever, but I must die. That's how you made me. In the daytime I can forget my sorrow, for the world is a pleasant place as long as the sun is shining. But when night falls I become sad. The darkness makes me think of death. So why shouldn't I pass the night singing how sad I am that I must die?'

Fidi-Mukullu's face was grave:

'It's true I give people life only to make them return to darkness in the end. That is a god's privilege. And it's your privilege to sing of sorrow, for you're a man, and mortal.'

'Why must we humans die?' asked the old man.

'Why not? You eat, drink and sleep. Do you call that living?'

'We hunt, we make war and fall sick. We build homes, adorn ourselves

and hold feasts. We sow and we reap, we make spears, we serve images and we cast spells. We love our mates and look after our children, and we tell them the old stories. We eat, we drink and we sleep.'

'And you die!' concluded Fidi-Mukullu. 'For without death, life would have no meaning. So sing on, mortal!'

So the old man returned to his village. And every night he sat in the hollow tree, and beat out a rhythm with his worn old hand, as he sang his lament of life and death.

THE IN-BETWEEN APE

Who rules the world, the strongest or the cleverest? Is it the lion or elephant or rhinoceros or crocodile? No, it is their weaker brother, man, because he can reason and talk and use tools. Animals have voices, but they do not use language or reason the way we do, and they cannot make a spear, shoot an arrow, or light a fire. Man and beasts may be brothers, but they are by no means equal. One is rich, and the others are poor.

But one animal can use its fingers like us, and even reason a little: the ape. These things set it apart from its fellow animals. In a way it is neither man nor beast, but something in between.

When this story starts, people and animals were still preying on each other, as they had done since the dawn of time. People were starting to get the upper hand, but they were still afraid of some animals, above all the lion, the king of beasts. People had always eaten the flesh of animals, and in turn the lion sometimes dined on any human unlucky enough to cross his path. He feared nothing that walked, whether on four legs or two. When people heard his deep, throaty voice roaring through the forest or savannah at night, they trembled and huddled closer together round their fires.

'The king of beasts is hungry, friends,' they would say. 'Put more logs on the fire. It's the only thing he fears.'

One year so many people were living in a certain part of Africa that their crops ran out. The only other thing to eat was meat, and so they had to catch far more animals than usual. Every day they hunted the buffalo and antelope and other animals, catching one after another till there was hardly any prey left for the lion, or even carrion for the vultures. All the beasts thereabouts — those that were left — lived in constant fear. What could they do? In the end they went to the lion and begged for help.

The lion growled in distaste at the thought of these humans getting above themselves. People got on his nerves, and usually he kept away from them. Just now and then he would hide and wait for a human to come by, then pounce and drag the luckless victim off to his lair, where his wife and cubs would work up an appetite by playing games with their dinner. But this was only a drop in the ocean, as the lion well knew. He might eat a human now and then, but they were many, and when a group of them banded together, it was wise to keep one's distance. He always felt rather uncomfortable when he had to deal with people. Besides, a gazelle or a young kudu antelope was tastier. But now that the other animals were needing help, he knew that something must be done.

'The trouble is their spears, not to mention their bows and arrows,' he growled. 'We can't beat them unless we have weapons too.'

The animals' spirits sank when they heard this. The stork shook its head, the ibis clicked its beak, and the giraffe arched its neck in astonishment.

'What? Use weapons the way people do?'

'Fight them?'

'Why, the very idea!'

The animals would not hear of it. Only the ape had an open mind. It knew humans better than the other animals could ever hope to. After all, it was closer to mankind than any of them, and if anyone could learn human ways, it was the ape. Sometimes, when humans met it, they would talk to it and try to lure it closer, but it did not trust them. People were cunning and deceitful. It knew their tricks! There's not much you can teach an ape about people.

'We must attack their village!' said the ape. 'We must give them such a beating, they'll never dare hunt us again.'

'But how?' retorted the lion. 'I'll take on one human happily, but not a dozen.'

'The lion's right, you know,' added the elephant. 'I can trample one to death, but the others will make a trap for me, and if I fall in they'll kill me and take my skin and tusks. There's no way you can fight people when they gang up on you.'

The ape frowned in disgust. 'Well, the likes of you may be big and strong, but you're stupid too. I know I'm weak, but at least I'm clever. Leave it to me. I'm off now to the humans' den, and when I come back I'll make you strong enough to defeat them.'

The lion shook his head doubtfully, but the ape set off for the village. Once there it wandered all over the place, turning somersaults and making the children laugh. Little by little the villagers got used to it. It would sleep first in one hut and then in another. It watched everything carefully — an easy task for this inquisitive creature, which found everything fascinating. It walked upright like a human. It got hold of a club and had fun learning how to use it. It practised throwing spears and shooting arrows.

'You'd never guess it's a wild animal, would you?' laughed the humans. 'It acts just like us.'

The men of the village taught it some things, the women others, and it lived among them almost like a human. It would spend entire days watching them make weapons, lazing about on the ground and looking for all the world as if it was dozing in the sunshine. But in fact it watched and remembered everything its hosts did. It did not speak, but it took in

150

every word, hanging around the humans' meetings so that it knew all that was going on.

One night the village elders decided to organize a great hunt. The ape sat there stuffing its mouth with the nuts and bananas people had given it, and its ears with what they were saying.

'Listen, my friends,' said the chief. 'We need more meat. We must kill many, many animals if we are to eat well tomorrow. This is going to be a hunt to remember. Now listen carefully. This is my plan...'

Softly the ape slipped away from the meeting. It crept to a hollow tree that it had been using as a hiding place, and took out a bag full of tools and weapons it had stolen during its stay in the village. Then, under cover of the darkness, it slunk off to the savannah, where the lion was waiting.

'The time has come,' said the ape to its king. 'The human folk are getting ready for a big hunt. Tomorrow they mean to kill a great number of us. We must arm ourselves and take them by surprise.'

It shook the tools out of the bag and started making weapons with them. It picked out the most skilful of the animals and showed them how to help. And long before the dawn, the animals were ready.

'Show no mercy!' ordered the ape. 'The humans don't show us any, and they never will.'

The moon was full. By its clear light the ape led its army silently into the village. When the beasts heard the order to attack, they flung themselves savagely on the sleeping villagers, shrieking and roaring in their fury. The ape seized smouldering sticks from the remains of the fire and set light to the huts. Those humans who did not die in the fire or under the claws, teeth and weapons of the animals fled screaming in terror. They were too bewildered and terrified to defend themselves, and the beasts routed them completely without losing a single one of their number.

The elephant lifted its trunk and trumpeted to announce their victory, and squeals and roars of triumph filled the air.

When the sun rose, the animals retreated to the thickest part of the forest to celebrate. They all talked at once, boasting of their feats of daring, and drinking toast after toast to the ape who had brought them victory.

Only the lion remained silent, deep in thought. The ape, observant as ever, went over to him, and asked, 'Why aren't you celebrating, your majesty?' 'Now we've beaten the villagers, we can live in peace.'

The lion scratched his beard. 'We may have beaten them today,' he replied, 'but they'll be back before long. They'll get help from the other villages and come to take revenge. That's what's worrying me.'

Now it was the ape's turn to worry. 'What can we do?' it asked. But the lion could not say. He and the ape sat there thinking, alone in the middle of the joyful throng.

'Tomorrow the humans will still be trembling at the thought of us,' said the ape. 'But sooner or later they'll get their courage back and start thinking of ways to wipe us out. We've got to do something before then.'

'The best thing to do,' declared the lion, 'would be to make peace with the humans. Go back to the village and talk to them about it.'

Then the lion summoned the stork and ordered it to write down a declaration of peace. The ape returned to the village, clutching the precious scrap of paper in its paw. When he appeared the villagers cowered in fear. They were too scared to attack, but not too scared to tell the ape what they thought of it:

'Two-faced ape!'

'False friend!'

'Traitor!'

The ape was furious. 'Do you take me for one of you?' it yelled back. 'Aren't I an animal?'

'Nobody knows what you are!' they shouted. 'Why have you come back to plague us?'

By way of reply the ape made itself comfortable on the ground and unrolled its scrap of paper.

'Listen, humans! This is a peace treaty,' he announced. 'If you sign it, we shall leave you alone. But if you refuse, terrible things will happen to you!'

The women wept and the men trembled. 'He's right,' they said. 'We're completely defenceless.'

And so the chief took the ostrich plume the ape offered him, and signed the treaty. He swore a solemn oath never to attack the animals again.

'You are very wise,' the ape told them. 'Just one thing more: if people and animals ever fall out again, I, the ape, shall be the go-between.'

Then it returned to the forest, pleased with its work and determined to have nothing to do with humans ever again. But things did not turn out that way. Soon the treaty was broken, and the ape had to act as go-between again. And so it still does. Even now it shuttles back and forth from village to forest, trying to iron out quarrels between beasts and people.

Sometimes you can see the ape sitting on its own, clearly pondering some problem it cannot solve. It is trying to decide whether it is animal or human. It is confused, and this makes it sad, as animals are when they try to fathom out something which is beyond them. And so the ape sits alone, somewhere between the animals and human beings, neither one thing nor the other.

HOW DEATH BEGAN

This is the story of how death came into the world.

In the beginning the god Soko created first the turtles, then the humans and finally the rocks. He created a male and a female of each kind, turtle and human and rock.

Then he breathed life into the turtles and the man and woman. But even though they were alive they could not have children; for when these creatures grew old, Soko simply made them young again, and so there was no need for children.

But after many years Dagbachi the he-turtle came before Soko and said: 'Master, I want a child.'

'And why might that be?'

'You know how hard walking is for us turtles,' said Dagbachi. 'It's a great handicap for me and my wife when we have to go out. But if we had a child, we could send it to do our errands for us.'

Soko pondered. 'Hmm...' he said. 'It hadn't occurred to me to give you children. No, Dagbachi, I don't think it would be good for you in the long run.'

Dagbachi went back to his wife, feeling disappointed. Before long he was back bothering Soko again.

'Oh, noble creator, it would be so good to have a child — maybe even several. They would be such a help to us.'

Soko began to grow angry. 'Why must you keep coming here begging for children?' he stormed.

'Because they would be useful, master. They could help us and keep us company. And whenever I grow old...'

'I shall make you young again.'

'...whenever I grow old and I am waiting to be made young again, I can scarcely reach the water's edge. My legs just collapse under the weight of my body. Sometimes I have to lie and suffer for hours in the scorching sun because I don't have the strength to move. You must admit it's not an easy life for me.'

The god replied gravely: 'Don't you know, Dagbachi, that all those who bear children will sooner or later have to die?'

Dagbachi looked into Soko's eyes and nodded.

'Are you willing to die, Dagbachi, if I let you have children?'

'Yes, master,' he answered, seriously. 'Once my wife is pregnant, you may kill me.'

'Hmmm... send the humans to me.'

The man and the woman appeared before him. Soko cleared his throat and made his announcement: 'The turtles tell me they want children. What about you two? What do you think of this idea?'

The woman did not hesitate. 'I would love to have some, my lord. When my husband is out hunting, I have to stay at home on my own. If I had a daughter, she could help me round the house, and I wouldn't be so lonely.'

'And if I had a son,' went on the man, 'he could carry my weapons when I go hunting, and he could bring back the game. And when I am old and shaky, he could do the hunting for us. So you can see how useful children would be.'

'But are you willing to die if I grant your wish?' asked Soko.

'Yes,' was the reply. And the man said, 'Death will not matter if we have sons and daughters.'

Then Soko turned to the rocks, which all this time had just lain on the ground and said nothing.

'And what about you?' he questioned. 'Have you nothing to say? Don't you want to have children and die too?'

But the rocks expressed no such wish.

Soko thought for a time, and then announced his decision:

'It shall be as you desire!'

Soon Dagbachi's wife began to grow large and round. After three months, before his offspring entered this world, Dagbachi left it, but not before the future of his race was safe.

The woman too became pregnant. Soon there were many humans, and when her husband died she took another husband, for she could not feed her children alone.

Only the rocks have no children, and only the rocks do not perish.

156

THE FRIENDLY LIZARD

Lizards are found in legends in many parts of the world. They are usually thought of as friendly, and they are such alert, lively little creatures that it is easy to see why.

Here are three lizard tales.

The first is set in the Banat region of the Balkans, long ago when the Romans ruled most of Europe.

Ever since prehistoric times, different races have met and fought in the Balkans, which run from what are now Rumania and Yugoslavia down to Greece. The plain and mountains of the Banat — the very name means 'frontier province' — have been split between Rumania, Yugoslavia and Hungary since the end of World War I. The plain stretches north from the famous river Danube and east to the Banat mountains and the Iron Gate, a deep cleft in the great Carpathian mountains, through which the Danube flows on its way to the Black Sea.

Wave after wave of invaders ruled the Banat. Goths, Huns, Slavs, Magyars, Serbs and Turks had all been there when it passed to the mighty Austrian empire in 1718. The Austrian empress Maria Theresa called on people from many nations to live in the Banat: not just from the neighbouring countries, but Italy, France and even Spain. But most of all she brought people who spoke German, and since most came from Swabia (in south-west Germany) they were known as the Banat Swabians. Instead of adopting the local language, as immigrants usually do after a generation or two, the Banat Swabians went on speaking German for nearly two centuries, to the end of World War II, when most of them had to leave the Banat.

But all those races came after the Romans. In fact it seems that the plain of the Banat did not even exist when the Romans invaded the region. Instead there was the White Sea, full of fish, with thousands of birds nesting on its banks. The inland sea could not flow away down the Danube to the Black Sea, because the Carpathian mountains blocked its way. At that time the cleft of the Iron Gate cannot have been so deep, but then something must have lowered its floor so that the ancient inland sea emptied away. All that remained was a marsh where the middle of the sea had been; there, till quite recently, dangerous serpents (dragons, some said) were supposed to live.

What deepened the cleft? It may have been some natural disaster, but the Romans say it was done on the orders of their emperor Hadrian, who was governor in the area for a long time in the second century A.D., and

who wanted Rome's campaigns of conquest to give way to peace and prosperity. Whatever the cause, the fertile plain of the Banat saw the light of day. On it the Romans grew wheat to fill the hungry bellies of their legionaries and the servants of their empire.

But that was later, when they had finally defeated the native peoples of the Banat. First they had to wage long wars of conquest. This lizard legend goes back to that harder time, before the reign of the peaceful Hadrian.

One evening a century — that is, a hundred Roman legionaries — found themselves in a narrow valley deep in the Banat mountains when night fell. It was too dangerous to sleep in the open, but the legionaries managed to find a cave, and crawled into it to pass the night in safety. But unknown to them, their enemies had seen them, and had re-grouped on a hill nearby so that they could take the sleeping Romans by surprise next morning, catching them like rats in a trap.

However in the cave there lived hundreds of emerald lizards. At first light the little sun-loving reptiles would come out of the crevices where they slept, to look for worms, insects and little frogs, and to mate and breed. On their way out that morning, they scampered over the faces of the sleeping soldiers, who woke up with a start. At once the centurion saw the enemy and gave the alarm, and the Romans were able to beat them off. So the little lizards saved the hundred Roman legionaries from a dreadful death.

Tales of helpful lizards are found in many countries. Eight thousand miles away from the Banat, in the Marianas, Palau and the Caroline Islands of Micronesia, people tell of female lizards who bear little human babies and make good mothers all their lives.

Once upon a time, they say, there was a lizard's daughter who grew up into a pretty young woman. Soon she won the love of a rich young man, and they decided to marry. His family, of course, wanted to meet their son's mother-in-law, but the bride was ashamed of her animal background and so she always found an excuse to avoid introducing them.

One day, a few months after they were married, the young husband came home unexpectedly and heard a stranger's voice inside his home. He stopped a moment before going in, and listened.

'My daughter,' the voice was just saying, 'I have brought you something to eat.'

'Thank you very much,' replied the young woman, 'but I have all I want. My husband gives me everything I need.'

'But you're my daughter, and I want to be quite sure you have enough.'

This must be his new mother-in-law, come to meet him at last, thought the young man.

'You're very kind,' his wife was saying, 'but you needn't have worried. I'm grown up now, and everything is fine.'

'Ah, my daughter, a mother can never stop worrying about her child. Grown-up children may not need parents any more, but their mothers don't forget them, you know. So I keep on wondering how you are, and worrying whether you're hungry.'

Now the young man knew for certain that the visitor was his mother-in-law, and he hurried in to welcome her. To his amazement he saw she was a lizard. But he hesitated only a moment. Her words had moved him, and soon he was deep in conversation with her, paying no attention at all to her animal looks. His wife was delighted, and was never ashamed of her animal family again.

Many of the lizard legends are about lizards who appear as women, or the other way round. The last of these three lizard myths is one which the

Djauan aborigines of northern Australia tell about a strange stone figure at Batuda, not far from the town of Mainoru.

The aborigines say that the figure comes from the dawn of time, soon after mankind came to earth. At that time there was little difference between man and beast, and humans could still change into animals, and animals into humans.

One day a number of young women and girls were stretched out in the tall grass of the bush, lazing in the sun. While they were talking, joking and laughing, along came the old, old medicine man Nagacork, with his bag on his shoulder. Now Nagacork was a very great magician. Only men were allowed to look at him, and no one at all could speak about him, or they would die. If a woman's glance fell on him, she would drop dead on the spot.

As Nagacork went past, one of the young women heard a noise.

'Wasn't that a dingo barking?' she asked, and jumped up to see. But the grass was taller than she was, and so she had to perch on a rock in order to see out over the bush.

'Look out!' she yelled. 'There's a huge dingo on the prowl. It wants to eat us up!'

All the others rushed to a rock and climbed it as fast as they could to escape from the wild dog. But at that instant Nagacork the magician changed them into lizards, and there they stay, fixed to the rock for ever.

To this day you can go to Batuda and look at their rock. A little way off, all by itself, stands a block of stone which people say is the young woman who was first to see the dingo. But what it was she really saw, nobody knows.

THE STORY OF AENEAS

The Flight from Troy

Zeus, the father of the gods, looked down from his Heaven, which the Greeks called Olympus. He cast his eye over the wealthy cities and fertile fields of all the countries around the Mediterranean Sea — Greece, Italy, North Africa and the Middle East — and saw to his dismay that although they looked beautiful and prosperous, the people living in them were not happy. Joy was mingled with sorrow, and peace was threatened by war.

Even on Mount Olympus, things were not as they should be, because Zeus's wife Queen Hera was at loggerheads with his daughter Aphrodite. In a competition to decide who was the fairest of all the goddesses, Paris of Troy had chosen Aphrodite instead of Hera, and as a result she was eaten up by jealousy. She had taken a violent dislike to the people of Troy, and in particular she hated Aphrodite's son Aeneas, who was a Trojan prince. She did everything she could to make his life miserable.

One day Aphrodite went to see her father, her beautiful face clouded with sadness. 'O Father, what has my son Aeneas done to deserve such misfortune?' she asked. Zeus looked uncomfortable, for he knew very well Aeneas was being made to suffer. 'I have planned a glorious future for him,' he answered, a little sheepishly. Aphrodite smiled sadly. 'Forgive me if I don't believe you, Father! So far he has no reason to hope for a glorious future! The city of Troy has been destroyed and many of his countrymen killed — I don't see much glory in that!'

'The war was in a good cause,' replied Zeus. 'The defeated deserve as much glory as the victors, and we should honour the dead as much as we honour the survivors.'

Aphrodite tossed her head angrily. 'Glory for the defeated, and honour for the dead!' she retorted. 'What good does that do them! We gods and goddesses are immortal, but men have to die eventually. Why should they be condemned to misfortune and unhappiness during the few years they spend on earth? I saw my son Aeneas wandering through the ruins of Troy, searching for survivors. I saw him escape leading my grandson Ascanius by the hand and carrying his poor father Anchises on his back. Look at me, Father! I am eternally young and beautiful! But did you see Anchises being carried through the flames?'

'I saw him,' said Zeus.

'He was old and feeble. Eighty years for him is just a twinkling of an eye for me. When I gave birth to Aeneas, Anchises was as youthful as I was, yet now he has reached the end of his life. I find that very sad. Why can't men live for ever?'

Zeus glanced down towards the earth. 'They are born to live on earth, and that means they have to die.'

'The Romans call me Venus,' his daughter continued, 'and the Greeks call me Aphrodite, the goddess of love. They believe in me because they yearn for love, but although they all long for it, hatred still seems to rule on earth.'

Zeus was silent. Aphrodite continued:

'After Troy was destroyed, just imagine how I felt about Aeneas! I saw him gathering all his fellow-survivors around him and protecting them from the vengeance of the Greeks. I watched them building ships to escape in. They set sail for Thrace in the hope that they would be able to

162

build a city and start a new life, but the people of Thrace declared war on them and again they had to flee. O lord and father, is that what you call a glorious destiny?'

Zeus was silent.

'Then Aeneas sailed to Delos and for a while he and his men were happy there. But the oracle of Apollo commanded him to sail on to Crete and build a fortress and a city. His people worked hard on the land and built up flourishing farms, but the sun scorched the fields until they were barren, and half the men, women and children died of the plague, leaving the others to grieve for them. O lord, is that what you call a glorious destiny?'

Zeus remained silent.

'After that, the oracle told him to go to Italy. His people took new heart and set sail, hoping at last to find a better life. But what happened? A terrible storm hit them at sea, and howling winds drove them off course, so that they had no idea where they were. When at last they reached land they were set upon by the Harpies, horrible monsters who snatched and dirtied their food and deafened them with ghastly screams. Their life was made unbearable. The Harpies cursed them and vowed they would be punished. Punished for what? For surviving the storm? O lord, is that what you call a glorious destiny?'

Zeus still remained silent.

'Again they had to set sail. They were cold and hungry, and many of them fell sick, and they were miserable and disappointed at not being able to find a home. Then they sighted land again and rejoiced, but the waves carried them away to face the dangers of the whirlpool Charybdis, which sucks ships and men down into the depths of the sea. When they escaped from Charybdis they were very nearly shipwrecked on the reefs of Scylla, where many ships have been destroyed. At last they caught sight of Sicily, the promised land, their destination — and what happened there? Old Anchises, the father of my dear son, died, worn out by the strains of the voyage. More anguish for Aeneas — is that what you call a glorious destiny?'

Zeus sighed. 'It was time for Anchises to die, daughter. His time on earth was over.'

'Please don't make my son suffer any more,' begged Aphrodite. 'I know perfectly well that it's Hera who hates and persecutes him because she is jealous of me. Behind your back she ordered the god of the winds to send a storm which drove Aeneas away from Italy again. The sea raged like a wild animal, the lightning split open the night sky, the ships were tossed up into the air and then plunged into the depths. Only seven ships survived, and when Aeneas and his companions reached the shore, they found themselves on the coast of Africa and not in Italy as they had hoped. Will they ever each Italy? Will their next voyage be any more successful that the others? What is your promise worth, O god of gods? I'm afraid for Aeneas!'

Zeus's hands trembled as he caressed his daughter's face. 'My promise will hold as long as gods are gods,' he told her gently. 'Don't be afraid. Aeneas will reach Italy, and there will be a war for the city of Laurentum which he will win, and he will found a new dynasty of rulers. Your grandson Ascanius will make Alba Longa the capital city of a great empire, and for three hundred years the descendants of Anchises will rule over the country, until Romulus creates a new city. Julius Caesar, the greatest Roman of them all, will be a descendant of your son, and when he dies he will ascend into Heaven and live among the gods. And men shall live in peace for evermore. That is my decree.'

Aphrodite gave him a dazzling smile, and with a light heart she made her way down to earth, to the coast of Africa. She disguised herself as a huntress and went to meet her son Aeneas, who was walking through the forest with his friend Achates, exploring the unknown land he had reached. He did not recognize his mother in her disguise and told her that he and his men had been driven off course by a storm. He was looking for someone who could tell him where he was.

'You are in Libya,' she told him, 'in the land of the Phoenicians, who are ruled by Queen Dido. She came here from Tyre, where she was married to Sychaeus. Her brother Pygmalion hated Sychaeus and wanted his money, so he murdered him, but Dido managed to escape with the treasure and fled to Africa, where she bought some land along the coast. She has built a citadel at Carthage, and if you continue along this road you will soon come to it. The gods go with you.'

Aphrodite turned away, and then the light that shone from her and the scent of divine hair revealed that she was a goddess. As she vanished, Aeneas realized that she was his mother. 'Why do you always appear to me in disguise?' he cried out. 'Why can't we talk to each other when I know who you are?'

Dido and Aeneas

Aphrodite wrapped Aeneas and Achates in a thick mist so that they would not be stopped or questioned on their way to Dido's city. When they reached Carthage, they found the builders still hard at work, digging a harbour, laying foundations for a theatre, hewing pillars from a quarry, all working at their various tasks like bees in a hive. In the market-place, the elders were choosing officials of state, councillors and law-makers.

On a raised throne sat the beautiful Queen Dido, proclaiming laws to her people. Aeneas and Achates were delighted to see some of their Trojan companions in the crowd. They had given them up for lost and thought they had been drowned when their ships were separated from Aeneas's own vessel during the last terrible storm. The Trojans had come to beg Dido for protection, and to ask her men for help in repairing their damaged ships so that they could continue their voyage to Italy. Dido welcomed them warmly, and gave them all they asked for. Then Aeneas and Achates left the protection of the misty veil and went to introduce themselves to the queen.

Aphrodite had seen to it that Aeneas looked particularly handsome. His face and shoulders, his hair and eyes had something of his mother's divine beauty, and Dido was struck by his appearance as well as by the story of his terrible adventures, which she had already heard from the other Trojans. Although she was devoted to the memory of her dead husband, she could not help falling in love with the handsome stranger. And this was not surprising, because Aphrodite had decided that Aeneas would be safer if Dido loved him. So Dido rose and welcomed Aeneas with great honour, and led him to her palace, together with the other Trojans, who were happy beyond measure to have their leader safely restored to them. She ordered a splendid banquet to be prepared, and an equally lavish supply of food and drink to be sent the Trojans whom Aeneas had left encamped by the ships on the seashore.

Inside the palace, a hundred serving-maids and manservants bustled about, laying the tables and loading them with wonderful food and bowls filled to the brim with wine. There were lamps hanging from the gold-panelled ceiling, and candles blazed everywhere. Singers, accompanying themselves on the lyre, sang of the glories of creation and the deeds of heroes. Dido asked Aeneas all sorts of questions about the Trojan War and about his travels and misfortunes.

Aeneas stayed a long time in Dido's palace. Summer passed and winter came, and there was no more talk of sailing on to Italy. Zeus's plans for Aeneas seemed to have been forgotten, and Aeneas was totally bewitched by Dido's beauty.

The partly-built towers of Carthage did not grow any higher, the young men no longer practised using their weapons, and building work on the harbour came to a stop, while Dido spent all her time with Aeneas, listening to his stories.

But this happy state of affairs was not to last. The goddess of Rumour began wagging her thousand tongues, murmuring and hissing, mixing

truth and lies, never resting until she had spread through all of Africa the story of Dido and Aeneas, of how a stranger from Troy had bewitched the Queen of Carthage until she had no thought for anything but him. The rumours grew and grew, reaching every city and village, filling everybody's ears, of how Dido was neglecting her duties as Queen of Carthage.

Finally the rumours reached Iarbas, the king of another African country, who had wanted to marry Dido but had been refused by her. He was the son of Zeus by an African nymph, and so he went to see his father and make an indignant complaint. 'I have built a thousand temples in your honour and I sacrifice to you continually, O Zeus! Am I, your son, to be rejected in favour of a stranger by a woman who came to my country seeking my help? Please do something to help me, O father!'

Zeus was moved by Iarbas's prayer, and he remembered what he had told Aphrodite about his plans for Aeneas. In order to put matters right, he sent his messenger Mercury down to earth. Mercury laced on the winged sandals which carried him like the wind, took up his wand decorated with twined snakes, and went to look for Aeneas. He found him dressed in a rich robe of purple cloth which Dido had made for him and wearing a sword thickly encrusted with jewels, and he mocked him, saying, 'Why are you dressed like an idler, with a sword that is an ornament rather than a weapon? Surely you're supposed to be founding an empire, not hanging around making eyes at a woman! Even if you don't care about yourself, think of what you owe to Ascanius, who is destined to rule in Italy, not Africa, remember!' After delivering his message, Mercury vanished into thin air. Aeneas was stunned by this vision. He began to realize that he had acted foolishly in letting himself become so attached to Dido. He loved her more than anything else, but that was not a good enough reason for giving up his responsibilities as leader of the Trojans. He gave orders for his ships to be made ready for departure, but he kept this secret from Dido, because he could not bring himself to tell her that he had decided to leave her. He knew that she would beg him to stay, and the thought of making her unhappy after she had been so kind to him made him feel very uncomfortable.

All the same, Dido suspected that something was going on. She loved Aeneas deeply, and she was terrified at the idea of losing him. Even if he had said nothing about it to her, Rumour would have told her that the Trojans were preparing to set sail once more. So she asked him directly: 'Is it true that you are getting ready to sail away, without saying a word to me?' When Aeneas reluctantly admitted that he felt he must take his men to Italy, she grew desperate. 'Traitor!' she cried. 'Did you really think that you could leave me? Don't you think you should consider my feelings? I made you welcome, I gave you shelter, a home, and everything you asked for. Don't I deserve a better fate than just to be thrown aside and left? I took care of your men — have they no gratitude to me? Do you really not need me any more?'

Aeneas was very unhappy, but he had to remember that Zeus's commands must be obeyed. 'I can't alter my destiny,' he said, taking Dido's face in his hands. 'I never pretended that I could stay with you for ever. If I had not been forced to leave Troy I would have stayed there after the war and helped to rebuild it. But now the gods have decided that I must start a new empire in Italy, and I have no choice in the matter.'

With flushed face and tears streaming down her cheeks, Dido begged and entreated him, but Aeneas was firm in his resolve. Then she became angry. 'You are very cruel, and I don't believe for a minute that the gods have ordered you to leave me! It's just an excuse!' she cried. 'You'll be punished with high seas and sharp rocks, and when I die I will haunt you so that you'll never be able to forget how badly you've treated me!'

With a sad face Aeneas returned to his ships and made sure that the keels had been freshly tarred, that new oars had been made and supplies for the voyage loaded up. Meanwhile, Dido was making her own preparations. At first she tried to use magic to keep Aeneas in Carthage, but the wine she poured out as an offering turned to blood, and she knew this was a bad omen. Then she decided that she would make a bonfire of Aeneas's clothes and weapons and the bed she hoped would be their marriage bed.

The following morning, Mercury again appeared to Aeneas and told him he must delay no longer or trouble would befall him. Aeneas was frightened by the warning, fearing some punishment, and he ordered his men to embark and raise anchor. When Dido awoke an hour or so later, she saw that the harbour was empty and the shores deserted. Then she cursed Aeneas, and she cursed herself for her unfaithfulness to her dead husband and her folly in letting herself fall in love with a stranger.

She gave orders for the bonfire to be lit. Everything that had belonged to Aeneas was placed on it. The flames roared up, and suddenly Dido rushed out towards the blazing pyre and hurled herself on to it. She was carrying a Trojan sword, and as the flames rose around her she plunged it into her heart.

Aeneas, now far out to sea, looked back at Carthage, and saw the flames. He did not know what they meant, but felt they were a bad sign.

The War for Laurentum

The winds carried Aeneas's fleet to the coast of Sicily once more. A year had passed since Anchises had died there, and Aeneas organized a festival of games in honour of his dead father. There were boat races, foot races, boxing and archery, and the sport was enjoyed by everybody, but while the men were amusing themselves in this way the Trojan women wandered sadly along the shore, wondering if their sufferings would ever end. Hera, always ready to do Aeneas an ill turn, sent Iris, the goddess of the rainbow, down to play a trick on the Trojans. Iris disguised herself as one of the Trojan women and suggested that they should set fire to the ships so that they would not be able to set sail again. She told them that she had had a dream in which the gods had ordered her to do this. At first the women hesitated, but then Iris cast off her disguise and soared upwards through the sky on her rainbow wings. This convinced the women that her orders were indeed the wish of the gods and, screaming like mad creatures, they carried torches from their hearths and dry leaves and brushwood to keep the flames alight.

Aeneas was watching the games, with no idea of what was going on down on the shore. When the news was brought to him that the ships were burning, he rushed to the shore, but in spite of all his efforts the fire continued to spread, taking a firm hold. Then Aeneas prayed to Zeus for help and scarcely had he finished his pleas when the skies opened and rain came pouring down. The ships filled with water, the charred timbers hissed, and soon the fires were out. Only four ships were totally destroyed, but it was still a bitter blow for Aeneas.

One of the Trojans suggested to Aeneas that this setback was perhaps a sign from Heaven. 'Let the old people and women who have small children, and anybody else who is weary of travelling, stay here. They can make themselves a home in Sicily while those of you who are young and strong can continue on towards Italy and found a new city there. Life is bound to be difficult for you at first. There may be more battles and you will be forced to fight once more. It would be better for you not to be burdened with the old and the weak,' he said.

This seemed to Aeneas to be good advice, and he set about carrying it out. Soon the day of parting arrived, and many tears were shed, both by those who were leaving and those who were left behind. The women and children stood on the shore and waved sorrowful farewells.

So Aeneas set sail again, and this time his ships reached the mouth of the river Tiber without misadventure. Soon they reached the country of Latium, whose king was called Latinus. He had no son to succeed him, and only one daughter, Lavinia, who had many suitors, for she was very beautiful. Her mother wanted Prince Turnus of the Rutulians as a husband for her, but an oracle had foretold that Lavinia would marry a foreign prince who would arrive on the shores of Latium with an army.

Aeneas landed his ships safely and then sent messengers to Latinus with gifts, and olive branches as a sign that he had come in peace. As soon as Latinus heard of Aeneas's arrival he realized that this must be the foreign prince his daughter was destined to marry, and he sent messengers to Aeneas thanking him for the presents and offering him

Lavinia's hand in marriage. On seeing this, Hera, still consumed by jealousy, could not bear the thought that Aeneas would fulfil his ambition of founding a new city in Italy, so she decided to turn Lavinia's mother against him and also to poison the heart of Prince Turnus by telling that he was about to lose Lavinia.

As a result the jealous Turnus set out to kill Aeneas. He led his army against the Trojans, and fierce battles took place, with many dead on both sides. King Latinus shut himself in his palace, saying he would not rule if he was prevented from obeying the predictions of the oracle.

One night when Aeneas, weary with the fighting and worried about the fate of his men, was resting by the Tiber, the river-god appeared to him and said: 'Have no fear, this will be your home. You will build your city on my banks. But do first of all make a sacrifice to Hera and see if you can win her favour, because otherwise you will never be able to live in peace. After doing that, go to Evander, king of the Arcadians, who is a sworn enemy of the Latins and the Rutulians. With his help you will defeat them.'

Aeneas did as he was told and took two ships upstream in search of the promised allies. While he was away, two important things happened. First, Aphrodite, anxious for her son's safety, begged her husband Vulcan, the god of fire, to use his magic skills and make a special armour for Aeneas to keep him safe from attack and protect him from all danger. She also asked Vulcan to forge a sword and a lance with special powers that would defeat every foe. By dawn next day, the finest and most beautiful armour was ready for Aeneas, and beside the armour on the ground lay a sword and a lance, ready for the Trojan hero on his return. In the meantime, in Aeneas's absence Prince Turnus had led a fierce attack on the Trojan camp. The camp had been well fortified and the Trojans were able to defend it, but their ships lay unprotected on the shore. 'Bring your torches!' shouted Turnus to his men, 'and we will have a fireworks display!' So his soldiers seized any form of fire they could find and rushed towards the ships, intent on destroying them. This Zeus would not allow, however; he gave an order and the ships broke away from their moorings, plunging down into the water and rising into the air again, for all the world like water-nymphs swimming through the waves.

This sight struck terror into the hearts of the Rutulians, for they realized that there had been divine intervention, but Turnus encouraged them to continue the fight and they surrounded the Trojan camp, once again trying to break through the fortifications.

Then Aeneas returned with reinforcements, not only from Evander and the Arcadians but from the friendly Etruscans as well. As his ships

170

sailed down the river towards the battleground they were helped on their way by the water-nymphs who only a little while earlier had been ships themselves. Now it was the turn of the Trojans and their allies to triumph, and Turnus and his men were driven back towards the city of Laurentum.

Zeus and Hera were watching the fighting from Olympus. The father of the gods now decided that the time had come to award the victory to Aeneas. Hera had been pleased by Aeneas's sacrifice to her, but she had still not forgiven Troy for her humiliation at not being chosen the most beautiful of all the goddesses, and although she now agreed to allow Aeneas to defeat his enemies she made one condition. 'Let the language and customs of Latium remain as they are now, and not be replaced by those of the conqueror,' she said. 'I want Troy and its ways to be forgotten for ever.' Zeus agreed to this condition, and Aeneas was victorious. He sent messengers to Latinus and Turnus offering terms for peace, but when Turnus found out that these terms included Lavinia's hand in marriage, he would not hear of it. 'Let the war be decided by a duel between Aeneas and me,' he proposed. 'The victor shall take Lavinia as his wife and the loser shall make his peace.' Aeneas agreed to this proposal, and a duelling-ground was made ready outside the city. At this point, Hera could not resist interfering again, and without telling Zeus she ordered Juturna, Turnus's sister, to stir up the Rutulians to attack the unsuspecting Trojans. The truce was broken by this surprise attack, and Aeneas began searching the battlefield for Turnus to see if he could put an end to the fighting once and for all. Juturna, still with Hera's help, was driving Turnus's chariot so cleverly that Aeneas was never quite able to reach him. Aeneas was on the point of giving up when he suddenly realized that, although the battle was raging outside the walls, the city itself was undefended. Quickly he gathered his captains together and gave orders for scaling-ladders and archers to be rushed to the city walls. The archers fired flaming arrows over the walls and soon had the buildings ablaze and the inhabitants of the city in a panic. The queen, seeing so many Trojan soldiers and no sign of Turnus, hanged herself in despair, believing her chosen son-in-law to be dead. Turnus meanwhile was far away, pursuing stragglers and still enjoying the fight, protected as he was by Hera. But suddenly he became aware of the sounds of distress in the distance and he called to his sister to rein in the horses, just as a messenger arrived with news of what was happening in the city. Immediately Turnus leapt from his chariot and rushed to the city walls, shouting to his men to stop fighting. This time he was determined to face Aeneas in single combat.

When Aeneas heard Turnus calling for him, he sought out a clear space where the final decision could be reached. The two rivals first threw their spears at each other, and when these missed they ran forward with raised swords. There was clashing and crashing of blade against blade and they seemed evenly matched until Turnus, striking a blow with all his might, broke his sword against Aeneas's shield. When he realized that his sword was broken, he turned and fled. As Aeneas ran after him in pursuit, he found the spear he had hurled at Turnus at the beginning of the combat, and he wrenched it out of the ground and flung it at his enemy again. Straight as the flight of a hawk it sped, and this time it found its mark. Turnus sank to his knees, and Aeneas buried his sword deep in Turnus's breast.

So Lavinia became the bride of Aeneas and there was great rejoicing among the Trojans who had found a home at last. Aeneas founded another city, as he had been commanded to do, and he named it Lavinium after his wife. Trojans and Latins lived peacefully together and became the nation we know as the Romans.

TALES OF WATER FOLK

For thousands of years there have been legends about creatures which live in the water but look like humans, at least in part.

Some come from ancient Greece. Triton, son of the sea god Poseidon, had a man's body and a fish's tail. The roar of the sea, said the Greeks, was the sound of Triton blowing into his great conch shell, and to this day we call those shellfish tritons. He would blow to calm the waves when the sea was stormy, or to frighten his enemies.

Poseidon's servants, who were also sometimes called Tritons, liked to amuse themselves by frightening pretty nymphs or even humans, and would even carry them off into the depths of the sea.

Wherever there are seas or lakes or rivers, in fact, people have told stories of water folk like these, who may be dangerous to humankind. Only the bravest of people would venture alone into the deep waters where they were thought to live. Some looked human, wearing beards and dressed in green from top to toe. Others had frogs' heads and webbed feet, which they had to hide if they wanted to mix with humans. Not all were hostile. Many wanted to be friends with humans.

One was the water sprite of the river Dill, whose sad tale is told in the German province of Hesse. He lived north of Frankfurt near the town of Wetzlar, where the Dill met the river Lahn.

One fine spring evening the water sprite saw a sweet young girl with golden hair. He came out of the river to talk to her, and they fell in love. All through the spring and summer he would sit on the riverbank at twilight and wait for her. When she came, they would sit there side by side, silent but happy.

One evening in midsummer the sprite brought his sweetheart a present, a necklace he had lovingly made her from little shells and pebbles of every colour.

'Wear this for me,' he said, placing the necklace round her neck. 'And don't ever forget me.'

The girl loved the pretty thing, and promised to wear it always.

Month after month went by, and at last the summer was over. On the first day of autumn, the girl looked sad when she came to the riverbank. The sprite put his arm round her comfortingly.

'Autumn is here, my love,' he said to her tenderly. 'The time has come for you to come away with me and be my wife.'

But the girl burst into tears.

'My parents won't let me,' she wept. 'They've just told me I have to marry a young man from Asslar on New Year's Day. They've agreed it all with his family.'

The sprite could not believe his ears. Just when he had hoped to win his sweetheart, he was to lose her forever. His face filled with sadness.

'Then I must go, and we must never see each other again.'

'You know it's you I love,' said the girl with tears in her eyes. 'But what can I do? A daughter has to obey her parents.'

'Yes, we must part,' replied the sprite. 'But you will wear my necklace and remember me forever.'

He kissed her tenderly. Then he turned and dived into the river, never to be seen again.

The girl went sadly home to her parents. She did what she could to prepare for her wedding, but try as she might, she could not take off the necklace, nor could she forget her lost love. Week after week she pined for him, till at last, on the day before her wedding, just as the Old Year was breathing its last, she found peace in death, and took the necklace with her to the grave.

There are water sprites too, they say, in Slovenia, the part of Yugoslavia that borders on Austria.

The river Ljubljanica, from which Slovenia's capital Ljubljana takes its name, was said to hide a friendly water sprite who delighted in human company. Many a boatman or fisherman would tell how it had come out of the river for a chat, and then vanished again under the water. Such tales are found in many regions, and some saw water sprites even come into villages to shop, or to fetch a mid-wife when their wives are having babies.

One story tells of a curious thing which happened in 1547. Every year the traditional summer festival was held on the first Sunday in July, under the lime tree in the old market-place. That year too people were gathered round long trestle tables, eating and drinking, talking and laughing, and dancing the old folk dances as the fiddlers played.

Suddenly an elegant young stranger walked proudly into the square. Courteously he doffed his hat, greeted the happy throng and wandered among the tables, shaking hands as he went. His eyes were clear and green, and his handshake was so cold and limp that it made people shiver.

Prettiest and merriest of the young girls at the dance was Ursula Schaefer, who was just sixteen. Soon she was dancing with the stranger, and after that they did not miss a dance. The pretty Ursula was radiant. Her eyes were shining, and she could not take them off her partner. Her long blond hair swung out as she whirled lightly round the market-place. They made a fine couple, and everyone stopped and admired them. But as they watched, a feeling of uneasiness crept over people, for a curious coldness seemed to come from the stranger.

Ursula did not seem to notice it. She had eyes for no one but the stranger who held her in his arms. Around the market-place they danced, then into the alleys beside it, on and on down the hill, moving ever nearer the river.

There on the bank some fishermen hauling in their nets heard laughter and dancing feet. They turned just in time to see the couple, still closely entwined, dance into the river and disappear beneath the water. Ursula was never heard of again, and neither was the water sprite.

In Bohemia, which is part of Czechoslovakia, there is a town called Budějovice, or Budweis, home of a famous beer. At one time the region, which is near where the rivers Moldau and Malše meet, was haunted by a very special water sprite. Whatever the form he took (and they were many), he always rode in a green coach drawn by four huge black cats with eyes of jade.

One day the sprite left the river's depths in the guise of a young man and went to where some children were playing. He drew out a flute and began to play such lovely merry tunes that the children stopped to listen, and when he began to walk away the children danced after him without stopping to think. Soon the procession reached a lake. The sprite touched the water with his flute, and it opened up before him. Down he went into the depths, with the children close behind.

But one timid little boy had hung back, and when he saw his friends disappearing into the lake he ran off to tell his parents. The people of Budějovice were beside themselves with grief. What could they do? Soon they had a plan.

For days they laid in wait for the sprite. When at last he came out of the water, they grabbed hold of him and dragged him to a stake they had driven into the ground. They tied him to it, then stacked wood round it.

'If you don't promise to bring our children back safe and sound,' the people threatened, 'we'll set fire to the wood and burn you to death!'

Water sprites were terrified of fire, as they well knew. Trembling all over, the sprite gave his solemn promise to bring the children home.

The people set him free, and he kept his word. Soon the waters of the

lake parted, and out came the sprite with his carriage full of children. The children leapt out and ran to their waiting parents with cries of joy. The water sprite turned his carriage, drove it under the water, and was never seen again.

There are even more tales of female water sprites than male ones. Beautiful young girls with pale skin and great sad eyes, they usually brought bad luck. Creatures like the blonde Lorelei who, disappointed in love, turned into a siren with a fish's tail and sat on an echoing rock in the river Rhine near St. Goarshausen, luring fishermen to their deaths.

Though they took human form, they did not have immortal souls like a Christian's unless they married a mortal. One who did was the fair Melusine in the old French legend.

Melusine was a water sprite who married the first Count of Lusignan. They were very happy, and as Melusine could take off her sea-serpent's tail whenever she wished, her husband suspected nothing. But the day came when Lusignan surprised his wife in her real form. Terrified, poor Melusine ran to the river and vanished beneath the water. She was never seen again, but for hundreds of years her voice could be heard lamenting on the battlements of her castle when death threatened the Counts of Lusignan.

One of the Counts was the ancestor of the Plantagenet kings of England, including Richard the Lionheart and King John. When the Plantagenets quarrelled among themselves, as they often did, the English used to blame it on the blood of Melusine.

The legend of Melusine also crossed the river Rhine and spread quickly to other parts of Europe. This is the way it is told in the German province of Baden.

In the forest of Stollen, on the Stollen mountain, lie the ruins of an ancient stronghold, not far from Castle Stauffenberg, home of the Stauffenbergs who were one of the great families of Swabia, in south west Germany. Once upon a time one of that family, who was steward to the Dukes of Swabia, had several sons. The youngest of them used to spend his time wandering in the woods, looking at the wild animals and listening to the birds.

One fine morning he heard a woman's voice coming from the Stollen mountain:

'Save me, save me!
Three times kiss me!'

So sweet, yet so sad was the song, and so appealing, that the young

Stauffenberg could not resist climbing the mountain to see where it came from. At the summit, near a place called Twelve Rocks, sat the most beautiful young woman. Blonde hair rippled to her shoulders, her eyes were greener than the ocean, and her lips were red as cherries. Yet she had fins instead of hands, and her body was a serpent's.

'Who are you?' asked the young man in wonder, and the young sprite replied:

> 'Melusine it is you see,
> Daughter of the sky and hills.
> Kiss me, please, it's not too late,
> Kiss my cheeks and kiss my lips.
> Do not fear, but set me free —
> Treasure and I shall be your prize.'

In spite of her fins and her serpent's body, the young man felt no fear of the pretty sprite, and he gladly kissed her the three times. At once she disappeared, but Stauffenberg waited impatiently in the hope that she would return.

And return she did the next day. To his surprise, she now had a dragon's tail, green scales on her serpent's body, and two golden wings on her back. She sang even more beautifully than before, though he could tell from her voice that she was weeping:

> 'Save me, save me!
> Twice now kiss me!'

He kissed her, and her kisses were burning with fever. After the second kiss she rose into the air at once, and disappeared into the forest with a rustling of wings.

The young man's heart was filled with longing. He could not sleep, but stayed on the mountain, waiting for the dawn. Then at last he heard the sweet song coming from the place near the Twelve Rocks:

> 'Save me, save me!
> Just once kiss me!'

But when he saw her, the fair Melusine had turned into a terrible monster, with the body of a horned dragon, a fish's tail, the talons of a bird of prey and, worst of all, the head of a tortoise, holding up swollen lips for him to kiss. Stauffenberg's hair stood on end. Terrified, he ran down the mountain as fast as he could, never to return.

Some time later he married a pretty young girl. But as he was sitting with his guests at the great banqueting table, the wood of the ceiling above him opened a crack, and a little drip of liquid fell onto his plate. No one noticed, but when young Stauffenberg picked up the piece of meat onto which the drip had fallen and put it into his mouth, he was dead immediately. And as the guests looked up, they saw the tail of a reptile disappearing into the crack. Such was the revenge of Melusine.

At the same time a pine tree with two interlacing trunks started to grow at Twelve Rocks. People called it Melusine's tree, and it stood for more than a hundred years before being struck by lightning.

There is another legend of Melusine. That is the legend already told in this book under the title *Fair Melusine and the Treasure of King Helmas*. But that, of course, is another story.

THE BIG FISH AND THE FLOOD

This is a story of Vishnu, the Hindu god of life, who was a great friend to mankind.

Vishnu, all in gold, sat in the heavens on a splendid throne, among lotus flowers flooded with light. With him was his ravishingly beautiful wife Lakshmi, goddess of love and happiness. He often used to visit the Earth, descending swift as lightning in a golden chariot pulled by demons, with the bird god Garuda flying beside him. Sometimes he would go in the guise of an animal, so that he could come close to men without being recognized.

Once upon a time the Dravidian people of India were governed by the wise king Satyavrata. He was a good and just man, who lived the life of a saint and took no food but pure water.

One day King Satyavrata was leaning over a stream, drawing water to offer as a sacrifice to the god Vishnu, who he worshipped devoutly.

Suddenly he felt a tiny fish wriggling in his fingers. The holy man was just going to throw it back into the water, when he heard a tiny voice, clear as crystal.

'O King, you're usually so kind to animals,' said the fish, 'so why are you treating me like this?'

'Because I want you to be free again, little fish,' replied King Satyavrata. But the little fish started to weep.

'That kind of freedom is for the strong, not for those who have something to fear,' it said. 'If I stay in the stream, the bigger fish will eat me, or a fisherman will catch me and cook me. I don't call that freedom.'

'Oh,' said Satyavrata in surprise. 'I'd never looked at it that way.' And he put the fish in a bucket of water instead of the stream. There it thrived and grew, and in no time at all the bucket was much too small.

'Give me somewhere bigger to live,' ordered the fish, and the king put it in a pool behind his palace. Yet in a few hours the strange thing had grown so large that its head and fins were out of water.

'Help me, holy man!' moaned the fish. 'I can hardly breathe.'

So King Satyavrata moved the miraculous fish to a small lake, then to a big lake, and finally to the sea, because the monster grew to a fabulous size, as though by magic. A thick horn appeared on the top of its head, and its scales glistened like pure gold. It was a splendid sight. But the fish was still not satisfied.

'King, why are you abandoning me?' it complained again. 'Do you

want me to be swallowed up by the terrible monsters of the ocean?'

Satyavrata thought for a while.

'You are bigger than everything else in the ocean,' he pointed out. 'Surely there is something supernatural about you. Are you a god?'

Vishnu revealed himself at last.

'Now I recognize you,' said the king of the Dravidians, bowing low. 'You are Vishnu, the eternal and the fortunate. What do you want of me, Lord?'

'Brahma the great creator is going to sleep, and the world will be drowned,' replied the fish. 'But you, Satyavrata, will be saved, and will be king in the new era. In seven days the sky and the air will fall into the sea. I shall bring you a ship. Take the seven wisest of your people, and go on board. Take seeds, and fruits, and healing plants, and one pair of every kind of animal. Then when the waves grow large, I will save you from death.'

Satyavrata did as he was told. He gathered together the seven sages, the seeds, fruit and healing plants, and a pair of every kind of animal. After seven days, the waves grew large, and torrents of rain fell from the sky. Vishnu returned, a fish again, pulling an enormous ship behind him, and king Satyavrata went on board with his precious cargo.

The sun became dark, and blackest night spread over the world. For

182

thousands of years, as long the sleep of Brahma lasted, the refugees travelled in their ship over the ocean that covered the world. Satyavrata put his trust in Vishnu, who never ceased to pull the ship along.

Then one day Brahma woke at last, a new sun climbed into the sky, and the earth was flooded with light. Vishnu pulled the ship towards the Himalaya mountains, and spoke to the Dravidian king.

'The water is starting to go down,' he said. 'When the highest mountain peak appears above it, throw out your anchors. Then, as the water goes on falling, take the animals and plants, go down from the mountains and give life back to the new world.'

Then Vishnu returned to the sky in his golden chariot, with the bird god Garuda flying beside him.

Satyavrata did as the god had told him. Trees and plants grew from the seeds, and the animals multiplied and spread to all parts of the world, and so did mankind. A new era had begun.

DOCTOR FAUST AND THE DEVIL

Once there was a learned man who practised magic, both black and white. His name was Johann Faust.

They say he was born in Germany in about 1480. Was it in the west, perhaps in the mountains of the Black Forest or near the university town of Heidelberg? Or in the east, in the province of Thuringia?

No one quite knows.

Wherever it was, Johann grew up into a teacher called Doctor Faust or Faustus. He did not last long as a schoolteacher and then led a rather shady vagabond life, doing conjuring tricks in the streets. His skill as a magician made him famous far and wide, but he was as much feared as he was admired.

Many were the tales told of Doctor Faust, even in his lifetime. This story is one.

Little Johann, some say, was born to a peasant family in the little village of Rod in Thuringia. Even as a boy he was very clever, and his rich, childless uncle in the city of Weimar paid for him to go to school and university. Soon he became a master of theology, and then professor. But his thirst for knowledge was never satisfied; he never felt he had got to the bottom of things.

His lectures at the university drew students from hundreds of miles around, but for Faust this was not enough. He was after nature's innermost secrets: he wanted to be the one to solve the world's mysteries. He kept to his study and laboratory for years at a time, studying one subject after another and doing endless experiments. First he tried to find the philosophers' stone, which would turn base metals to gold. Then he sought the elixir that would make humans immortal, and so he studied medicine and began a long quest for the hidden mysteries of life.

At last Faust had read all the old books of magic and science, and yet he seemed to be no nearer his goal. Was there no way he could discover the secrets of Heaven and Earth? If only he could fly, like Daedalus and Icarus, who made themselves wings to escape from the labyrinth of ancient Crete... Faust resolved to do likewise, but whenever he tried to take off into the air he seemed rooted to the ground.

Faust was in despair. His thirst for knowledge was greater than ever, and there was only one thing left to try. For a long time he wrestled with his conscience. Then he spoke the magic formula that would call up the Devil. At once the demon stood before him. Now the Evil One has many names — Satan, Beelzebub, Lucifer — but in the Faust story he is called Mephistopheles.

'Why have you summoned me, Doctor Faust?' asked Mephistopheles.

'Because I want to fly,' answered Faust.

Mephistopheles could not help smiling. 'Then give me your soul,' he said quickly, 'and your every wish will be granted.'

'If you can make me renounce God for the rest of my life,' said Faust, 'my soul is yours for eternity.' And he made a pact with the Devil, and signed it in his own blood.

'Now name your wish, and I'll make it come true.' Mephistopheles laughed a sly, grating laugh.

'I want to fly up into the heavens.'

'That's easily done,' said the messenger from Hell, and under the Doctor's very eyes he turned into a winged horse.

'Get on my back,' said the magic charger, and he flew like the wind up from the earth and away into the heavens.

'Which way?' asked the horse.

'To all the great cities,' cried Faust.

With great beats of his wings the demonic mount bore Faust across Europe. First they visited all the big German cities of the time. They flew to the North Sea ports of Bremen and Hamburg, and along the Baltic coast from Luebeck to Stettin, Danzig and Koenigsberg (in what are now Poland and Russia). They swept inland to see Berlin and Magdeburg, Hanover and Muenster. Then they left Germany behind and flew farther afield, to Paris, Vienna, Rome and even the great Turkish capital of Constantinople.

'Take me down there,' ordered Faust. Using magic powers the Devil had given him, he took on the likeness of the prophet Muhammad and appeared in the Sultan's palace. The Turkish ruler bowed low before the impostor, and they had a long and learned discussion.

'And now, the heavens!' commanded Faust. This time the Devil sent to Hell for a chariot of fire, harnessed to twelve fierce dragons. Faust and Mephistopheles climbed in, and the Devil's team roared into the air in a cloud of smoke. They streaked through the heavens like a comet, leaving a dazzling trail of sparks. Soon they were so high Faust could see Europe, Asia and Africa in a single glance.

'Higher!' he cried, drunk with the excitement of the spectacular climb. 'Higher!'

The Earth receded with horrifying speed. Soon it looked as small as a barrel, then a child's ball, then the merest pinhead. Faster and faster the chariot went, till it was almost on the sun. Scorching vapours swirled

down from the blazing star, and red and yellow flames began to lick the chariot. Faust could hardly breathe, but the Devil puffed out his cheeks and blew a cold breeze over him.

Yet no matter how high Faust rose into the heavens, he did not find Heaven itself, or see the face of God. The sun's heat was nearly stifling him. An idea struck him.

'Not even Hell can be worse than this,' he said. 'Take me there.'

The chariot of fire plunged abruptly back to Earth, where it dived into a great abyss. Thick smoke rose from its depths. Half blinded by glowing flames, Faust glimpsed monstrous forms wandering miserably in the shadows, but he could not see any souls of the damned in agony.

'Where are the damned?' he asked. 'Is this really Hell?'

'Yes,' replied Mephistopheles, 'this is the entrance to Hell.'

'But it's Hell itself I want to see,' demanded Faust.

Mephistopheles frowned. If Faust saw the terrible sufferings of those

186

who sold Mephistopheles their souls and were damned for all eternity, he would not renounce God, and his soul would not go to the Devil. It was time to persuade Faust to bring his visit to Hell to an end.

Quick as lightning, Mephistopheles made a deep chasm open up at Faust's feet. Startled, the Doctor staggered and slipped. He tumbled over the edge, and everything went black.

When Faust came round, he could hardly move. Long hairy arms, half human, gripped him like a vice. An ancient ape, ugly as sin, had caught him in mid flight.

'Where am I?' cried Faust.

'With the beasts,' answered the ape, 'where you belong.'

Faust's blood ran cold. Surely he was more than an animal.

'Never!' he screamed. 'Save me, Mephistopheles! Take me back to Earth!'

He returned to the world of man as fast as he could, and Mephistopheles was able to continue tempting him.

KAE AND THE WHALE'S NEPHEW

In the South Seas many stories are told of Hina, the great and lonely goddess of the moon. One of these legends tells how Hina, or Sina as some call her, fell in love with a priest called Kae.

At that time Hina was queen of an island inhabited only by women. Kae, they say, was a priest in New Zealand.

One day Kae went out sailing and was caught in a terrible storm. Buffeted by gales and mountainous waves, he was blown far away from home. At last he managed to land on Hina's island. Some of Hina's women found him in the beach, and took him before their Queen.

Now Kae was by no means a young man, or a handsome one. In fact the crooked teeth that stuck out of his mouth in all directions made him look very ugly. But there were no other men on the island, and the Queen decided to marry the strange priest. Kae was overjoyed to have such a beautiful bride, and the marriage took place at once.

After some time Hina gave birth to a son, whom she loved and cared for devotedly. Soon he grew into a fine little boy.

But Kae felt a great longing to see his homeland again. What is more, he could feel himself growing older, while his wife still kept all her youth and beauty. Kae could not understand this, for he did not know that he had married a goddess. But he had noticed that every now and then she would go down to the beach, and each time she would come back looking younger and more beautiful.

One day Kae decided to spy on her. He saw how she picked up a board, took it into the sea and rode it out over the waves (as they still do in Australia and the South Seas). Again and again she did this, and each time she came back lovelier.

'Look at Queen Hina!' the women marvelled. 'She's as fresh as a spring day.'

And so she was. Kae, with his ugly face, was made uneasy by his wife's youth and beauty. Having a young and beautiful wife was naturally something he liked, but it also made him all the more aware of his own advancing age. In the end he could bear it no longer.

'The time has come for me to return to my homeland, Hina,' he said. 'I have to go there to obey the commandments of my god.'

The goddess frowned. 'What commandments are these?' she said.

'A man with a son must do three things,' he replied. 'He must build his son a house, make him a garden and dig him a lake. All these things I must do for our child. I am a priest, and must do as the gods say.'

So Hina agreed, and told her women to prepare for Kae's departure.

Now Hina's brother was Tunua-nui the whale. All whales were descended from him, and so whales were sacred on Hina's island. Not so on Kae's. Kae and all his people were very fond of whale-meat, and an evil plan had formed in the priest's mind.

'Do you think you could lend me your brother, Tunua-nui?' he said to his wife, slyly. 'If I go on his back, it will take me next to no time to cross the sea and do those three things.'

Again Hina agreed. But before Kae climbed on the whale's back, the Queen warned him: 'Be sure to turn Tunua-nui round when you reach land. Without your help he won't be able to swim again.'

And indeed a huge whale cannot turn itself round if it is lying in the shallows with its head towards the shore. Kae promised his wife to do as she asked, and set off.

When he reached the shore of his homeland, his people shouted for joy: 'Kae is back! He has brought us a whale!'

The priest stepped down from the whale's back. Now this was the moment when he should have carried out his promise to turn the whale round, so that it could go home. Instead he did nothing of the sort.

'Kill it!' he cried to the other men.

Yelling with excitement, the tribesmen fell upon the whale and killed it. Then they cut great chunks from its flesh and roasted them over an open fire, and a great feast was held in honour of Kae.

Next morning Kae ordered his servants to build a house, lay out a garden and dig a lake. For though he was not a very honest man, as we know how he repaid the kindness of Tunua-nui, he was anxious to fulfil his sacred duty to his son.

Back on Hina's island his son went on growing up carefree and happy, like most children in the South Seas at the time.

But in one way he was different from the other children he knew. Because it was an island of women, there were no men there now that Kae had gone, and the other children were descended from trees.

One day, when he was playing with the other children as usual, they came to blows. Kae's son was strongest, and so he won. The others were angry, and to get their own back they yelled:

'Your father was a foreigner!'

'That's a lie!' answered the little prince, furious. 'Anyway, I've got a mother just like the rest of you, and what's more, she's the Queen. So there!'

But the boys went on teasing him, and eventually he ran in tears to his mother to tell her what they were saying.

'It's not true!' said Hina. 'You don't have a father and you don't need one.'

But in the end she told the little prince the truth, and after that his greatest wish was to meet his father. Hina could not say no to her son and agreed to let him go after Kae.

Like his father before him, he was to go to his father's island on the back of a whale. This time the whale was the boy's cousin, son of Hina's vanished brother, Tunua-nui.

When he was about to climb onto the whale's back, Hina made him make the same promise as his father: he must turn the whale round as soon as he reached land, so that it could swim home. Then they set off across the sea.

When they reached the shore of Kae's island, the little prince climbed down and at once pulled the whale round to face the sea. But some men had seen them arrive, and ran up shouting at the tops of their voices. They wanted to drag the whale up onto dry land and kill it, for they remembered the taste of the whale that Kae had brought them.

'Stop!' cried the boy. 'You have no right to kill him. He's my cousin.'

The men just laughed and pushed him aside. They rushed forward to seize the enormous beast's tail, to drag it out of the water. But to the boy's delight the whale flexed its great body and, before they could let go, flung the men into the sea and drowned them. And so the son of Tunua-nui avenged his father's cruel death, and swam away.

At once the little prince started to search for his father. He asked the people of the island. Everyone knew Kae, the high priest, and they told him to make his way towards the middle of the island.

He walked a long, long way, but finally he came to a large garden. He saw a lake, and dived in to refresh himself. He found a pig running about in the undergrowth, so he caught and killed it, roasted it over a fire and had a hearty meal. Then he ate some juicy fruit he found growing on a tree, and lay down to rest.

But just then some servants came along.

'You have broken into the sacred garden,' they cried angrily, 'the garden of the high priest's son. There is only one penalty for this. You must die.'

When he heard this, the little prince was filled with terror and tried to run away. But the servants held him firmly and took him before Kae.

'You have committed a terrible crime,' said the priest sternly. 'The punishment for it is death.'

'I did not know,' replied the prince. 'I am a stranger here.'

'What is your name?' demanded the priest. 'Where do you come from? Who were your parents and grandparents?'

190

The prince, though small, was very proud. Head held high, he listed his noble ancestors, many of them gods or demi-gods. Kae listened without a word. Then, excitedly, he embraced the boy.

'You are my son,' he said, deeply moved. 'I was married to your lovely mother, Queen Hina.'

'Does that mean I don't have to die now?' asked the prince.

'Of course you don't,' smiled Kae. 'You have done no wrong.'

The boy did not understand. 'I bathed in the sacred lake, I killed a sacred pig and I picked the sacred fruit,' he said, puzzled. 'Your servants tell me all this is forbidden.'

But his father replied: 'The lake is your lake, the garden is your garden, and the fruit is your fruit. What you did would have cost another boy his life, but for you it is different. Those things are yours by right.'

And so the little prince was happy, and he stayed on Kae's island until he grew up.

THE RAT AND THE CUTTLEFISH

Once upon a time a man called Manumanu, who lived on the Pacific island of Funagu, made himself an outrigger canoe.

He was very proud of it — and well he might be, for it was a fine craft and thoroughly seaworthy. Then he had an idea. He would make a great voyage, taking with him one of every sort of animal there was.

Just then a frigate-bird flew by.

'Good day, my friend,' called Manumanu. 'Where are you off to?'

'Over the sea and far away,' answered the big black bird with a shake of its forked tail. 'When I find the island where I want to hatch my chick, I'll lay my egg. Then I'll go and steal fish from the other seabirds.'

'Now isn't that a stroke of luck!' said Manumanu. 'Why don't you come along in my boat?'

'Why not indeed?' said the bird.

'All right,' said the man. 'But what will you do if my boat sinks?'

'I'll fly away,' answered the bird, who was an excellent flyer and had no fear of the open sea.

'And what about the other birds I want to take?'

'They'll fly away too.'

'That's all right, then,' said Manumanu.

Then a crab came by. 'Will you take me too, captain?' it asked Manumanu.

'Of course,' the man replied. 'But what if the boat sinks?'

'I'll swim,' answered the crab.

Soon a great crowd of animals had collected.

'You're all welcome on my boat,' Manumanu told them, 'but first you must think what you'll do if it sinks.'

All the animals spoke at once. 'I'll swim,' said some. 'I'll run along the ocean floor,' said others. Only the rat said nothing.

'And what about you, friend rat?' asked Manumanu.

'I'll swim,' replied the rat.

The animals climbed on board, Manumanu set sail and the breeze quickly carried them out into the ocean. The animals made a terrible noise. You never heard such a barking, miaowing and chattering, cheeping and croaking, mooing and bellowing and grunting. They crawled, waddled and fluttered, jostled, clambered and jumped about until Manumanu could stand it no longer.

'Be quiet and keep still,' he shouted, and after that they settled down peacefully for the voyage.

But suddenly the wind grew stronger, and a storm blew up. The boat began to fill with water. Higher and higher the water came, until at last the boat sank. The birds rose into the air and flew away. The land animals dived to the bottom and walked to the shore. But poor Manumanu was not so lucky: he drowned and was never seen again. As for the rat, he started swimming. And he was making good speed, for rats swim strongly when they have to. But when a cuttlefish crossed his path, he jumped quickly on to its head. Why tire himself if someone else could do the work? The cuttlefish, of course, had other ideas, and tried to get rid of the uninvited guest.

'Please let me stay,' pleaded the rat. 'My grandparents are waiting, and they'll be worried if I don't get there soon. Won't you take me to them, dear friend?'

The cuttlefish was soft-hearted, as molluscs are. 'Oh well,' it sighed. 'If your grandparents are waiting, I don't mind.'

Then it opened its mouth, swallowed a gulp of water, and squirted it out at its other end so that it shot forward like a rocket.

The rat had been travelling for quite a while now, and was very hungry. But he didn't like fish, so he began nibbling the hairs on the cuttlefish's head. The rat ate greedily, and the cuttlefish soon noticed its hair vanishing. Thinking some enemy was attacking it, it squirted out black ink to camouflage itself.

'What are you doing?' asked the rat.

'Something is trying to eat my hair, so I'm squirting this ink to put it off.'

The rat chuckled to himself and said, 'Well then, you'd better put some speed on.' The cuttlefish took a great gulp of water and accelerated. It was far too busy rushing along to notice what the rat was doing. At last, when only a few hairs were left, the mollusc felt cold and realized that something was wrong.

'Hey, rat, what are you doing?' it asked.

'Why, nothing,' answered the crafty rat. 'Anyway, you can slow down now. I see we've nearly reached my grandparents' beach.'

And there indeed was an island. Soon the rat was able to leap on to dry land.

'Goodbye, dear friend,' he cried. 'Off you go.' The mollusc turned and made for the open sea. But it heard a parting shot from the rat: 'Feel your head!'

'Whatever for?' enquired the cuttlefish.

'Oh, nothing, I was only joking,' laughed the rat.

'What a stupid rat!' the cuttlefish muttered to itself as it swam on. But in the distance it heard the rat again:

'Feel your head, cuttlefish. You've gone bald!'

Thunderstruck, the cuttlefish put some tentacles to its head. Not a single hair was left. It nearly fainted. Then it flew into a rage.

'You unspeakable creature!' it stormed. 'I give you a ride and this is how you repay me — by gobbling up every hair on my head!'

Quickly it swam in to punish the rat. Too late: the villain had escaped inland, where the cuttlefish could not reach him. But the mollusc could not take such an injury lying down. It lurked under the shore waiting for the rat.

Before long the rat came back. It found a hole left by a crab, and crawled in looking for food. Cautiously the cuttlefish slipped a tentacle in to catch the rat, but the rat saw it and sank his teeth into it.

'Ow!' shrieked the cuttlefish, but it sent out another tentacle. This time it managed to seize the rat, and soon the sly rodent who had tricked it was no more.

Ever since then the cuttlefish has been bald, and cuttlefish parents have told their children: 'Look what the rats have done to us. If you see one, show no mercy.'

And the people of Funagu know the cuttlefish are sworn enemies of the rats, and whenever they want to catch them they put out a bait that looks like a rat. They join two brown shells with a piece of string, add a little shell for the head and twig for the tail. And when a cuttlefish comes to the shore and stretches out its tentacles to grab the rat, the fisherfolk of Funagu seize it and pull it out on to dry land.

THE LONELY DOLPHIN

This is one of the many South Sea tales of girl creatures like mermaids who come out of the sea at night to spy on men as they dance.

One evening two young dolphin girls were swimming near Rota, one of the Marianas Islands, and saw the men's fires. Then they heard chanting, and felt the pulsing rhythm of the men's dance. Inquisitive like all dolphins, they slipped out of the water, hid their flippers in the mangrove trees, and ran to spy on the men. The music, dancing and warm darting flames fascinated them. Not till dawn did they go back to the sea.

After that they came again and again. One day a young man saw their tracks and wondered what they were. He hid and waited. Sure enough he saw the dolphin girls arrive. One was so lovely he fell in love with her at once.

He watched them hide their flippers in the mangroves and run off towards the music. Then he took one of the flippers of the girl he thought so lovely, wrapped it in palm leaves, and hid it in his roof. He went back to the beach and waited.

At dawn the girls returned. When she discovered the theft, the lovely one burst into tears and threw herself sobbing to the ground. Her sister, panicking, could do nothing but flee to the comfort of the waves.

Then the young man came out of hiding and went up to the girl.

'Why are you crying?' he asked her tenderly.

'I can't go back to my family,' she sobbed. 'I'm so lonely.'

'There, there, don't cry,' he comforted. 'Let me take you home and give you something to eat. Then you'll feel better.'

After a while he made a proposal. 'It worries me that you're all alone and can't go back to your family,' he said. 'I would like to look after you instead. Would you like to be my wife?'

The dolphin had nothing else to do, and no one to turn to, and she thought he was very kind. So she married him gratefully. In time they had two children, and she brought them up very lovingly.

She seemed quite satisfied with her lot. Only when her husband went fishing would she rock her children in her arms and sing a soft lament:

> 'How sad is my soul, and how bitter my heart,
> In this alien world where my tears seek the sea.
> For life and contentment and joy pass me by
> As I shoulder my burden of sorrow alone.'

One year a bird nested in their roof. When a chick fell from the nest one day, the young wife picked it up gently and put it back. As she did so, her hand brushed a bundle wrapped in palm leaves. Still inquisitive as any dolphin, she looked inside.

There was her flipper. At last she could go back to the dolphin family she missed so sorely, back to the sea where she belonged. But what of her children? For many months she was in anguish, but in the end the call of the sea was too strong for her. She called her children to her.

'My darlings,' she sobbed, hugging them tight. 'I must leave you now. I will never, never forget you, but I cannot live without the sea any longer. Just make me one promise. Never eat dolphin meat, for if you do you will kill your mother, and she loves you dearly.'

'We promise, mother,' answered her children, with tears in their eyes. 'We shall think of you often.'

Sadly the young mother picked up her flippers and walked down to the shore. Turning, she waved a last goodbye. Then she dived into the waves, and was never seen again.

GOG AND MAGOG

Once upon a time, and a very long time ago it was, lived the great emperor, Alexander of Macedon. No one could defeat him, and he conquered all the world, or as much of it as was known about in those days. He loved making war, indeed, it was what he liked doing most, and as he went through the world in his career of conquest, he gathered around him all the best fighters and the bravest warriors.

After many victorious campaigns he came at last to the end of the world, and then he, who had been afraid of nobody and of nothing, at last knew what fear was. For there he met two races of beings who were so strong and so murderous that even he and his stalwart men trembled. One of these races was called Gog and the other was Magog.

These two peoples were worse than the fiercest and most savage animals. They were always thirsty for blood, and they would swallow

their enemies whole — skin, bones, hair, armour, even their boots. Some of them were giants who had one single eye in the middle of their foreheads, others had three eyes and could see round corners. Some of them had only one leg and yet could run quicker than the swiftest horse, others had three legs and were even faster. These Gog and Magog people were truly horrific.

When Emperor Alexander of Macedon had watched and spied on these creatures for a time, he determined not to fear them any longer, and boldly he launched an attack against them. Surprisingly enough, once Alexander and his warriors advanced to do battle, the Gog and the Magog took to flight. The emperor's forces pursued them over mountains and across rivers, through marshes and through forests, and finally he trapped them in the remotest desert. There they disappeared without trace. Alexander and his men searched for them high and low, but in vain. What was he to do next? What would you have done?

Alexander made the tops of the high mountains round about the place where the Gog and the Magog had vanished bend right over until they touched, and then, where the mountain peaks met, he fixed some hollow pipes. And then he went home to Macedon.

Whenever the wind blows over those pipes it produces a horrible howling noise, like the sound made if you blow across the top of a milk-bottle, but a million times louder. This fills the Gog and Magog with terror, and they groan, 'Woe! woe! Alexander of Macedon has come again!'

They are more afraid of Alexander than of anything else, and they will tremble at the very thought of him until the world comes to an end.

THE FLYING ELEPHANTS

Once upon a time, an ancient legend from India tells, there was a sun bird which laid an egg, the Original Egg. From this egg came the sun, to light the world.

Brahma, the all-powerful god, held half of the eggshell in each hand, while he sang the chant of creation. At the end of each verse, a cow elephant sprang from his left hand, and soon there were eight elephants. From his right hand sprang eight bull elephants. The first of these was Airavata, on which the god Indra rode.

Of all creatures the elephants were the gods' favourites, and at that time they could move freely in the sky as well as on earth. They had wings to fly, light as clouds, but whenever they wanted they could resume the elephant form we know and return to earth.

If the elephants had been more careful, they would still have had wings today. One day they were flying north over the mountains of the Himalayas, when they saw an enormous fig tree. Its branches made a huge dome, a mile across. The elephants perched on one of the great branches, to rest and look at the earth. After a while they decided they wanted to walk on the ground, but when they took on their earthly shape, the branch broke, and down they fell. Now the fig tree sheltered the hut of a hermit, who was at that moment meditating with a messenger from Brahma. The elephants fell on the hut, crushing it so that the people in it died, and as he died the holy man cursed the elephants.

'From this moment,' he warned, 'your bodies shall be heavy and cumbersome. You shall stay anchored to the earth like other animals, and the sky shall be closed to you for ever. You shall be nothing but beasts of burden. Humans will ride you, and when they labour, you will carry their loads.'

Elephants have always played an important part in the legends of India. The universe, they say, is carried by sacred elephants, and one of the Hindu gods even wore an elephant's head. This was Ganesha, of whom many tales are told.

Ganesha was the son of the god Shiva and his wife Parvati, and he lived with his mother and his brother Skanda in the royal palace. His father Shiva was always away travelling, doing all the things a god has to do.

One day Shiva returned after being away for a very long time, so long that his children did not recognize him. When he arrived at the palace gates, Queen Parvati was out in the garden, bathing in a pool, and it was young Ganesha who saw the stranger.

'You've no right to come in here,' he warned the god.

Shiva did not recognize his son, and he was amazed to have some child barring his way.

'Get out of my way!' thundered the god.

'It's no good, I won't let you pass,' replied the young prince defiantly.

Now no one dared to disobey the great god Shiva. In a fit of rage, the god drew his sword and cut off Ganesha's head. Hearing the voices, Parvati came running up. When she saw what had happened, she fell to her knees by her son and screamed in anguish.

'What have you done, you monster?' she cried to her husband when at last she found her voice. 'You have sacrificed your own son Ganesha!'

The god groaned in horror at what he had done. Then he called his huntsmen, and ordered them to find another head at once, so that his son could be brought back to life.

The huntsmen set off and hunted desperately, but all they could find was an elephant. They cut off its head, and brought it back to Shiva. The god placed it on Ganesha's body, and he came back to life at once.

So after that Ganesha had an elephant's head. It was much too big for his body, of course, and once he noticed that, he started to fatten himself up. Soon he was very fat indeed.

Some time later Shiva decided that he should give one of his two sons the gift of everlasting life, to make him equal with the gods. Which son should he choose? He did not know, and so he arranged a competition. He decided that the one who could travel round the world the fastest would win a place among the gods.

At once Skanda climbed on his mount, a swift-footed peacock, and set off at a rapid pace. Ganesha, however, stayed miserably where he was. With his weight, how could he possibly win the race and become a god? He crouched down on the ground, his elephant's eyes full of tears.

Suddenly a little mouse popped out of a hole nearby.

'Why are you crying?' asked the little creature. 'Look, there's your mother, Queen Parvati. Isn't she the wife of a mighty god, and mistress of the world? If you run round her it will be just the same as running round the world.'

Ganesha looked at the mouse in delight. 'Thank you, clever little mouse,' he said.

He lumbered once around his mother, and joined the ranks of the immortals, long before Skanda came back exhausted from his journey round the world.

Since then Ganesha, son of Shiva, has been the Hindu god of wisdom, with the title of 'Remover of Obstacles'. The clever little mouse has been his travelling companion, and to this day the mouse and the elephant are often shown together in Indian art.

MORPIDE THE DRAGONSLAYER

Some time between 1157 and 1174 a priest in Bayeux, in the north of France, wrote a 'History of the Normans'. One of the stories he told was about the last adventure of King Morpide of Northumbria, the ancient land which stretched across what is now northern England and southern Scotland.

Morpide was a Norman, a strong and handsome man, a bold

horseman and courageous knight. But he could also be harsh and tyrannical. He oppressed not only the conquered inhabitants of Northumbria, but even his own Normans, the new rulers. Yet he was devoted to them: he was a protector as well as a tyrant, and as he grew older he became wiser and kinder, though his people could never forget his early harshness.

One day a knight from the west coast galloped to his castle. His horse was on the point of collapse, dripping with sweat and foaming at the mouth. The rider burst into the great hall.

'Disaster, my lord!' he gasped, and fell exhausted to the floor. 'A terrible disaster!'

Morpide frowned. 'Speak, man. What has happened?'

'A dreadful dragon has come over the sea from Ireland, my lord. A loathsome monster. It is a terrifying sight, with a misshapen body as high as a mountain and a head of unbelievable ugliness. Enormous fangs. Claws like hooks of iron. It is eating up everything in its path — cattle and horses, men, women and children. People are fleeing as if the devil himself were at their heels, leave their farms and houses wherever the dragon appears. The people beg you to help them, Sire!'

Anger filled Morpide's face. 'Where are my Norman knights and soldiers? Are they men of straw, that they fear a mindless monster?'

The messenger wrung his hands. 'It is not their fault, my lord. Swords and lances shatter against it like glass. It tramples buildings underfoot. You are our only hope — if you do not come soon, we shall all be lost.'

Morpide rose. 'Bring me my arms,' he commanded, angrily. He put on his armour, sheathed his sword, filled his quiver with arrows and took up his spear. Gathering his men together, he galloped towards the west.

In the distance they could already see whirling clouds of sulphur rising into the sky. The trees were threshing from side to side. On the road they met a sobbing crowd of people stumbling along in terror, a procession of human misery. It was as if the land had been devastated by a terrible earthquake.

At last the dragon loomed into sight. The King spurred on his horse, firing his arrows as he rode. They did not even scratch the monster's scales, but it reared up angrily. Then Morpide hurled his spear with all his might, but it glanced off harmlessly. Enraged, he plunged his sword into the monster's side, barely avoiding a deadly blow from its claws. Without pausing for breath he attacked again. Blood spurted from the panting dragon, but it would not give way. The King, beside himself with rage, leapt from his horse and flung himself on the dragon. Clinging to its neck, he plunged his dagger into its throat. As he did so the monster, with a last effort, opened its mouth, seized him in its fangs, crunched him up and swallowed him down.

Petrified with fear, none of his men dared come near. But the monster rolled over, blood pouring from its wounds, and died. The danger was past. The people ran forward, dancing and shouting for joy: 'The dragon is dead! The dragon is dead!' No one seemed to care that their King was dead, for they had still not forgotten his old harshness. And this is how the old chronicler finished his tale:

'At the King's death there was only joy, with no thought of how he had given his life for his people. But the most wondrous stories were told about the dragon for many a year to come.'

THE TURTLES OF KORO

In the Pacific Ocean around the islands of Fiji live many sea turtles. If they come on land, people say, they will bring good luck.

The villagers of Nakamaki, on Koro, one of the islands, have the gift of calling the turtles out of the depths of the sea on to dry land. They put on fine clothes and garlands of flowers and perform an ancient ritual, singing and dancing on the shore till the turtles come out of the sea and clamber up the beach.

Once upon a time the law decreed that the villagers must leave the beach as soon as the ritual was over, and not come back till the next day.

'Never watch the turtles at night,' warned the wise men of Nakamaki. 'Their secrets are not ours to know. Whoever watches them will suffer the most terrible misfortune.'

But the day came when one of the men of Nakamaki decided he did not believe all this. 'It's only a stupid superstition,' he said to himself. 'Why shouldn't I watch the turtles? I'll watch them all night if I choose. After all, they're only humble sea creatures.'

So he decided to break the rule and find out the turtles' secret. As soon as the ritual dance was over, he hid behind a tree. His companions hurried back to the village to drink the peppery kava and celebrate the turtles' return. When they had all gone, the man found a new hiding place so that he could see all the beach, and then he settled down to wait and watch.

From the distance came sounds of singing and laughter. He knew they were feasting in the village, and he began to feel lonely on the beach. Was he really safe here alone in the dark? He shook himself.

'Don't be silly,' he told himself firmly. 'Nothing's going to happen.'

But at that moment something did happen. A strange shape glided out of the sea and came up the beach. Slowly, veiled in mist, it moved along the shore. The man was frightened now, but his curiosity got the better of him. He followed silently to see what the thing was going to do. Suddenly it turned. The man stopped dead in his tracks, terrified.

'Poor wretch,' it said to him. 'I am the god of the turtles. By spying on me you have disobeyed your wise men and broken the law. I must make an example of you, so that no one on the isle of Koro ever does that again. I shall turn you into a tree, and the stones of your fruit will look like turtles. Whenever people see these stones they will think of the proud unbeliever who refused to obey the law.'

The man was paralysed with terror.

'No, no! Have mercy!' he begged. 'What will become of my family? Spare me!'

'You should have thought of that before,' answered the god of the turtles, coldly. 'It is too late now. You chose to break the law, and now you must be punished.' And with that he turned his back on the wretched man and disappeared into the mist.

Unable to believe what he had seen, the man from Nakamaki tried to rub his eyes, but he couldn't lift his arms. He wanted to run away, but he couldn't move his legs. He wanted to scream for help, but his lips wouldn't obey him. He felt himself stiffening. His heart beat slower and slower, a great weariness overcame him, the mist enveloped him. The horizon faded out of sight, twilight descended on him bit by bit, and he became unconscious. As the night went on, roots grew from his feet and sank deep into the ground. By the time dawn came, he was anchored fast.

Next morning the villagers of Nakamaki came back to where they had danced the day before. They were amazed to find a strange tree that had not been there when they sang to the turtles.

'How strange,' they said to each other, puzzled. 'And just look at its stones. They're like sea turtles.'

They had already noticed that the man was missing, and now the wise men soon guessed what had become of him, and warned the people not to be unbelievers like him.

And the vono trees which flourish on the isle of Koro to this day are the descendants of that strange tree, into which the god of the turtles turned the unbeliever.

THE CROCODILE PEOPLE

In the south of Papua New Guinea, not so very far from Australia, lies an island called Kiwai where the people are supposed to be descended from crocodiles. This is how the story goes.

Long, long ago Ipila, the creator of the world, decided it would be a good idea to create the human race. For a while he wondered how to set about it, but at last he took a piece of wood and a knife and began to carve a man. He put a lot of care into it, and when the man was finished Ipila was very pleased with his handiwork.

'That'll do nicely!' he said to himself. 'I'll call him Nugu, and make him come to life.'

Ipila took a coconut, poured in some flour from the sago palm, and mixed it with the coconut milk to make a paste. With this he coated the wooden man's face.

At first Nugu stayed stiff as a poker, but after a while his eyelids twitched, his nostrils quivered, and he began to breathe. Then he opened his eyes and looked all around. Finally he opened his mouth.

'I'm alive!' said Nugu, and puffed like a crocodile.

Nugu was a little bit simple. He didn't really understand very much.

'You're not very bright, are you?' said Ipila after a while. 'I think I'd better show you how to do a few things.'

'Whatever for?' said Nugu. 'I can eat sago, I can drink water, I'm alive. What more do I want.'

'Even animals eat, drink and are alive,' scolded Ipila. 'You want to be more than an animal, don't you?'

'No!' retorted Nugu. 'What's wrong with being an animal?'

And nothing Ipila could say would change Nugu's mind. Ipila was very disappointed.

Some time later Nugu went to see his creator.

'I'm very lonely, Ipila,' he complained. 'Make some more men, to keep me company.'

'Certainly not!' said Ipila. 'Why should I make men if they don't want to learn anything?'

But Nugu kept asking, and in the end Ipila gave in. He carved a man and two women, brought them to life with sago paste, and sent them off to find Nugu. They made friends at once.

'That's much better,' said Nugu. 'Now I'm not alone any more.'

He and one of the women decided to marry, and so did the other couple. A happy, lazy honeymoon followed.

But it could not last forever.

Soon Ipila went to the humans and said, 'I'm going to teach you some very useful things. I'll show you how to make fire, and sow seeds, and make clothes, and lots of other useful things as well.'

'Don't listen!' Nugu warned the others. 'He wants to educate us, come with me.'

And he took the others off into the bush to laze around. Ipila was furious with them. Every day they did nothing — and every day they ate sago. Before long the other man was bored to tears.

'Sago, sago, sago! Morning, moon and night! I can't eat another mouthful.'

'Yes, why doesn't Ipila give us something else?' grumbled his wife.

Her husband turned to the others.

'Come with us,' he urged. 'We're going to catch an animal and eat its meat.'

Nugu blinked. 'Don't do anything of the kind,' he warned. 'Ipila hasn't given us permission to eat meat.'

'That doesn't matter a bit!' The other man and his wife brushed Nugu's objection aside and ran off. Soon they captured a kangaroo, killed it and began their meal. But as they ate, they began to change. Their bodies stayed human, but their heads became like crocodiles' heads. Back they went to Nugu and his wife.

'Go away!' cried Nugu the moment he caught sight of them. 'We don't want you here. You're not real humans any more.'

So the crocodile people parted from the people of Nugu. They lived all alone, catching animals and eating them. As long as meat was a novelty, they lived quite happily. But little by little the lack of company began to bother them.

'Let's make some companions for ourselves,' said the crocodile man to his wife. And they took some wood and tried to carve some crocodile men, just as Ipila had carved the people of Nugu.

But it did not suit Ipila to have more crocodile people in the world, and as fast as the crocodile folk carved people in their image, Ipila turned them into real humans. Today the Papuans of Kiwai are the descendants of these creatures, and indeed people say their ancestors were crocodiles.

And what of the people of Nugu? Ipila was still furious with them. After all, they didn't want to learn, and they had turned their backs on him. But he blamed Nugu most. If Nugu hadn't been so lazy, the others wouldn't have been bored and killed animals.

'I'm going to punish him,' he decided at last. 'Nugu, come here!'

Nugu appeared before his creator.

210

'Your brother and his wife weren't content to eat sago,' Ipila said to him. 'They ate meat.'

'That's not my problem,' said Nugu.

'Oh yes, it is,' contradicted Ipila. 'In fact it's all your fault, Nugu, because you wouldn't do as I said. I wanted to give you fire and teach you lots of useful things, but you couldn't be bothered to learn. Now I'm going to punish you. From now on you can support the world.'

So Nugu's lazy days in the bush were over, and instead he laboured under an enormous burden — he had to carry the whole world on his shoulders.

MOTHER BEAVER
AND THE GRIZZLY BEAR

Of all the animals in the forests of the Rocky Mountains, from Alaska to Yellowstone Park, the one most feared was Hoorts the grizzly bear. When they heard Hoorts' angry growl, all the other animals trembled. When he roamed through the forest on his heavy paws, they hid or fled in terror. He was so strong, and his anger so terrible, that not a single animal could stand up to him.

And Hoorts knew it. He was so powerful that he could kill the strongest enemy with one blow of his great paw. And he was not only very strong, but very big, so he was for ever looking for food to keep up his strength. The only time of year when the other animals were safe from him was the winter, for while the snowstorms raged outside, the grizzly stayed curled up in his cosy den, and did not stir till spring.

One year, when winter had been specially cruel and long and spring came very late, Hoorts woke up starving. Never before had he been so hungry. His empty stomach was rumbling loudly. Hoorts got on his feet and lumbered outside. He sniffed the fresh air, felt the sun tickling his nose, and gave an enormous yawn, so loud that the other animals jumped with fright.

'The grizzly has woken up, friends,' they whispered to each other. 'Get away while you can.'

'Oof,' groaned the grizzly, 'I'm so hungry, I'm going to eat every single thing I can find.'

He stretched his stiff limbs and went off into the forest. And indeed he did kill and eat every little animal he came across. Soon the forest floor as far as the eye could see was littered with bones. There they lay bleaching in the spring sun, where the bear had gnawed them and thrown them down.

Yet still Hoorts was hungry. Terror spread through the animals, and they fled as fast as they could. But no matter how fast they ran, Hoorts caught them up.

'Watch out, here comes the grizzly!' cried the birds, watching in horror although they themselves had nothing to fear. 'Run, the killer is coming!'

'Wretched chatterboxes!' Hoorts grumbled up at them.

And still he killed and ate. Soon all but one animal had gone. Even the father beaver and his little ones had fallen prey to the grizzly's greed.

212

Only the mother beaver was left. Weeping, she vowed to avenge her family's death.

'I'll make Hoorts pay for this,' she vowed. She sat to work and built a trap for him near her dam. Then she stood in the middle of the path, and whistled to attract the bear's attention.

Soon he was after her, and at the sight of this plump morsel his mouth began to water. Cautiously he approached her.

'Come on then!' shouted the mother beaver, drawing herself up to her full height. 'Come and eat me!'

An angry glint came into Hoorts' eyes, and he forgot his caution. He reared up on his hind legs and hurled himself at the beaver with a great leap. But she dodged nimbly aside, and Hoorts blundered straight into the trap.

And there he stayed. What on earth had happened? Why was he in pain? What was gripping his paw so tightly? Yelping, he tried to fight his way out, but whatever he did, he could not pull free of the trap. Now he went mad with pain and rage, beating the air with his other paws and roaring at the top of his voice.

'Well?' mocked the mother beaver. 'Don't you want to come and eat me?'

'I'll get you for this!' raved Hoorts, and he struggled even harder. But the more he struggled, the more the trap bit into him. In the end he was exhausted. Looking down at his paw, he saw blood, and at last he realized there was nothing he could do. He sank down, overcome with despair.

Mother beaver sat there at the entrance to her home, watching.

'That's what you get for being greedy,' she said. 'You're going to die, Hoorts.'

'No, no!' begged Hoorts. 'Please free me.'

'No, you're going to die,' repeated the mother beaver.

Soon the bear became so weak that he could hardly speak.

'Have you no pity?' he moaned. 'Help me!'

But the mother beaver replied coldly: 'You have eaten my husband and my children. You have filled our forest with terror. Instead of being content with your fair share of food, you always wanted more. More and more. You were never satisfied.'

'Mercy!' begged the grizzly bear.

But the mother beaver turned away. Again and again Hoorts begged and cried and sobbed and wailed, but nothing could change the mother beaver's mind. The reply was always the same: 'You're going to die.'

And at last he did. Hoorts the strong, the great, the invincible died because the little mother beaver had so decided.

THE NOBLE SWAN

Majestic and untamed, the swan has long been revered.

People of many cultures have honoured it as the companion of gods and kings. Hindus believe that the god Brahma came down from heaven on a swan's back. One Greek god, Apollo, had a swan which could foretell the future. The son of another, the war god Ares, was raised by a swan and known as Cycnos, 'the swan'. Later, as king of Colonus, he was killed by the great Heracles, then turned into a swan by Ares and placed in the sky as the constellation Cygnus.

Some believe that the swan bears souls away at the moment of death. When the swans sing, the Norse legends say, death is calling. They sing before they die, and they will sing when the world is about to end. Anyone who has heard the swan's uncanny voice will understand that belief.

When Norse warriors died in battle, too, the Valkyries (the god Odin's handmaidens, sent to bring the heroes' souls to Valhalla) might come in the guise of swans. Maidens in swan's feathers, indeed, often appear in myths.

In the Middle Ages many knights bore swans on their coats of arms, including the Dukes of Cleves, Geldern and Reineck. The emblem comes from the tales of knights and swans of olden days. This is one such story.

The Duke of Limbourg and Brabant, in what is now Belgium and Holland, had a lovely daughter, Elsa, who meant more to him than all his wealth and power. When the Duke knew that his death was near, he sent for his most trusted knight, Sir Frederick of Telramond.

'Soon I shall die,' he said. 'You have served me well and loyally, Sir Frederick. Will you do me one last service after I am gone?'

Telramond promised faithfully to carry out his master's last wish, whatever it might be.

'Look after my daughter,' said the Duke. 'She is still young, and she has no husband to protect her. Unless I know she is in safe hands, I cannot die in peace.'

'As long as I live, my lord,' vowed Telramond, 'your daughter shall be safe.'

After the Duke's death Frederick did indeed care for Elsa and governed her lands well on her behalf. But after some time he fell in love with her, and also with his new-found power. Now he wanted to be Duke himself, and he asked Elsa to marry him.

'I am honoured by your request, my lord,' replied Elsa, 'and I shall never forget what you have done for me. But alas, I do not love you, and I cannot marry you.'

Telramond was bitterly disappointed. His hurt pride and ambition demanded revenge. Some days later he called the nobles of Brabant together.

'Princess Elsa promised me her hand in marriage,' he announced. 'Now she has broken her word. Such an act brings shame on the House of Brabant.'

Elsa was horrified at his treachery. She swore on her father's grave that Sir Frederick was lying, and that she had never made such a promise. Her courtiers did not know who to believe, and they decided to lay the matter before their king, Henry I, nicknamed the Fowler.

'This is a very grave accusation,' said the monarch. 'God himself must judge who is telling the truth. Let some knight come forward to fight Sir Frederick of Telramond for the honour of Princess Elsa. If he wins, she is innocent.'

At that moment the young knight Lohengrin heard the bells begin to ring at the castle of Montsalvat, where the Holy Grail was enshrined.

'Lohengrin, son of Percival,' said the bells, 'you shall fight for Princess Elsa.'

As the knight stood listening, a boat came floating down the river. It was pulled by a noble swan, its feathers like snow in winter sunlight. Lohengrin stepped into the boat, and the swan flapped its great wings and set off down the river.

For five days it swam, till at last it reached the court of Brabant. Elsa was taking a walk by the river with her retinue. Lohengrin leapt on to the bank and bowed low.

'I have come to serve you, Princess,' he said.

Elsa, amazed and overjoyed, took him at once to the king.

'Sire, I have found my champion,' she said.

The next day Lohengrin faced Sir Frederick of Telramond in armed combat. The fight was long and fierce, but at last Lohengrin won, and Elsa was declared innocent. Its task fulfilled, the swan floated majestically away.

Another tale of a knight and a swan is set in the time when the Emperor Charlemagne ruled much of Europe. Duke Godfrey of Brabant had died, leaving his lands to his wife and daughter. The Duke of Saxony, his brother, then claimed the lands, saying they could not be left to women. The dispute was laid before the Emperor, who summoned the dead man's relatives to Nijmegen, on the Dutch river Waal.

216

While they were gathering there, a swan appeared on the river, wearing a band of silver round its neck. It was pulling a boat in which there lay a knight in shining armour, his head resting on his shield, and his helmet at his feet.

As the swan drew near the bank, all the men and women of the court ran forward to see this strange sight. The Emperor invited the unknown knight to take his place among the nobles of the court.

Soon the Emperor announced that the right to the dead Duke's lands would be decided by armed combat. The Duke of Saxony was a mighty warrior, who had never been defeated. Who would dare champion the widow's cause? For a moment she was in despair, but then the Knight of the Swan came forward and offered to serve her.

Long and valiantly they fought. The Duke was strong, but the Knight of the Swan was mightier still, and at last the Duke was defeated.

Overjoyed, the Duchess offered the knight her daughter's hand in marriage.

'I am honoured to accept, my lady,' said the knight. 'But one thing I must ask: my wife must never ask who I am, or where I came from. All I may tell you is that my name is Helias.'

His bride gladly agreed never to question him, and the wedding took place. At Cleves, near the river Rhine, just over what is now the German border, the Duke of Brabant's family had an ancient castle, first built by the Roman emperor Julius Caesar. In that castle, now renamed the castle of the swan, Helias and his young wife went to live.

They had two children, and for a long time they were very happy. But Helias' wife could not help wondering about her husband's past, and in the end she could not contain her curiosity any longer.

'My love, we have been married so long now,' she said to him one day. 'Surely you can tell me now who you are?'

Sorrow filled his face at once.

'With that one question you have thrown our happiness away,' he answered sadly. 'Now I must leave you and our children for ever.'

Without another word he embraced them for the last time. Once again the swan appeared on the river, trailing the boat behind it. His wife and family watched with tears in their eyes. Soon the swan disappeared into the distance, and Helias was never seen again.

218

THE LAND OF DEVILS

Far, far away there lies a place called Wumbu, the Land of Devils. Behind its name lies the strange tale of the Devils of Marm.

In the mists of the ancient dream-time, before the dawn of history, Wumbu was ruled by a blind old she-devil called Marm. She lived on a rock in the shadow of trees in the Monjajawa area, near a place called Cave Creek. All around, for mile upon mile, stretched the empty bushland, where the woial fruit grew.

One day, when the rainy season was just beginning, Marm summoned her maidservants.

'Quick!' she ordered. 'I need woial fruit. Run and fetch me as much as you can carry.'

The girls ran off into the bush, laughing and giggling among themselves. They filled basket after basket and ran back with them, but it was not enough for Marm.

'More, you stupid girls!' she screeched angrily. 'I need far more than that.'

And back the girls ran into the bush as fast as they could. Again and again they filled their baskets, till at last Marm was satisfied.

The old she-devil set to work. Taking a big stone in her hand, she crushed all the fruit. She worked so hard and so long that she wore a hole in the rock.

When at last she had crushed all the fruit, she summoned the girls again and made them eat it. For it was magic, and at once they turned into she-devils like herself: the Devils of Marm.

To this day they haunt that area, and in a place called Jaleetjee, where the devil is said to live, you can still see what they left of Marm's fruit, beside the hole that she wore in the rock when she was working.

If you go there, you will soon find out what the devils get up to, the natives say. Just pitch your tent near the rock of Jaleetjee, and you will hear singing.

Where is it coming from? Out of the earth or down from the rock? You follow the sound hither and thither, till at last you think you know where it comes from, but just as you reach it, it stops.

At that moment you hear the noise of an axe in the opposite direction. Someone is cutting down a tree. You hurry over there, but find you are all alone.

And all alone you stay, except that there are devils there too.

So it goes on. At last, tired and lonely, you lie down to sleep in the back of your tent. But there through the trees a fire is glowing, and you can hear girls' voices as they talk and laugh. For though not a soul has seen them, the bush all around you is filled with the Devils of Marm.

THE DOGS OF THE MOON

In the night sky of the southern hemisphere there are few stars, but the moon shines with a beautiful yellow light. Balu, they call her, the friendly round moon. People love her, because she shows them the way when they walk across the bush, and shines her light on the ground when they feast.

When humans are asleep, Balu plays with her animals. Three in particular are always round her, and she calls them her dogs. But they are not dogs: one is called Black Serpent, another Death Adder, and the third Spotted Cobra. People are frightened of the dogs of the moon. And this is not surprising, because they are very dangerous.

'If one of Balu's dogs bites you,' they say, 'you'll turn into a black stone and fall to the ground, and there you'll stay, stiff as a poker. Not even the sorcerer can help you. So you'd better keep away from the dogs of the moon.'

One night, while Balu was playing with her animals, she looked down to Earth, to where the Australian aborigines lived. More and more brightly she shone, as she always did when she looked at the Earth. Then she could see better who was out at night instead of in bed, and what they were doing.

This time Balu saw a river, and black men walking in it. She saw twice five men walking in the river.

'Hey, men!' she called.

The ten black men lifted their eyes to the moon.

'What is it, Balu?' they asked.

'Listen, men,' said the moon. 'You're strong. Wouldn't you like to carry my dogs over the river?'

'What?' cried the men, trembling, 'carry Black Serpent, Death Adder and Spotted Cobra over the river? Never!'

They knew what Balu's dogs really were. Sometimes she sent them down to Earth, and they would run into the grass and play. When a dog came, poor wretch, they would catch it. When a human came near — a black man or a Lubra woman — the serpents would bite. The aborigine sorcerers had no cure for the serpents' venom, and soon people would be wailing, 'Dead, the black man! Stone dead, the poor black lady!'

'No, Balu,' cried the men to the moon. 'We love you dearly, we love to look at you and we'd gladly help you. But we can't carry your dogs over the river. Don't ask us to do that.'

221

Balu's face darkened. Lines wrinkled the round face of the full moon.

'So you won't do it?' she grumbled.

'No, in the name of the good spirit of the sky! What if your dogs bite us?'

'They won't bite you.'

'But what if they do?'

'Your dogs bite too, but you're not afraid of them.'

'Our dogs may snap or even bite,' replied the black men, 'that's true, but they don't kill anyone. Your dogs are different. Anyone they bite is a dead man. You must admit that, Balu.'

The moon thought it over.

'Well,' she said at last, 'I suppose one of my dogs might bite you. But if you'll do as I say, I'll give you a present.'

The men looked at Balu warily. 'What use is your present to us if we are dead?'

'If you die,' answered the moon, 'you'll come back to life. That's what my present is. Watch this.' She took a piece of bark and tossed it into the river. The bark sank, but a moment later it was back on the surface.

The men looked at each other in surprise. They did not know what to think.

'Is that your present, Balu? A piece of bark?'

'In a way,' said the moon. 'If you carry my dogs over the river, you see, the same thing will happen to you as happened to the bark. You'll sink, but then you'll come straight up to the surface again and go on living.'

Amazed, the men watched the piece of bark as it danced on the waves in the light of the moon. They wavered.

'And what if we don't carry your dogs?'

A shadow appeared on the moon's face.

'Then the same thing will happen to you as happens to this stone!' she said, and she threw a stone into the river. 'When you're dead, you'll never come back to the surface. You'll never be seen again.'

The men hummed and hawed for a long time, but at last they made up their minds.

'It's all very well to talk of presents, Balu. But it's us who have to carry your dogs over the river, and we're just too scared to do it.' And indeed they were shaking so much that they could hardly move.

The moon's face was darkening.

'Fools!' she said. 'I'll show you how easy it is. My dogs are quite harmless, you'll see.'

And Balu came down to Earth. Black Serpent, Death Adder and Spotted Cobra were coiled round her neck and shoulders, chest and

222

arms, hissing and darting out their tongues. Terrified, the men shrank away.

Quickly Balu carried her dogs over the river. On the far bank she turned, and threw a stone into the water.

'You're cowards, all of you!' she shouted at the men. Her voice was menacing. 'So you'll never come back to life when you die. You'll stay forever where you're buried. Soon you'll be nothing but bone, and you'll become part of the ground like a stone. Fools! You had the chance to die and come back to life, again and again for ever, but you threw it away. Now it's too late.'

Her face now quite black, Balu turned and disappeared into the bush. For a while the men could still hear the hisses of Black Serpent, Death Adder and Spotted Cobra, but then they died away.

'The snakes are terrifying,' they told each other when at last they dared to breathe. 'We must kill them, or we'll never be safe.'

Ever since then the black men have killed all the snakes they meet. But that night when the men would not carry her dogs, Balu made a vow: 'As long as there are men, there will be snakes to remind them that they would not do as I asked.' And so she sends more snakes, and more, and more.

And it is so to this day. Australia is the only place in the world which has more poisonous snakes than harmless ones, and the Black Serpent, Death Adder and Spotted Cobra are among the deadliest of all.

THE EVENING STAR
AND THE BLACK BIRD

Long, long ago the Karasha Indians of South America were still nomads who spent all their time roaming through the forests, hunting game, fishing in the great river Beracan, and gathering roots and berries. At that time they did not know how to grow crops.

Once upon a time there were two Karasha sisters, Imakro and Denake. The elder, Imakro, was a proud, haughty girl with high ambitions. The younger, Denake, was kind hearted, modest and good-tempered, quite the opposite of her hard sister.

In the evenings Imakro used to sit outside their hut and look at the Evening Star. Tajnakan, the Karashas called it. It shone out in the night sky with a golden light, so bright and beautiful that the girl could hardly take her eyes off it. In the end she fell quite in love with it, partly because it was so beautiful and partly, perhaps, because it was so far away.

Was it really out of reach? One evening Imakro sat down in front of the hut and sighed deeply.

'What's wrong, Imakro?' asked her father. 'Why are you sighing?'

'Oh father,' replied the girl sadly, 'every night I look up and see the beautiful Tajnakan shining in the night. If only I could go up into the sky to join it.'

'It's a little too far away, Imakro,' answered her father, smiling. 'No one has ever been able to reach up there.'

'But father,' said Imakro, 'I'm so sad, and I haven't been able to sleep since I saw how beautiful Tajnakan was.'

'You still can't reach it, my child. So you'll just have to put it out of your mind.'

Yet Imakro shook her head. 'How can you expect me to forget something so lovely?'

So her father tried to comfort her. 'Perhaps if you pray hard enough,' he said, 'the star will come down to you.'

Imakro stood up and held her arms out to the star.

'Lord Tajnakan, the great and good,' she cried. 'Come to me, I beg you. I am waiting for you.' Then she went into the hut and lay down with the rest of her family. Soon she was fast asleep, dreaming of the Evening Star and its beautiful golden light.

All at once she woke up. A hand touched her shoulder, and she saw someone leaning over her.

'Who are you?' Imakro asked the stranger. 'I am Tajnakan,' replied a deep voice.

Imakro was afraid. 'You?' she stammered. 'Is it really you, the Evening Star I've so longed to see?'

'Yes, Imakro,' replied the stranger's voice. 'You called me, and I heard you. I've come to ask you to marry me.'

Imakro felt a wave of joy rushing over her. She jumped up.

'Wake up, everyone!' she cried, her voice trembling. 'Tajnakan has come to me, and he wants to marry me. I'm the happiest woman in the whole wide world.'

She ran to the fire and threw on some logs. Up leapt the flames, and the glow lit up Tajnakan's face.

But Imakro could scarcely believe her eyes. Her beautiful Evening Star was an old, old man bowed down by the years. His hair and beard were white, and his face deeply wrinkled. Horror stricken, Imakro covered her face to shut out the sight of him.

'Go away!' she shrieked. 'It was the lovely Evening Star I called, not you. You're just an ugly old man. I want to marry a fine young man, someone tall and strong, not a miserable old skeleton like you!'

Tajnakan bit his lip, and his face grew dark and bitter. Without a word he turned away and went to leave the hut. But Denake, Imakro's younger sister, took pity on the poor old man. She was ashamed of her sister's biting rudeness, and her kind heart could not bear to see the stranger treated so cruelly.

'Please stay, sir,' she said to Tajnakan. 'Don't let us part so unhappily.' And turning to her father, she went on: 'If you will let me, father, I will marry Tajnakan instead.'

Tajnakan smiled, and he took Denake's hand. A few days later the marriage took place, with much feasting and joy. Only Imakro mocked her sister for marrying such an old man.

Tajnakan built a hut, and he and Denake settled down together happily. One day Tajnakan decided to go out.

'You see to the house, Denake,' he said. 'I'm going out to work.'

'What are you going to do?' Denake asked.

'You'll soon see,' her husband replied smiling. 'I'm going to sow plants you've never seen before. No one here has ever seen them. You're going to be glad you married me.'

Denake was puzzled.

'What does "sow" mean?' she asked.

'Sowing is doing what the wind does,' answered Tajnakan. 'I take the seeds and put them in the earth. Then the plants grow and bear fruit, and afterwards you can gather the fruit and eat it.'

226

Denake's question was not as silly as it sounds. As we know, the Indians of the forests had not yet learnt to grow crops.

Tajnakan left Denake in the house, and went away to where the wide river Beracan flowed over rapids. There he stepped into the water and whispered a magic spell:

'Tajnakan, Evening Star, shining on high,
to the great Beracan river does cry:
Carry me roots now, and plants too, and seeds,
that I may fill the poor Karasha's needs.'

All at once, swirling down the river, came grains of maize and wheat, sugar-cane plants, tapioca roots and pineapple plants. Tajnakan caught them as they floated down, and bore them off to the bank.

Then he made a clearing in the forest, turned over the patch of earth, sowed the seeds and planted the roots and plants. He had made a field.

It was a big task, and took quite a time. Denake, waiting at home for her husband to return, began to worry.

'Perhaps he's ill,' she said to herself. 'My Tajnakan is old, and not very strong. I hope nothing has happened to him.'

In the end Denake could wait no longer, and she ran into the forest to find him. After a long and anxious search, she found the new field, and then she caught sight of her husband. She gasped in astonishment.

Tajnakan was no longer a frail old man, but a fine, handsome youth, with arms so strong that he was uprooting trees from the ground. He was wearing the jewelled ornaments of a tribal chief, and wondrous symbols were painted on his body. Denake could not believe anyone could change so much, but her husband smiled at her. 'Yes, I'm really Tajnakan,' he said.

'Does that mean you're not old after all?' asked Denake, amazed.

'I'm as old as when you first saw me,' replied Tajnakan. 'But at the same time I'm as young as you see me now.'

Denake ran into his arms. Then she took him back to show him to her family. As they entered the village they met Imakro, who stared in astonishment.

'Who's that with you?' she said to her sister.

'It's Tajnakan, my husband,' replied Denake proudly. 'Isn't he handsome?'

And so he was. Imakro was speechless with envy. Why, oh why had she refused him? Eaten up with longing and jealousy, she pushed Denake aside and whispered in Tajnakan's ear.

'Denake's simple and stupid. What's she to you? Wasn't it I who called you, I for whom you came down from the sky?'

'That's true,' said Tajnakan.

'And wasn't it I you came to marry?'

'That's true too,' said Tajnakan.

'Then you belong to me. You're my husband.' And she took Tajnakan's arm and tried to drag him away.

Denake stood to one side, watching silently while this was going on. She saw Imakro's eyes gleam in triumph. But Tajnakan pulled his arm from Imakro's grasp.

'When I was an old man, you refused me,' he said sternly. 'You, Imakro, will never understand how age carries youth within it, just as youth already carries the seeds of age. You cannot see through to the heart of things. You see only the outside, but Denake saw my heart. Go away!'

Imakro let out a piercing shriek. She lifted her arms to the sky and tore her hair. Then she fell to the ground, foaming at the mouth and shaking through and through. The villagers came running up.

'What's happened?' they cried. 'Has an evil spirit got into her?'

Denake tried to go to her sister, but Tajnakan held her back.

'Don't touch her,' he said. 'She's lost. It's too late to help her now.'

When Imakro's parents ran to help their daughter, she had gone. No one had seen it happen, but where she had lain a black bird was standing, flapping its wings and wailing. The sound was sad as sad could be, and at the same time it had an evil ring to it:

'Kree-ah, kree-ah! Are you there? Are you there?'

Imakro had turned into the black bird. Ever since then the bird has wandered through the night, crying to Tajnakan, because Imakro cannot forget him. When people hear it wailing, their blood runs cold. Sometimes, when lovers walk in the forest at night, the bird flies down and pecks at the girl's head again and again, trying to drive Denake away and win back Tajnakan — Tajnakan the great, who taught the Karashas to grow crops, because Denake's love was stronger than Imakro's selfishness.

'Listen,' people say when they hear the bird wailing in the night. 'It's Imakro, still longing for Tajnakan.'

And far away, high in the night sky, the Evening Star goes behind a cloud.

THE ROAD TO ANÁHUAC

This tale is partly legend, but it also contains more than a grain of truth. The great migration of the Aztecs in search of their new home really did take place.

In the year 1160, when the migration began, the Aztec tribes were still in their Dark Ages. They lived like barbarians, rough and uncivilized. Some historians trace their old homeland to northern Colorado, in what is now the United States. The old Aztec legends call it Aztlán, the White Land, and say that it was surrounded by water. But wherever it was, another Land by the Water, Anáhuac, was waiting for them far away to the south.

One day, the legends say, a strange bird told the Aztecs to leave their country. It flew over the White Land crying 'ti-hui, ti-hui,' which are the Aztec words for 'we must go'.

'What can this mean?' cried the puzzled people. They quickly gathered together. 'The bird is calling us,' said the priests. 'He wants us to follow him.'

The bird flew off towards the south. The tribes chose one of their number, Tecpaltzin, to lead them. 'We shall go,' declared Tecpaltzin. 'A new homeland awaits us!'

And so it was decided. The men set to and built boats, and soon the Aztec people were able to cross the water.

The legend also tells us that eight tribes of the Nahuas Indians came from the Ancestral Cave. These tribes had settled on the southern bank of the river Colorado, and were amazed to see the Aztecs arriving in their boats.

'Where are you going?' the princes of the Nahuas asked them.

'To find a new homeland,' replied Tecpaltzin. The Nahuas were very excited.

'May we come with you?' they asked eagerly. The Aztecs agreed, and so they set out together.

The Aztec tribes decided to make a statue of their sun and war god Huitzilopochtli. Then the god spoke to them through the statue:

'I shall lead you. I shall fly with you in the shape of a white eagle, with a serpent in my beak. Follow me wherever I go. Where I settle, build a temple to me, with a bed for me to rest on. Build your houses round the temple, and destroy the villages you find there. Worship the eagle and the tiger, and be a brave and warlike people. That is my command.'

So spoke the god Huitzilopochtli. He had given the Aztecs a great task: to be noble, fight for the truth, and keep order in the world. His words were symbolic. But the Aztecs misunderstood, and thought they were to enslave other people, occupy their countries, destroy their homes and behave like tyrants. And that is what they did.

The Aztecs praised their god, and swore to obey him. They set off on the great journey with the Nahua tribes. Three priests and a priestess bore the god's statue on their shoulders on a bed of reeds. On they went until they reached a suitable place to set up camp.

It was getting towards evening. The Aztecs built a mound of earth and set their god on it. But before they could eat they heard cries coming from the tree. Alarmed they looked up at the top of the tree, and at that moment it split in two. They were terrified, for they knew this must be a sign from their god. They fell to their knees, weeping. Suddenly the god began to speak:

'Wait, my Aztecs. You must part from the Nahua tribes. Call them here and tell them they must make their way alone.'

Tecpaltzin summoned the Nahua chiefs. 'Our god has spoken,' he announced.

'We are listening,' replied the chiefs.

'He has ordered us to wait. The time has come to say goodbye.'

The Nahuas were very sad. 'But what about us?' they asked.

'You must go on without us,' Tecpaltzin told them.

'Can't we stay with you?' asked the Nahuas sadly.

But Huitzilopochtli had forbidden it, for he did not wish his people to share the promised land with the Nahuas. So the Nahuas parted from the Aztecs and went on their way alone.

The Aztec tribes stayed for some time at that place and it is said that the chiefs of the tribes gave the people a test. They offered them two bundles, one of jewels and the other of sticks and memorial stones. 'Choose!' ordered the chiefs. Those who chose the sticks and stones showed more wisdom, for people who are to conquer other nations must value useful things more than beautiful ones.

The long caravan of wanderers set off again. After some time they came to a land where acacia trees and cacti grew. Suddenly they heard cries, and saw a band of sorcerers who had fallen from the acacias and been caught on the cacti. They had tried in vain to free themselves, but the spines had torn their clothing, scratched their faces and hands, and held them fast.

'Save us,' cried the sorcerers, 'or we will die.'

Huitzilopochtli spoke to his people:

'Set them free. Let them obey you as their masters, and serve you from now on!'

232

So these were the first of the Aztecs' subjects. The tribes were on their way to founding a new empire.

It was at this spot, too, that Huitzilopochtli gave them another important order: 'It is my will that from now on you call yourselves not Aztecs, but Mexicans.' And his people obeyed him.

Some of the Mexicans continued straight on towards Anáhuac, the central plateau valley of the great country we now call Mexico. But the others were to continue their wanderings for years to come. They reached the place called 'Where the Huaxtecs wept', and then, eventually, they came to Coatlicamac, and their sacred rite of kindling the New Fire was celebrated on the mountain of the snake Coatepec. Then, for some years, they lived at Tollan, which people now call Tula. Up and down over Mexico, hither and thither they wandered. Not until the year 1216, after a migration that had lasted for nearly 60 years, did they come upon Anáhuac, the high plateau valley.

They stopped, dumbstruck. Far below stretched the high plateau, dotted with lakes and bordered by mountains. It was, the ancient legends tell, a 'Field of Dazzling Whiteness'. Everything seemed to be a brilliant white: the trees, the reeds, the meadows, the water — even the fish and the frogs. Were they really all so white, or was it simply that the new Mexicans were blinded by the beauty unfolding before their eyes?

The people fell to their knees and prayed. The chiefs and the priests wept for joy.

'At last we have come to our sacred land,' they told the Mexicans. 'It is Anáhuac, the Land by the Water. Our wishes have been granted. Rejoice, everyone. Rejoice, for our god has led us to the promised land.' But could their wanderings really be over? Anxiously they awaited a sign from their god.

And suddenly the voice of Huitzilopochtli thundered forth.

'Stay, Mexicans! With all your strength and all your wisdom, make this country your own. Though you sweat blood and tears, you shall win what you have been seeking. Gold and silver, precious stones and splendid finery shall be your reward. You shall harvest cocoa, and cotton, and many fruits. Beautiful gardens will delight your eyes. This is your country!'

The Mexicans praised their god and vowed again to obey him. Down they went into Anáhuac, the lake-dotted Valley of Mexico. Here the Mexican chiefs sent messengers to announce their arrival, and then entered to do homage to the King. But the King was clever enough to recognize that these would be the new masters of his country, for he knew that his own star was on the wane.

'Noble lords,' said the king to the chiefs of the Mexicans. 'My house rests not only on me, but on my son. He is now of an age to take a wife. Honour me by choosing one of your daughters to become the queen of Zumpango.'

A girl was chosen, and the wedding took place. From that marriage sprang the royal house of Mexico, whose 300-year reign was to end only with the arrival of Hernán Cortés and the Spanish conquistadores. Moctezuma II, last of the line founded at Zumpango, was the mighty Aztec emperor we know as Montezuma.

Yet when the 'White Gods' sailed in from the eastern ocean, Montezuma welcomed them joyfully, for an old Aztec prophecy had predicted their coming. His trusting people were betrayed and slaughtered, his empire plundered and destroyed.

THE JAGUAR PRINCESS

This is a tale the old folks tell among the Lenca Indians of Latin America.

Many, many years ago (two centuries at the very least) a noble princess came to the Lencas from far away. Her arrival marked a turning point in their history, and they called her Comizahual, or 'Flying Jaguar', after the mighty jaguar which is so much feared and respected among the Lencas.

Comizahual was a woman of great dignity and extraordinary beauty. Her people adored her, and they were happy to obey her, for she was a natural leader. She was a sorceress, and worked wonders with her magic arts. She differed from the women of the Lencas and other Indian tribes in all sorts of ways; but the strangest thing of all was the whiteness of her skin.

When she first appeared in the land of the Lencas, she travelled far and wide. Followers flocked to her banner. Then she built a palace in Cealcoquin, the loveliest and most fertile part of the land, and began to rule. She was a strict ruler, with many servants and soldiers, but anyone could appeal to her if they felt they had been treated unjustly.

For some time there were still tribes holding out against her, but Comizahual led her troops into battle and defeated them, so that they too became part of her empire.

Comizahual's magic powers made her all the stronger. One day she rose into the sky and disappeared for many hours. When she came back she was carrying a rock with three outcrops that looked like faces, a magic talisman that put her enemies completely in her power. There were rocks with faces all over Cealcoquin, some like people and others like animals, many of them pumas. Pilgrims came from far away to pray to them, and the most revered of all were the puma heads.

Comizahual never married, but she had three sons, bearded men who loved her dearly and held positions of great power among the Lencas. They had white skins like Comizahual, and some say that they were her brothers, not her sons.

Many years passed, and the Jaguar Princess grew old and weak. In the end she fell sick, and people feared that she would die. She still issued orders from her bed, but she could no longer get up and walk. At last she felt death draw near, and called her sons and loyal chieftains to her. Sadly they all gathered round.

'Soon I must leave you,' she told them. 'My sons shall govern my

realm between them. Their rule shall be strict, but fair, and my people shall obey them as they obeyed me. Do not quarrel, my sons. For you can preserve your kingdom and protect your subjects only as long as you live together in harmony. You must neither give unjust orders, nor tolerate injustice in others. Help the poor, my sons, and make my country rich and strong.'

Her sons could not bear to think of losing their mother.

'Stay with us, mother,' pleaded the eldest, stepping forward. 'Our people need you.'

'No, my son,' replied Comizahual, gently but firmly. 'My time on the Earth is over. Fate wills it so. Here, take my crown, and carry me into the streets so that I can take leave of my people.'

The servants raised the bed and carried it outside. When the people saw their Jaguar Princess, they rushed out and surrounded her, weeping and asking her blessing.

Suddenly a bolt of lightning split the sky, and the air shook with thunder. Everyone threw themselves to the ground. And at that moment Comizahual vanished, and a bird with colours like the rainbow blew up into the sky.

'She has turned into a bird and gone to heaven,' cried the Lencas, full of fear and awe.

Ever since then the Lenca Indians have worshipped Comizahual as a goddess, and every year they hold a great festival in honour of their Jaguar Princess.

THE GIANTS FROM
OVER THE SEA

Somewhere in Peru they are supposed to have found skulls and bones which must have belonged to people much bigger than ordinary humans. So big are the bones that their owners' arms must have been as long as a normal Indian is tall. Peruvians think they were the giants who, in an ancient legend, came to Peru from over the sea.

Once upon a time, a very long time ago, some Indians spotted a fleet of boats out in the Pacific Ocean. Nearer and nearer came the fleet, and soon it was in the Indians' own bay. The boats were made of reeds, in the same way as those the fishermen of Lake Titicaca use today. Who could the strangers be? They looked very tall, but it was hard to tell from a distance, and the Indians ran down nearer the beach to get a closer look at them. Sure enough, the people coming ashore were real giants. Some were naked, some dressed in skins. All had square shoulders, long hair, and gleaming eyes which lit up their harsh faces like lanterns. When they spoke, it was like the roar of thunder, and the natives of Peru, trembling, hid themselves away from the new arrivals.

The giants explored the bay quickly, then picked the most beautiful spot, high up on rocky ground, and built their homes. They had strange tools, tools the Indians had never seen: they could carve wood and cut stone. Another thing surprised the Indians as they watched from their hiding places. Why, they wondered, had the giants built their village on rock where there was no water? Then they saw them digging holes deep down into the rock, and drawing water from them. The remains of these wells, some Indians say, can still be seen.

Still from a safe distance, the natives kept watch. Would the invaders be friendly or hostile? Carefully the Indians watched them, trying to guess how they would behave. Something struck them at once. The giants were the greediest eaters they could imagine. When they saw what huge amounts of meat and fish and plants the giants devoured, the Indians could hardly believe their eyes. Yet the invaders showed no sign of preparing to grow their own food, as the natives did. This was worrying. Soon the giants would have eaten everything that grew wild in the bay, and what would happen then? The Indians feared the worst.

Sure enough, the giants were too lazy or stupid to grow crops, and before long they were plundering the country far and wide. They hunted the game, stripped the fields of the crops the natives had grown, and caught whole schools of fish with enormous nets. Yet even this was not enough. Further and further into Peru went their pillaging parties, emptying the peasants' stores and mercilessly killing any who stood in their way.

The Indians, of course, were terrified. The moment they heard the cry 'The giants are coming!' they would run and hide. But they were too small and weak, and soon the giants caught them and made them their slaves.

And worse was to come. Not only were they forced to work for these strange new masters, but when the hunters and fishermen didn't bring back enough food, the giants would eat some Indians instead. They loved the taste of human flesh, particularly women's.

Horrified and disgusted, the Indian tribes all along the coast met to discuss how they could get rid of the appalling cannibals. For many days the council of war went on, with much shouting and moaning. All sorts of plans were put forward.

'Let's attack them in their village at night and kill them all!' said one.

'No, we'll never manage that. But we can kill them one by one when we see them alone.'

'The sorcerer must cast a spell on them.'

'Our womenfolk can mix a deadly poison and put it in the giants' food.'

But none of this had any effect. What could these puny men do against such huge giants? The Indians' arrows hardly scratched their skin, and magic had no power over them. And who was going to poison them when it meant almost certain death for themselves?

So the Indians lost heart and lived in utter despair, while the strangers remained as powerful as ever. Many families left their tribes and the region altogether and went far away to begin a new life, further along the coast or on the high plateau up in the Andes mountains. Better a poor life far from the country of their birth, they thought, than to live at home without hope, always in terror, and to meet a terrible end in the belly of a greedy cannibal.

Those who stayed lived in constant fear. Nothing had any effect on the giants, and their behaviour became more and more revolting. They had no shame, and feared neither the devil nor the gods. Years went by, and it seemed the tyranny would never end.

Then at last something completely unexpected happened. The giants had gathered in their village for one of their great feasts. They were drinking fiery brandy, and as usual they had captured some Indian women, killed them and roasted them over a huge fire. All the giants

240

drank and drank. They made a huge din, and their menacing laughs could be heard for miles around through the quiet of the night.

Then, quite suddenly, flashes of lightning slashed across the sky, and thunder came crashing over the bay. The earth trembled with the noise. At that moment a huge ring of fire ran round the giants' village, and in the midst of the fire a shining angel appeared. His face was lit with an unearthly light, and in his right hand he carried a sword of flame.

The giants were dazzled, and for the first time in their lives they felt fear. They threw themselves on the ground, begging the angel for mercy.

But the angel had no more mercy on the giants than they had had on the poor Indians. With one blow of his sword, he killed them all, drunk and grovelling as they were. The fire consumed their bodies, and soon all that was left of them was a few bones, which on the orders of the gods were scattered in the wind.

And so the gods punished the giants for their crimes, and saved the Indians of the Peruvian coast from the most terrible nightmare. But it was many a long year before the Indians forgot their fear of the giants from over the sea.

THE HUMMINGBIRD'S FEAR

In the Andes mountains of South America, there is a strange legend about the hummingbird, that tiny jewel of many colours.

The Indians of the Andes say that the bird, however beautiful, is evil through and through. To them it is a messenger of death, and they avoid it whenever they can. It is itself afraid of death, they say, and this is why it does not settle like other birds, but flits about all the time above the flowers. This too is why it whirrs its wings so fast, and why it sleeps not in trees but in dark caves, hanging from the rock.

Sometimes, after a very hard winter, the tiny birds freeze to death in the caves, and when spring comes they can still be seen hanging there. If just one hair of a person's head is carried off by a hummingbird, say the Indians, he will die like the bird: one day he will be found hanged. The birds, they believe, are always looking for human hair, and when the Indians cut or comb their hair they take great care to bury every hair that comes off. People with hearts as evil as the hummingbird's will steal their enemies' hair, and throw it away so that the bird will find it and bring the victim bad luck.

This belief goes back to a legend of the age when the Incas ruled much of the Andes. At that time an Inca prince ruled over the province around Mount Litran, where he had a wonderful palace set amid fertile terraces. He was a tall young man, and very powerful too.

On Lake Paimun, not far from Mount Litran, lived two sisters, Painemilla, which means Blue Gold, and Painefilu, or Blue Serpent. Both were dazzlingly beautiful, but Blue Gold was gentle and kind, while Blue Serpent was proud and selfish.

One day the prince was passing by their hut with a troop of soldiers when he caught sight of the two sisters. He thought they were the most beautiful girls he had ever seen.

'I shall marry one of you,' said the prince to the two girls. 'Stay here till I decide which of you it shall be.'

Blue Gold blushed, and lowered her eyes, but Blue Serpent looked up at him boldly, her eyes shining with desire.

'It's me he'll marry,' she said to her sister when the prince had gone. 'I'll be the queen, because I'm more beautiful than you are.'

Blue Gold said nothing, and Blue Serpent began to prepare her wedding finery. But imagine her rage and shock when at last the Inca prince returned, and he took Blue Gold to be his bride. The sweet girl's gentleness had touched his heart.

For days on end, Blue Serpent wept and brooded, full of bitterness. Her family could do nothing to comfort her. Secretly she vowed that her luckier sister must die.

After some months, Blue Gold was overjoyed to find herself pregnant. The prince summoned the priest, who was also the court fortune-teller.

'Will our child be a boy or a girl?' he asked the priest.

'The queen will give you two children, my lord, a boy and a girl,' answered the priest, 'and both of them will have golden hair.'

When the time came for the queen to have her babies, the prince was away fighting the Incas' enemies. Blue Gold sent a messenger to her sister Blue Serpent, asking her to come to the palace to be with her.

Blue Serpent came at once. Outwardly she was kind and helpful, but inside her only thoughts were of revenge. When the time came for the babies to be born, Blue Serpent sent away all the servants, and delivered the twins herself: a boy and a girl, both with golden hair just as the priest had said. Then Blue Serpent laid the babies in a wooden box bound with iron, and stole out of the palace to lake Paimun. She threw the box into the water, and at once a strong current carried it away. Then she ran to the kennels, killed a bitch which had just had puppies, and took two of the pups to Blue Gold.

'Where are my children?' Blue Gold asked her sister anxiously.

Blue Serpent began to laugh, and she put the two puppies on the queen's breast. 'Here are your children. Feed them!'

Blue Gold burst into tears. But as the two tiny puppies were nuzzling up against her, searching for their mother, she gave them her breast as though they were her own children.

When the prince came back from the wars, Blue Serpent was waiting for him.

'Your wife has given birth to twins, my lord. Come and see your children!'

Excitedly the prince ran into Blue Gold's chamber, but when he saw the puppies, his anger knew no bounds.

'You have deceived me,' he shouted. 'You were to bear me children with golden hair, but all the time you were nothing but a dog. From now on you shall live with dogs!'

In his anger the prince killed the puppies and shut his wife up in the kennels. The hounds bit her, and the only food she had was what they left. She hid herself in the farthest corner of the kennels, weeping, but still silent.

Blue Serpent stayed close to the prince, flattering him and hoping to become his queen. The prince let her stay at the palace, but to her great disappointment he did not marry her, and he just could not forget Blue Gold.

He called the priest to him. 'You prophesied wrongly,' he said accusingly. 'My wife gave birth to dogs.'

The priest froze, horrified. 'Forgive me, my lord,' he replied. 'The oracle spoke of children with golden hair. Do the dogs have golden hair?' Then he turned, and without another word he went back to the temple of the sun.

Meanwhile the box with the two babies had floated round Lake Paimun. A man walking on the opposite bank saw the box and took it out of the water. To his amazement he found the two golden-haired babies, and ran quickly home with them. His wife tried to give them food, but they refused it all. Yet they grew so fast that within a year they were as tall as ten-year-olds. The Indian and his wife were rather frightened of the children, who seemed to be more than human. The twins didn't eat or drink, and never laughed. They could see far into the distance and far into the future, and all the time they behaved like adults.

One day the prince came with his court to fish on the banks of Lake Paimun. For a long time he had had doubts about what happened when the dogs were born to his wife, and he had often questioned the priest. The priest had consulted the old legends and found two prophecies.

'The water will bring the gold,' said the first mysteriously. 'The kennels will open and the prince's heart will rejoice,' ran the second. So doubt and hope nestled side by side in the prince's heart.

Suddenly, as he was fishing on the lake, he saw two golden dots shining in the sun, far away in the water.

'What's that shining over there?' he asked his servant.

'It's two children, master,' replied the servant. 'They're bathing in the lake, and it's their golden hair you see shining in the sunlight.'

The prince's heart leapt. 'Bring them here,' he ordered.

The men of his retinue brought the boy and girl before the prince. Golden indeed was their hair, and gleaming. The prince was sure he had found his children, but he forced himself to hide his feelings.

'Do you know who I am?' he asked the twins.

'You're the prince,' replied the boy, and the girl agreed.

'Are you afraid of me?'

The children shook their heads. 'No, we're not afraid of you,' answered the boy. 'But we don't love you either,' said the girl.

'Why aren't you afraid of me?' asked the prince. 'After all, if I'm your prince, you're my subjects.'

'Because you're our father,' said the girl.

'But if I'm your father, why don't you love me?'

244

'Because you have punished our mother, who deserves your love, not your anger,' answered the boy. 'She should be living in the palace, but you shut her up in the kennels. She should be happy by your side, and yet she is unhappier than any dog. It is your doing that she suffers so. Should we love you for that?'

So the prince learnt the truth from his children's mouths. Moved to the depths of his heart, he took them by the hand and led them to the palace. But when they reached the door, they refused to go in.

'Do you want us to live in the palace like princes while our mother stays in the kennels like a dog?' they said to their father. 'If you don't free her and give her back what is hers by right, we'll leave you, and you'll lose your throne and your life.'

Gladly the prince sent for Blue Gold. He begged her forgiveness, and restored her to her throne. With tears running down her cheeks, the princess gathered her children into her arms.

Blue Serpent watched all this in hidden fury. She tried to wheedle her way back into her sister's affections and win over the children. But the prince's son pointed an accusing finger.

'She's the one who made all this happen. I'm going to punish her.'

He had her brought in front of the palace gate, and tied her to it. Then he took a magic stone, and placed it between Blue Serpent and the sun. The stone was so thin as to be transparent, and the sunlight falling on it was focused into a burning ray.

'You are evil, Blue Serpent,' said the prince's son. 'Every last bit of you must go. You shall become ashes, scattered in the wind.'

Blue Serpent begged for mercy, but the boy called on the sun, and she began to burn. Because the child, like his father, was descended from the sun, it shone for him with all its force. Higher and higher licked the flames, and soon Blue Serpent was no more. When nothing but ashes remained, the boy scattered them in the wind.

But he had not noticed that a tiny piece of Blue Serpent's heart was left beneath the ashes. That fragment turned into a hummingbird, which whirred hastily away for fear of being discovered. But as it came from an evil heart, it was to die a miserable death, like Blue Serpent herself.

Hummingbirds know that, and that is why they are so restless and sad. They may be able to deceive people, with their jewel-coloured feathers, but they cannot deceive themselves. In their hearts, which spring from the heart of Blue Serpent, they know they cannot escape their sad fate, and that is why hummingbirds can never find peace.

THE DARK MONSTERS
OF ANCIENT GREECE

The Greek myths are full of legendary animals. Many were creatures of hell, monsters who lived deep in the earth. They are not like the sky gods of Greece's golden age, but go back to darker myths from farther east.

Some, with gargoyle faces or many heads or arms, came from gods and demons which are found in Indian religions. Others were winged lions and bulls, or lions with human heads, which belonged to the myths of Egypt, Assyria and Babylon.

Dogs of Hell, giant boars, vicious birds, winged horses, mighty lions, fire-breathing dragons and terrifying sea serpents: somehow the dark monsters found their way into the Greek myths, to be pursued to their deaths by the ancient heroes.

Many of the creatures sprang from the monsters Echidna and Typhon. Echidna was half serpent, half woman. Her husband was a gigantic beast whose eyes breathed fire and whose limbs ended in serpent's heads. Zeus killed him with his thunderbolts and buried him under Mount Etna, which still breathes fire today. One of their brood was the Sphinx, part woman and part winged lion, who asked riddles of passing travellers, and killed them when they could not answer. Others were the Nemean lion and the two-headed guard dog Orthos, both slain by the great hero Hercules.

Here we shall tell of the man-eating Stymphalian birds, and also of four of Echidna's monster offspring: the Lernean Hydra, the hundred-headed dragon Ladon, the dog Cerberus which guarded the gates of Hell, and the terrible Chimaera. Most of these stories are about Heracles or, as the Romans called him, Hercules.

To become immortal, Hercules had to perform twelve labours for his cousin, the cowardly tyrant Eurystheus, King of Argos. One of these tasks was to kill the hideous Hydra of Lerna. This was a serpent with the body of a dog and nine snaky heads (though some say five, or even a hundred). One of its heads was immortal.

No one could overcome it but Hercules, son of Zeus, the king of the gods. Even that mighty hero dared not attack it alone, but took his brave nephew Iolaos with him as his charioteer.

The intrepid pair hastened to the marshes of Lerna, where the monster lived beside the seven sources of the river Amymone. Hercules leapt from the chariot, and Iolaos tethered the horses.

'Come out, monster,' cried Hercules. 'Show your foul face!'

They waited, but all was silent.

'Coward!' jeered the hero. He lit a fire, wrapped his axe in rags, plunged it into the flames and hurled it into the monster's lair, which filled at once with thick dark smoke. Coughing and choking, the monster came out, still hissing and spitting fire. Its nine heads were weaving to and fro ready to attack.

Hercules hurled himself on the beast with all his might. The Hydra coiled itself round his right foot, but he braced himself on the left one and grabbed hold of the nearest head. His club whistled through the air and severed the serpent's neck. The second head followed, and the third and the fourth. Down they fell onto the ground, and thick brown blood spurted from the stumps.

But what was happening? Iolaos watched in horror.

'Look, Hercules!' he shouted.

Hercules felt a shiver of fear go down his spine. As if by magic, new heads were rising from the stumps. And that was not all: for every severed head there were now two, foaming with rage and more menacing than ever.

'It's hopeless!' groaned Iolaos, and he hid his face in his hands. 'We'll never kill it.'

At that moment Hercules gave a yell as pain shot through his left foot. He looked down and saw an enormous crab, moving fast and nimbly on ten feet, its iron claws poised to attack him again.

Roaring with pain and anger, Hercules crushed the armoured attacker with one blow from his club.

Seeing the crab die, Hera, queen of the gods, wept bitterly. She had brought up the Hydra, and she hated Hercules. It was she who had sent the crab to the Hydra's aid, and in gratitude she placed the unlucky crab in the sky, where it took its place in the Zodiac under the name of Cancer.

But the crab's death helped the hero only a little. As fast as he cut off the Hydra's heads, they grew again.

'Iolaos, help me,' he cried.

The young man sprang forward at once.

'Light a torch, brave nephew. Set fire to the forest, and bring me burning branches. Hurry!'

No sooner said than done. Hercules was moving so fast, Iolaos could hardly believe his eyes. As his right hand severed one of the Hydra's heads, his left burnt the stump with one of Iolaos's blazing branches, destroying the monster's nerves and blood vessels forever so that no more heads could grow.

248

At last Hercules had almost mastered the terrifying reptile. But the last head, the immortal one, still survived.

'Dig a deep pit, Iolaos,' ordered the hero.

Then Hercules cut off the last head and threw it into the pit. Quickly the two companions filled the pit with earth and dragged a huge rock over it. The last head would never die, but they made sure that it could not leave its prison.

Now Hercules cut the Hydra's body in two, and dipped his arrows in its poisoned blood. From then on the slightest scratch from those arrows would be fatal. Every warrior dreamt of having weapons like these, from whose wounds none could recover, but only to the valiant Hercules did the gods give this priceless gift.

At one time the area round the marshy Lake Stymphalis, in the lovely land of Arcadia, was plagued by the terrible Stymphalian birds. Big as cranes and sacred to the war-loving god Ares, they filled the forests round the lake, stripping the trees of their fruit. Their droppings poisoned the fields, the lake and even the underground streams. Worst of all, they attacked humans, killing and devouring them.

The birds had iron claws, beaks and even wings. Their beaks were so sharp that they split the soldiers' armour easily; and they could throw their feathers like arrows. Weapons were useless against them, and their victims were beyond number. Sometimes the flocks were so dense that they blotted out the sky. When the birds dived towards the ground, men and beasts tried to flee, but they were paralysed with fear. The whole region was in mortal terror, and the only hope was to appeal to the famous Hercules.

The hero came at once. Tired after a long, hard journey, he paused a moment in the forest beside Lake Stymphalis.

Looking up from its bank, he could not believe his eyes. The sky was black with the birds. They were everywhere. It was like a great advancing army of soldiers, shoulder to shoulder, row upon row. What could even Hercules do against all these millions of evil birds?

All at once he was blinded by a flash of light from the sky. There before him stood Athene, goddess of wisdom, with an owl on her shoulder and two enormous bronze cymbals in her hands.

'Take these cymbals, Hercules,' she said. 'The god Hephaestus has forged them for you.'

Relieved, Hercules dragged the heavy cymbals up a neighbouring hill and began to clash them together. The noise he made would have wakened the dead. Terrified, the Stymphalian birds flew away in all directions with shrill harsh cries.

Arrow after arrow came from Hercules' bow, fast as lightning. Every one found its target, and the birds that survived flew swiftly away, never to be seen again.

The eleventh of the death-defying labours that Hercules had to perform for his cousin Eurystheus was to steal the golden apples of the Hesperides. The earth goddess Gaea had given these as her wedding present to Zeus and Hera, king and queen of the gods. The apples grew on a tree which Hera planted in the garden of the gods 'on the west coast of the great sea of the world', which meant at the western end of the Mediterranean. The garden was said to be in north west Africa, not far from the Atlas Mountains. The apples were guarded by the Hesperides, the three nymphs of the evening, daughters of the ancient Titan Atlas and Hesperus, the evening star.

As they watched in the garden, the three nymphs sang sweet melodies. They in turn were guarded by Ladon, the hundred-headed dragon, son of Typhon and Echidna. Ladon never slept, but mounted guard proudly and constantly, his hundred pairs of eyes ever watchful. His hundred throats bayed, shrieked and yelled like his father Typhon.

When Hercules was ordered to go to the garden of the Hesperides, he was at the opposite end of the Mediterranean. Before he reached it, and even before he found out where it was, he had many battles and adventures, but at last some nymphs showed him the way to the home of Proteus, the prophetic old man of the sea, who tended flocks of seals for the sea god Poseidon.

'Proteus is wise. He knows everything,' the pretty daughters of the waves told Hercules. 'But he will only tell if you grip him fast, so the best thing is to surprise him when he's asleep.'

It was easier said than done. True, the strange old man was a wise and good being who could not lie if he was asked a question. But first he had to be caught, and he could take on any shape he liked at a moment's notice. Hercules learnt this to his cost. He hesitated too long, and Proteus woke and slipped from his grasp. In an instant the old man had become a ram, then a goat. This in turn changed into a cuttlefish, then a crab. The crab turned into a snake, the snake into a weasel, the weasel into a wild boar and the boar into a stag. At last the stag turned back into a man, but Hercules was ready for him. He pinned Proteus to the ground, and once trapped, the old man told him the way to the garden of the Hesperides.

It was a long, long way, many hundreds of miles. Hercules had to cross Egypt and all of Libya. But in the end, after many more adventures, he saw the garden.

Now he could hear the sinister chorus from the hundred heads of the great dragon, but he had no fear of it. He shot Ladon with his bow and arrows, and entered the garden. With the help of Atlas, the giant, he was able to carry off the precious fruit, and so to complete his eleventh labour for King Eurystheus.

The King made a gift of the golden apples to Hercules, but the hero dedicated them to the goddess Athene, and she had the apples returned to the three guardian nymphs, as it had been laid down by Fate.

The twelfth and last labour of Hercules was the hardest of all: to bring back from Hell the terrible dog Cerberus who guarded its gates.

This horrible monster, another son of Typhon and Echidna, had three heads, a serpent's tail, and on his back a multitude of serpent's heads which darted their tongues in every direction. The shade of every person who died had to pass before him before it could enter the gates of Hell. Cerberus would circle round them, lashing his serpent's tail, to inspect them before letting them through. But he would not let in any living person, and above all he would never let anyone out of Hell, for whatever reason. In Greece they said that the gatekeeper of Hell was so repulsive that any mortal who saw him was petrified with fear. Few indeed were the mortals who escaped his vigilance.

One was the wonderful singer, Orpheus. Orpheus married the beautiful nymph Eurydice, but that night she was pursued by the demi-god Aristheus, and she stepped on a snake. Its bite was deadly, and she had to leave for the eternal shadows of the underworld.

Grief-stricken, Orpheus fell into a black despair and even abandoned his beloved music. In the end his longing brought him to the gates of Hell, but how could he, a mere mortal, find a way into the underworld?

He took his lyre and began to play. His melodies were so enchanting that not even the dreaded Cerberus could resist them. He let him pass without a word, and Orpheus was reunited with his beloved.

Now it was Hercules' turn to confront the hound of Hell. He made careful preparations. At Eleusis, in Attica, the priest Eumolpus taught him the secrets of life and death, and initiated him into the mysteries of the world of the living and the dead.

Armed with this information, Hercules clad himself in the skin of the terrible Nemean lion, and made for Cape Taenarum, in the south of the Pelopennese, from which a passage led to Hell. There Hermes, the messenger of the gods, who guided the shades on their way to Hell, was waiting for him, cold and hostile. At last they reached the gates of Hell.

Hercules, the fearless hero, felt fear for the first time in his life. The shades of the dead were wandering aimlessly along the walls of Hades forever, plunged in silent sorrow. When they saw the living mortal coming, they fled in utter confusion.

But the Gorgon Medusa, whose head Perseus had once cut off, did not flee. She stared at the demi-god Hercules with the full force of her look, which carried in it all the hatred in the world. He seized his sword, but Hermes held him back.

'Your sword can do nothing to the shades,' he warned Zeus' son.

Then Hercules saw old friends, and he felt a sharp pang of anguish as he saw how longingly they remembered the light of day, which they would never see again. Their endless suffering so touched Hercules that he killed one of the oxen of the underworld to refresh the gasping shades with its fresh, warm blood.

Further on, in front of the gates of Hell, he was received by Hades himself, the god of Hell.

'You cannot enter here,' warned the god.

'Give me Cerberus, and I shall leave,' demanded Hercules.

Hades said nothing, but pointed imperiously in the direction of earth, where he meant Hercules to go. Hercules took a poisoned arrow from his quiver, and let fly, and the god of the underworld bellowed in agony.

'What is this pain?' he groaned. 'I can't bear it.'

'It's the suffering that every mortal must endure!' replied Hercules calmly. 'Now you know what men must suffer before they come to your kingdom. For many poor and desperate mortals, death means freedom and relief.'

Hades was uttering heart-rending wails and groans.

'Silence!' ordered Hercules. 'Are you going to give me your gatekeeper, or shall I shoot another arrow?'

Hades did not hesitate. 'Take the monster, but on one conditon: you must seize it with your bare hands.'

Hercules obeyed at once. The more he risked, the more glory there would be, he thought to himself. Empty-handed he went to seek the monster, and he found it baying, panting and growling at the mouth of Acheron, the river of woe. It was lurking in a corner, ready to leap, and its blood-curdling roars echoed round the cavern.

'Down!' ordered Hercules.

'The hellhound yelped and drew in its head. Hercules came at it. Cerberus put its serpent tail between its legs. With one almighty leap Hercules was on it, clamping its throat in his iron grip. He did not loosen his hold even when the animal's serpent tail bit him.

The pain was terrible, but he squeezed the monster's neck so hard that it could hardly breathe. He slung it across his shoulders, with its front paws in one hand and its rear paws in the other, and carried the fearsome dog, powerless at last, out of the underworld towards the land of the living.

252

When the brilliant light of the sun fell stinging on the monster's eyes, it shook with fear and foamed at the mouth. Where the foam dropped on the ground, there grew aconite, whose roots contain a deadly poison.

When Hercules presented Cerberus to King Eurystheus, the cowardly tyrant was so frightened that he sent the animal back, and set the hero free. Hercules carried Cerberus back into the underworld, before returning to earth for more adventures.

Another of Typhon and Echidna's monstrous brood was the fire-breathing Chimaera. 'Chimaira' is the Greek word for a she-goat, and indeed the head of the repulsive beast was a goat's, but its front was a lion's, and its back was a serpent's. The Chimaera was ravaging the lovely Greek kingdom of Lycia, causing havoc far and wide. No one, it seemed, would ever be able to kill it, and the people were in despair. Yet when the young hero Bellerophon attacked the Chimaera on the winged horse Pegasus, the hideous monster was to worry them no more.

Bellerophon was the son of King Glaucos of Corinth. One day he accidentally killed someone, and had to leave his father's kingdom. He was invited to the court of King Proetos of Tiryns, where the queen, Anteia, fell in love with him. When Bellerophon rejected her, she falsely accused him of attacking her. Proetos believed her and was mad with rage, but even so he felt he could not kill a guest. Instead he sent Bellerophon to Anteia's father, King Iobates of Lycia, with a letter asking him to kill the young man.

King Iobates welcomed Bellerophon warmly, and held a great feast in his honour. Many bulls were killed for the occasion, and nine days of feasting and sports passed before Iobates had a chance to read the letter. When he finally did, he was shocked to the core. Was he really expected to execute this pleasant young man?

For a long time King Iobates wondered what to do. He could not bring himself to have the young man killed, any more than Proetos could. At length he thought of an alternative, and he summoned the youth to his presence.

'Listen, Bellerophon,' he said. 'A hideous monster, the Chimaera, is laying waste my lovely realm of Lycia. You've enjoyed our Lycian hospitality. How would you like to fight the monster? You've no wife or land to lose — you're free as air.'

Bellerophon was young, and eager for glory. He agreed gladly and set off at once.

The way led through a shady forest. After a while he noticed a horse grazing by a spring. He looked closer: it was a winged horse, the immortal Pegasus which had sprung from the blood of the Gorgon Medusa!

253

It was so beautiful that the young hero could hardly believe it. He resolved to tame the splendid beast, and tried his utmost to catch it, but it was all in vain. Exhausted, he threw himself down by the spring and fell asleep.

Soon he became aware of a voice gently reproving him.

'Why are you sleeping, grandson of Sisyphus and great-grandson of Eolus?' It was the helpful goddess Athene, come to him in a dream. 'Take this golden bridle, and go and sacrifice a big bull to the god Poseidon,' the all-powerful goddess told him. 'Then you'll be able to tame the winged horse.'

Bellerophon woke up and rubbed his eyes. He looked about him, and there he saw a bridle studded with gold. Now he knew that it was really the goddess of wisdom who had appeared to him. He followed her instructions at once, sacrificed a magnificent bull to Poseidon, and built an altar in honour of Athene.

This time, when he found Pegasus to put on the bridle, the horse stood quietly, meek as a lamb. The youth jumped onto its back with cries of joy, and it answered with a resounding neigh. The splendid charger drummed its hooves so that the sparks flew, and with one great majestic beat of its wings, it rose into the air.

Bellerophon flew for miles through the sky and high over the mountains. At last in the distance he spotted the Chimaera. Pegasus dropped down swiftly, and Bellerophon aimed his arrows as they flew.

The awful monster roared out huge flames, and the serpent tail lashed out with its poisonous tongue. However, safely astride the winged horse, Bellerophon could soar up into the sky again out of danger.

At last the monster began to weaken and with one mighty heave Bellerophon hurled his spear down the monster's throat. With a dreadful cry the fire-breathing Chimaera rolled over and died. The fair country of Lycia was free of the menace at last.